AMO

Julien threw off his jacket and tie and addressed himself to the delicious task of undressing Suzette. He removed her frock, her shoes and her silk stockings. He placed at least a score of kisses on each part of her body and two or three times that number on her bare breasts. Suzette found it most enjoyable.

She was standing by the magnificent bed, naked except for her little silk knickers and her diamond bracelet. Julien was on his knees on the oriental carpet, kissing her tummy and thrusting his wet tongue into the dimple of her belly button. His big hands clasped the cheeks of her bottom through the thin silk of her knickers.

'Take them off, *cheri*,' she murmured, longing to feel his hot mouth between her thighs . . .

Amour Encore

Marie-Claire Villefranche

HEADLINE
DELTA

First published in Great Britain in 1994
by HEADLINE BOOK PUBLISHING

A HEADLINE DELTA paperback

10 9 8 7 6 5 4 3 2 1

ISBN 0 7472 4275 5

Typeset by
CBS, Felixstowe, Suffolk

Printed and bound in Great Britain by
HarperCollins Manufacturing, Glasgow

HEADLINE BOOK PUBLISHING
A division of Hodder Headline PLC
Headline House
79 Great Titchfield Street
London W1P 7FN

INTRODUCTION

Marie-Claire Villefranche is the daughter of the well-known writer Anne-Marie Villefranche, whose books are available in sixteen languages around the world. Marie-Claire's stories of Paris are as amusing and as outrageous as her mother's.

AMOUR ENCORE is set in Paris in the mid-1950s and continues the story of Suzette Bernard, a young and sexy night-club singer who becomes a star. But before she took up singing, Suzette was a show-girl at the Folies Bergère and has retained many friends from those days – and a few lovers.

On her way to the top she makes new friends and shares in their triumphs and fiascos, their preposterous lives and loves.

SUZETTE AT
THE CINEMA

Outside the cinema, on the Champs-Elysées, eight policemen were flourishing long white truncheons to hold back the eager crowd. Suzette loved every moment of it. She smiled at the crowd while her handsome escort helped her courteously from the shiny black Citroen limousine and took her bare arm to guide her across the broad pavement and into the cinema.

She knew she looked particularly ravishing – it had taken her the entire afternoon and much of the early evening to get ready for this moment. Her raven-black hair was swept up into a knot, her fringe was exquisite, her oval face made up to perfection. She was wearing a long white satin dress with gold and silver embroidery, delicate and magnificent, cut low to draw attention to her superb breasts.

Photographers pressed forward with large cameras and flash-bulbs popped. The fans cheered as Suzette swept across the pavement on the arm of Antoine Ducasse. They were not sure who she was, but she looked so stunning that she *had* to be a film star. Why else would she be at the premiere? Hands reached out to thrust autograph books at her, she smiled warmly and shook her head as she moved on.

1

Some of the fans thought they remembered the names of movies they'd seen her in. As for her companion, naturally he was her lover, what else? He too must be a film star, to be allowed to escort so great a beauty – but perhaps he was on the fringe of the movie business still, as no one could recall his name. What an honour to be *her* escort to the premiere that evening!

And to be her lover, what a privilege! The men in the crowd stared enviously at Antoine, then back to Suzette as she passed graciously by. They pictured his arms round her and his lips on hers, his hand roaming lovingly over the cheeks of her rounded bottom, outlined by the close fit of her satin frock.

In heated imagination they saw the frock gone, silk underwear stripped away, Suzette lying on her back, her long legs apart.

'*Ah, mademoiselle, je t'aime!*' cried a man's voice from the crowd, so desperate a passion in his tone that those closest to him on the pavement laughed out loud and nudged each other.

'He wants to *kiss* you, mademoiselle,' another called out, and Suzette giggled as she moved on. She was very well aware of the effect she had on men. Sometimes it was a nuisance if they were too importunate, but more often it was a source of pride.

Though the onlookers adored Suzette and cheered for Antoine a little, it was only a passing diversion, something to fill the time before the main event. The stars of the evening, the Big Names the fans were waiting to see, jostling each other to edge closer to the front and held back by the busy police, were Jean Gabin and Simone Signoret.

It was *their* movie, their evening, their glory. So *they*

2

would arrive last, after everyone else was in position and ready for their entrance, that was their right. So until *their* limousine pulled into the kerb, the lesser stars were cheered and feted.

Including Suzette Bernard and her escort. But in fact the beautiful Mademoiselle Bernard was not a film star, not even a starlet, nor an extra. And nor was her escort. His acquaintance with the cinema was the same as Suzette's, the same as those in the crowd cheering them – it was restricted to buying a ticket and sitting in the dark to watch the stars up on the screen.

This Antoine Ducasse was a stranger to Suzette – they had met for the first time an hour ago – and yet for a particular reason she felt he was not entirely a stranger. The reason for that feeling was that he strongly resembled a man she had known well not so long ago: Vincent Lafoye. It must be said, however, Vincent was taller and the resemblance was only in profile. When viewed full face, Antoine had a deeply dimpled chin, utterly unlike Vincent, and his eyes were a different shade of brown.

Vincent was very loving and open-handed. He was easy to like, Suzette was fond of him – but he had a most disconcerting habit of pulling out his male part at unexpected moments. Naturally, it was always stiff when he exhibited it, that was the point of his game. He was able to make it go hard at will, anywhere and at any time, just by thinking about it. And he thought about it very frequently.

Suzette could remember reading in a magazine – or perhaps it was a newspaper article – that on average men think about women three times an hour, every hour, whatever they are doing at the time. And though the article primly said *women*, it was clear it really meant men were thinking about sex. And on that basis she decided that

Vincent was not average. He seemed to think about it all the time!

To be precise, it was not making love itself that filled most of his waking hours. Whenever he flipped out his upright part, it was not a question of wanting to make love to Suzette – he often exposed himself in impossible situations, in public, when there were other people close by. Walking across a bridge over the Seine, for example, with traffic rushing past and pedestrians on the pavement nearby, Vincent would put an arm about her as they stood by the parapet, looking down at the river. With his other hand he would flip open his trousers. *Et voila!* Fifteen centimetres of hard flesh!

Like any true Frenchman, he was excessively proud of his male part. He wanted women to admire it. He wanted Suzette to admire it, that was why he pulled it out so often to show her. She was amused by this childish attitude and she gratified him by stroking it a little, until he knew he was becoming dangerously aroused, near to the moment of crisis – whereupon he would thrust it back into his trousers and wait for it to subside.

By preventing the natural outcome in this manner he was able to repeat the process many times during the course of a day. He impressed himself by the actual number of times. He claimed his record score was seventeen undetected public appearances in one single day. *If that's true*, thought Suzette, *he was on his own when he did it, or with another woman, it certainly wasn't with me*. But privately she thought he was exaggerating his prowess.

In a cinema queue after dark Vincent was incapable of leaving his personal property in decent concealment. Even though people were standing elbow to elbow with him, he would grin and turn to face the wall – and pull Suzette close. No one ever remarked on that, all Paris is full of lovers kissing, in cafés, at busstops, in the parks, on the streets. Vincent would want to do more than kiss her. His hand would be inside his raincoat, undoing his trousers, before he steered Suzette's hand in to touch him.

When he took her to bed, a frequent occurrence, to go all the way in love-making, he wanted Suzette to tell him that his part was big and strong. He wanted to be assured it was the biggest she'd ever seen – the longest and thickest she'd ever felt slide into her! None of this was true but because a simple lie gave Vincent so much pleasure she murmured the words for him.

The *affaire* between them was not long-lived. Suzette's sense of humour intervened eventually and this was fatal. There was nothing even faintly amusing for Vincent in his compulsive and regular exposures of male pride – only conceit and vanity. They parted, but as friends, and he went in search of a pretty woman who would be properly impressed by these impromptu exhibitions of his masculinity – one who would take his fifteen centimetres more seriously.

In profile Antoine Ducasse looked so very much like him that Suzette kept expecting to see a flash of pink down between his thighs as he displayed himself for her admiration. Antoine did no such thing of course, he was not Vincent, a passing facial likeness had no significance. Antoine's hands did not stray in the direction of his lap in the limousine that carried him and Suzette to the Champs-Elysées.

Although Suzette was not a film star, she was very beautiful. She was twenty-three years of age and a cabaret singer, not a famous one, it is true, but on her way to the top – that she believed very firmly. In truth, she had been singing in expensive night clubs for only about a year.

As a way to make a living it was precarious, especially after she had left a settled job for this gamble on fame and riches.

Her handsome escort for the evening was not aware of it, but until a year ago Suzette was a show-girl at the Folies Bergère. Because of the excellence of her face and figure she had been one of a line-up of lovelies appearing naked on stage. Naked, that is, but for a tiny gold-spangled *cache-sexe* and a plume of snow-white ostrich feathers a metre high on her head.

To be beautiful was Suzette's profession, so to speak. But it displeased her to be no more than living scenery, one of twelve beauties with perfect breasts and long legs – to say nothing of enchanting little belly buttons – who formed the back-drop for Big Name singers. She resented that and she had ambition to be a Big Name herself.

She had taken lessons, she had rehearsed for hours every day, she persevered in spite of all discouragement. And now at last she had one elegantly shod foot on the bottom rung of the long ladder that might one day lead to stardom and acclaim.

In the flower-filled foyer of the cinema her hand was kissed a hundred times by men she had never seen before, whose names meant nothing to her. They were film-company people: producers, directors, financiers. They bowed over her hand and stared down the front of her satin frock and thought their thoughts.

To be ogled did not discomfort Suzette at all. Not after her experience at the Folies Bergère, which had quickly accustomed her to being stared at by appreciative and heavy-breathing men in large numbers. Each evening as she posed under the lights in a *cache-sexe* no bigger than the palm of a man's hand covering the feminine charm between her bare thighs, she could feel hundreds of eyes on her.

She was always aware of those hot eyes staring. It was almost as if unseen hands were slithering over her body, caressing her nakedness, feeling her breasts, stroking her belly, sliding up her thighs. Ah, that hot gaze between her thighs – it seemed to her almost like invisible fingers attempting to snatch away her tiny *cache-sexe* and bare her last secret! And caress it!

They were unaware of who she was, these film people. But very possibly every one of them at the premiere had already seen her bare breasts and her beautiful bare thighs, in the days before she became a singer. It was reasonable to assume they had all at some time been to the Folies Bergère. But they did not make the connection in their thoughts between a gorgeous naked body on stage and the elegantly dressed beauty whose hand they were now kissing.

But even with her clothes on, Suzette could feel the intimate gaze on her body from the men about her. Naturally these cinema impresarios were wondering who she was and how they could meet her again in more private circumstances. The casting couch was in their mind as they stared at her, every one of them wanted to uncover her marvellous breasts, stroke them and kiss them.

They were experiencing certain fleshy stirrings down in their trousers, these middle-aged moguls, their blood was boiling at the idea of slipping a hand into her silk underwear to feel the warm softness between her legs.

One of the film moguls actually did recognise her, as he took her hand to kiss it. Not as a naked show-girl from the

Folies Bergère, that would have been too impossible a feat of memory, but more recently he had heard her sing in an exclusive club in the Avenue George-Cinq.

He had been greatly impressed by her singing and even more so by her stunning looks. He would certainly have liked to become more closely acquainted with Mademoiselle Bernard. But on that evening he was entertaining a pretty blonde would-be film star and he had taken her to the night club to discuss her future . . . or something like that. Whatever it was, it required him to put his hand on the pretty blonde's thigh under the table. Occupied in this manner, he was unable to invite Suzette to join him for a glass or two of champagne.

Perhaps he thought about her later that night, when he lay on the naked belly of the pretty blonde. Perhaps Suzette's breasts were in his thoughts, her belly under his in his imagination – but on the other hand perhaps not. Men can be versatile in love and switch their urgent and panting devotion from one woman to another, according to whose knickers they are taking down.

Yet there are inconveniences, even for a film mogul, and even here at the premiere he was not free to express his desire.

'Julien Brocq,' he whispered to Suzette, so that Madame Brocq at his side did not hear him. 'Telephone me at my office, there are important things we should discuss about your career, dear Mademoiselle Bernard.'

Suzette rewarded him with a most dazzling smile and instantly forgot his name. She could guess precisely the career he had in mind for her and it held no interest.

The cinema was sold out for the premiere, it was an important occasion and everyone who mattered was there, elegantly dressed and groomed. The men looked distinguished, or nearly so, while between them the women displayed thousands of square metres of semi-covered breasts. Suzette's escort was a little overwhelmed by it all and gave fifty francs to the middle-aged usherette who showed them to their seats, instead of the usual five.

Everyone was talking, commenting on everyone else, and no one was listening. With almost 2,000 persons in the huge auditorium the noise was astounding. Reputations were being destroyed or made as they noted who was accompanying who, and which couples were having affairs of the heart with each other. Eventually the Big Stars arrived and took their seats to tumultuous applause and soon after that the lights dimmed and the curtains swished slowly back.

Suzette had no ambition whatsoever to become a film star. In her opinion it was a career that depended on looks. Except for a very few who had a real talent for acting, female movie stars became famous by beauty of face and grace of body. And that was exactly the same as Suzette's old job at the Folies Bergère.

Antoine Ducasse, for example, this overly handsome young man she was with this evening, he was not a film star but he *was* an actor. He was not a well-known actor, not yet, but he had appeared in several important plays at proper theatres. The roles had been minor, it must be said, but to hear him talk he had more or less carried the plays single-handed.

But then, all actors talked like that. The two lines they had to speak were invariably the most important lines in the play, everything depended on how they spoke them! And how they stood or moved when they spoke them!

Antoine wanted to leave the serious theatre behind and become a famous movie star and monstrously rich. Suzette had not seen him on stage but she was convinced that his talent lay in his looks. Which meant he might do very well in movies. As was well known, intelligence was not required in movies, only good looks and the ability to speak clearly.

Sitting beside him in the dark she tried to interest herself in the film. She liked films and she admired Simone Signoret, a beautiful and talented woman. Naturally she adored husky-voiced Jean Gabin, with his beaten-up face and rough charm. She ought to have enjoyed the film immensely. But a premiere was nothing to do with enjoying the film being screened, everyone was there to be seen by others, to be envied, above all to be *noticed*.

It amused Suzette to compare Antoine with herself in the days when she appeared naked at the Folies Bergère. He had the looks to be a film star but that was all he had. There was a certain superficial charm of manner but his conversation was boring to the extreme, being almost entirely about himself. Very probably he didn't like women at all, seeing them as competitors for the attention of others. Ravishingly handsome actors all too often were left-handed, so to speak.

There were reasons why this thought came into Suzette's mind. When Antoine had called for her at her apartment he had kissed her hand briefly, that was all. He made no declaration that she was the most beautiful woman he had ever met in his life and he was honoured to take her to the premiere that evening. No question about it, he had been cool and just a little distant.

In the limousine on the way to the Champs-Elysées he had made no attempt to put his arm round her waist or to kiss her cheek or to put his hand on her knee! She could hardly recall a ride in a car or a taxi with a man who did not try to kiss her or to stroke her thigh or touch her breasts. But not Antoine Ducasse, he sat back easily in the seat, leaving space between them, his legs crossed gracefully, chatting of nothing in particular, all the way to the cinema.

And in profile he looked so much like Vincent Lafoye! If *he* had been with her in the limousine, his trousers would have been open before they had travelled a hundred metres, his pink stiffness rearing up for her to admire.

It was a quarter of an hour at least since the cinema lights had gone out and the film had begun. A whole quarter of an hour and Antoine had made no move to take Suzette's hand or to kiss her or to put an arm around her – even though she had liberally dabbed herself with an expensive perfume that made men giddy with desire – (or so the publicity said). And her superb breasts were half exposed by her evening frock. An ordinary man by now would be in a frenzy of passion – all the indications were that Antoine was left-handed.

There was a simple way to find out and it would be amusing if she disconcerted him. She laid her hand flat on his thigh, then slid it between them, about halfway up from his knees. His trousers were of an exceptionally fine material and she felt the nervous tremor that ran through his leg muscles at her touch.

There was another reason besides his coolness for Suzette to be displeased when he called for her at her apartment – he was in a white dinner-jacket. She had not expected that, she was in white herself. It was extremely annoying to lose the advantage of contrast – if she'd known he intended to wear a white jacket she would have worn black velvet.

In effect, she knew nothing about Antoine, for this evening was the first time they had met. The meeting was one of convenience pure and simple, nothing more. It had been arranged by Suzette's agent, dear fat red-nosed Emile, who seemed to transact all his business standing at zinc-topped bars. Emile was also Antoine's agent and he was trying to get him into movies. So he could be seen by all the right people, in the right surroundings, Emile had got a ticket to the premiere for him.

Or, rather, he had got a pair of tickets as it was out of the question for an actor with Antoine's looks and high aspirations to be seen in public without a beautiful woman gazing at him adoringly.

Antoine could have asked one of his many actress friends but fat Emile puffed and objected – and suggested he took the most beautiful woman he knew, one who had the added advantage of not wanting to be a film star herself and would not upstage him. So it was arranged that Suzette should go with him.

She heard Antoine exclaim softly in the dark as she smoothed her hand up the inside of his thigh. She considered the touch-test to be foolproof, he would react decisively, one way or the other, by the time her hand reached the join of his legs. It was of little consequence, his reaction, as she didn't especially want him. But his apparent indifference to her displeased her, she was determined to find out if her speculation was true.

She had her answer almost at once, for Antoine sighed faintly and moved his thighs apart on the cinema seat. Her hand reached the fork of his legs and her fingertips traced the outline of a bulge under the fine material of his trousers. He was already hard. This was another point of similarity with Vincent, apart from looks. Antoine also had the capability of instant hardness.

Nevertheless, he did not return the compliment. There

was no move to touch her while she explored with delicate fingertips the shape and size of the bulge that held her attention. Vanity plays an extraordinarily important role in men's emotions when this part of their body is in question and it was not just Vincent who entertained obsessive fancies. Suzette had known very few men who wouldn't be delighted to have some centimetres more than Providence had arranged, even the best-endowed of them.

The hard flesh in Antoine's trousers jerked to her touch. Not enormous, Suzette said to herself, but not small either – a good useful length and thickness. Too much was as bad as not enough. And evidently Antoine was not left-handed after all, he reacted in the usual way to being stroked by a woman's hand. In fact, he was more than ordinarily sensitive for he had become stiff the instant she put her hand on his thigh.

The reason for his previous indifference to her charms must be sought elsewhere. It was hardly a lack of confidence – there was no such creature as a shy actor. So perhaps he was in love with someone and had eyes for no other woman, not even one as desirable as Suzette. His male part had no such reservation – it grew hard without hesitation when she touched his thigh. Her curiosity was aroused.

'Do you want to see the rest of this movie?' she asked in a whisper, her hand sliding over his bulge affectionately.

'No . . .' he murmured, 'but we must be at the party afterwards, at Julien Brocq's, everybody will be there.'

'There will be plenty of time to get there,' Suzette assured him, squeezing his throbbing part between her fingers.

They made their way very quietly out of the darkened cinema, trying not to be seen or to disturb anyone. The policemen were still swaggering outside, though many of the fans were gone now they had seen the stars. The dementedly determined lingered on to wait for Gabin and Signoret to leave.

Antoine waved to a taxi. By some miracle the driver happened to notice him and pulled to the kerb.

The forlorn little band of fans raised a ragged cheer as the cab drove off with Suzette and Antoine in the back, waving with regal condescension. She didn't hear the address he gave to the driver, but when the taxi turned off the Champs-Elysées down to the Seine and over the Pont Alexandre III, it became obvious he lived on the Left Bank. Naturally, the Left Bank! Most people with artistic hopes and pretensions insisted on living there – as if the nearness of so many academies of learning would in some way breathe a certain authenticity into their work.

Antoine had an apartment not far from the river, it was halfway along the rue des Beaux-Arts. And throughout the taxi ride he was content to hold Suzette's hand in both his own, stroking it lightly, nuzzling her cheek, sighing faintly, breathing in her exotic perfume.

Suzette exercised no such restraint, she did not know if his uncertain ardour would last long enough to get to his apartment without assistance. She unbuttoned his white evening jacket and slipped a hand down the top of his trousers to clasp his stiff flesh. A delicate stroking kept it in a state of tension.

His apartment was up a flight of stairs. He unlocked the door and switched on the lights, took her hand and led her into the bedroom without hesitation. As indeed he should, she thought to herself, though he could hardly be described as ardent, judging by his passivity in the taxi.

The bedroom was large and pleasant, the bed was broad

and low, without headboard or footboard. It was a sort of divan, a platform for sleeping and making love on. What gave the room a character all its own was the huge gilt-framed mirror that almost covered one wall. The top of the frame almost touched the ceiling, the bottom was less than knee-high from the floor. How so huge a looking-glass had ever been carried into the room Suzette couldn't guess. She would have said it was impossible – yet here it was.

There was an antique look about the mirror, the style of the frame perhaps. For all Suzette knew it could have hung on that wall since the day the house was built, long ago. The thought was romantic – a rich man perhaps bought it for the bedroom of a *poule-de-luxe*! But more probably it was put there by Antoine and he rehearsed his movements and expressions in it before he appeared in the theatre.

He had left his white jacket unbuttoned when they got out of the taxi. Suzette stood close to him, kissed his mouth lightly while she reached down to unbuckle his belt and then slide the zip of his trousers down. She put a hand under his shirt, flat on the cool skin of his belly and stroked him. His arms crept round her waist, his hands lay on her bottom, gently caressing the cheeks through her thin frock and underwear.

'*Ah chérie,*' he murmured at the warm clasp of her hand around his stiff flesh. He seemed content to remain like that for as long as she would hold him. Suzette began to wonder if she had been mistaken about him after all. She murmured into his ear, a suggestion he should undress her.

He did it remarkably well. He removed her frock and then her flimsy brassiere with finesse. He kissed her breasts when he uncovered them, and flicked his tongue over their pink buds in a very competent sort of way, not exactly loving, but enough to send little tremors of pleasure through her.

He stroked her belly with a casual touch, that satin-skinned belly that had caused uncountable numbers of men at the Folies Bergère to sigh with desire and put their hands deep into their trouser pockets to touch their throbbing stiffness. He slid her ivory silk knickers down her legs.

Suzette's jet-black hair led her admirers to imagine she was as dark between the legs, that a shiny black thicket of curls would be revealed when they removed her underwear. In this they were wholly mistaken, the truth was more arousing even than the fantasy. Between her splendid thighs Suzette was shaven smooth and bare, a custom she acquired soon after she began to appear on stage very nearly naked,

The discovery of her nudity between the legs brought a little sigh from Antoine – a reaction at last! His fingers traced the length of the bare pink lips.

'How very graceful,' he murmured, 'a touch of refinement, how adorable, *chérie!*'

At last he did what was expected of him, he went down on one knee and kissed the delicious nectarine he had uncovered. Not a passionate kiss, Suzette noted, more a token of formal respect, as if he were kissing her hand! And while he was kneeling, he undid her suspender belt and slipped her silk stockings down.

Suzette was beginning to think she was in the wrong place at the wrong time. Antoine was still stiff – his upright part was poking out of his open trousers – but apart from that he seemed not to be excited at all by the sight of her naked body. It was ridiculous, didn't the idiot realise he was looking at the most beautiful woman he would ever see naked! What was wrong with the fool?

She pulled him to his feet by his ears, slightly exasperated and almost ready to put her clothes back on and go. But first she would make one last effort to rouse him to action. Quickly she stripped off his white jacket and his silk shirt, flicking a scarlet fingernail over his flat nipples, making him gasp.

When he was as naked as she was, she took his hand and tried to lead him to the waiting bed. But he murmured *Not yet* and turned her gently to face the enormous mirror on the wall.

'Look,' he said.

He stood close beside her now, his arm round her waist.

'We look well together, you and I, Suzette,' he said, and his free hand made a delighted little gesture at their reflections in the glass.

She could see how true it was, they were excellently matched. They were more or less the same height, they were equally long-necked and long-legged. But male and female, unambiguously so.

She cast a critical and admiring look at her own reflection, her sumptuous body, full beautiful breasts, smooth curved belly and superb thighs. The glass told her she was a marvellously desirable woman, as near to perfection as humanity permits. She turned her attention to Antoine, she looked at his reflection carefully, piece by piece.

He was slenderly built, no athlete, but well proportioned and attractive. His chest was broad and hardly hairy at all, just a small patch of brown curls. His belly was flat, his thighs long and strong, his male part pointed boldly upwards from between them. It was not over-long, not brutally thick, as some she had known, it was elegantly shaped, admirable for its purpose.

His hand moved delicately down her body to her belly, down to her thighs, his fingers touched the bare lips between and stroked them with warm fingertips.

'I shall kiss you here until you cry out in ecstasy,' he said coolly. *Yes!* she whispered, but he made no move to do so, instead his finger pressed carefully against the soft lips and slipped inside.

She thought he meant to caress her secret bud, but his finger stayed there without moving. Its firm presence alone was enough to excite her greatly and soon the fingertip became slippery with her arousal. His other hand was gliding lazily over the cheeks of her bottom, his warm palm smoothing over the satin flesh and sending tiny quivers of pleasure through her.

'Antoine!' she sighed in surrender and dreamily she thought *How delicately he touches me, he adores me after all!*

But adore her or not, Antoine certainly wasn't looking at her – he was staring into the big mirror, that was true, but he was observing the movements of his own hands in reflection. It was as if he still sat in a dark cinema, staring at the screen and the actions of lovers pictured on it. He was lost in wonder and in delight at what he saw; his mouth was open a little, to show gleaming white teeth.

In spite of the pleasure rippling through her body, Suzette realised that she alone was not Antoine's source of delight and inspiration. His gaze was fixed not just on her reflection, but on the *couple* shown in the mirror, himself and his own naked body as much as hers. What truly excited him was not Suzette's naked body, it was the sight of himself making love.

So, after all, you have more in common with Vincent than I saw at first Suzette thought *but you lack his daring.*

To observe himself in the act of caressing her beautiful body and to watch how his own body became more and more excited, his stiff part stretching upwards, jerking in nervous spasms – this was for Antoine a pleasure beyond imagination. His dark brown eyes reflected in the mirror were tender at the delicious sight of his own happiness.

Ah, egotist that you are! You actor! You little narcissist, Antoine! Suzette said to herself in realisation of his nature. She sighed as the fingers between her spread thighs started to move slowly and tantalisingly. She understood him now and she guessed how to exploit his nature for her own amusement.

She reached across his body to take hold of his upright part. He gasped to see, there in the mirror, her long scarlet-nailed fingers clasping his stiff flesh, sliding up and down.

'Suzette!' he sighed. 'Oh Suzette!'

His handsome face was flushed and his chest heaved. The sight of his own body being stroked had so intense an effect on him that Suzette decided, in a moment of inspiration, to see just how far it could be taken before Antoine realised his nature was being observed. She moved slowly backwards towards the big mirror on the wall, drawing him along with her by the grip of her hand on his throbbing stiffness.

She placed the bare cheeks of her bottom against the glass and leaned backwards a little, until her shoulder blades rested on it and she felt its coolness against her flesh. To Antoine it seemed that she and her reflection had merged together into one, he had been staring over her shoulder as she moved back to the mirror and he had seen the image of her graceful bare back coming closer, until image and flesh touched.

Her feet were well apart, his hands were on her rounded

hips and her fingers guided him to the smooth-shaven lips between her thighs. A quick lunge of his loins drove his hard flesh into her: a strong thrust that penetrated her to the marrow. And the sensations she experienced at that long thrust were astounding. She felt herself being overwhelmed and she surrendered totally to him.

His belly was pressed close to hers. She felt his stiff flesh sliding in and out. She sighed *Oh yes, yes, yes* . . .

Antoine thrust hard and fast, he made her belly convulse and quake with pleasure. Before she could dissolve into ecstasy he changed to a long and slow rhythm that made her belly throb and quiver delicately, then after some moments he again thrust hard and sharp for a while, then tenderly once more. He was changing rhythm at will, arousing her furiously by his capriciousness.

And all the time he stared not at her beautiful face so close to his own, nor into her eyes to enjoy her delight. He stared over her bare shoulder, at his own face in the mirror. Antoine was making love to himself and never knew it.

Suzette was wide open to him, her thighs apart, her long legs splayed, her belly pressed against his to let him penetrate as deep as he could. Through the intense tremors of pleasure that racked her she could hear herself sighing and laughing and gasping as the climactic moment approached ever closer.

She felt the cheeks of her bottom squirm on the smooth glass of the mirror, the wildness of the sensations that gripped her were at the point of becoming insupportable.

'Antoine, Antoine!' she moaned. 'More, more, more!'

His hands tightened their grasp on her hips. His breath was ragged in his throat. In another instant Suzette was swept into a shuddering ecstasy more violent than she could have guessed. Ferocious spasms of delight raced through her body, making her twist and jerk against the glass behind her. She shrieked and sobbed, her eyes and mouth wide open, her shaking belly close up to Antoine's to drive his hardness impossibly deep into her.

'*Oh you, you!*' he sighed in deep adoration at his moment of crisis, his cheeks dimpling in delight.

The hot gush of his passion flung her into fresh paroxysms of sensation and his words at the supreme moment went unheard and unconsidered. Which was fortunate for both those concerned, for this tender moment was in all truth pure comedy. Suzette might well have asked herself to whom the adoring but ambiguous exclamation was addressed. Did he mean her, or himself, by that *you*?

Perhaps she would not have found it difficult to answer the question. Then she would have shrugged and dismissed it as of no importance, Antoine had served his purpose and pleasured her marvellously well, though a trifle oddly. In different mood she would not have been quite so understanding, but would ask him outright if his love-making had really been directed to her, to see his confusion.

But she had not heard his moaned *Oh you!* though she knew his gaze had been fixed on himself and not on her while he was sliding in and out of her beautiful body – a privilege for which other men less self-absorbed than Antoine would fight each other. But what of it? Her mood was one of great content, she had no wish to disconcert him. At least, not this time.

When they had recovered a little they sat side by side on the bed and drank a glass of cognac to restore their strength. And before long Suzette was eager and ready to resume their curious love-making, to see what new discoveries were to be made about this actor. She lay full length on the bed to show her body to good advantage, her upthrust breasts and round belly, her satin thighs and the long bare pink lips between.

But Antoine was of a different mind. His self-esteem had been wonderfully boosted by the entr'acte against the mirror, he was ready to conquer the world – or at least the world of film-acting.

'We must dress and go,' he said, bending to kiss her thigh in a gesture of finality. 'The party will be in full swing by now, everyone of importance will be there.'

A GIFT
FOR SUZETTE

Halfway through her second song, Suzette saw a familiar face in her audience. It was a man sitting alone – a circumstance highly unusual in a night club – a distinguished-looking man. He was at a table right on the edge of the tiny dance floor. She couldn't think of his name, or when or where, but she was quite sure she had met him somewhere before. His interest in her was very evident.

In the normal course of events one of the regular club girls, blonde Zoe or big-bosomed Regine, would slither into a chair at the table of a man who came in alone. Just to drink with him and to make sure he wasn't lonely, of course. If he wished to continue her acquaintance in more private surroundings, that was for him to decide. The middle-aged Monsieur in the grey suit was alone by choice, he had declined the club's regular company, and there was only one possible reason – he was waiting for someone.

Suzette had never troubled to ask Regine or Zoe how much they charged as a fee for closer friendship but she was sure it would be high. Both were good-looking and this was an exclusive club, not a noisy *café-dansant* in Pigalle where the girls started by asking too much and could be argued down to half.

The club where Suzette was engaged to sing that month was in the Avenue George-Cinq. Needless to say, only those with plenty of money could afford its prices – those who frequented it were celebrities and some of them were even important.

Mostly they stopped talking when Suzette sang. Men who hadn't put a hand up their girlfriend's skirt to caress a stockinged thigh were now moved to do so. Suzette's songs had that effect, they were sophisticated and tender, sensual and chic.

The one she was singing was a favourite of hers called '*Palais Garnier*'. It told of a young and beautiful woman descending from her shiny black limousine at the Opera. She was wearing a Dior ballgown and a kilo of diamonds. Her lover was a tall handsome man in tails and top hat, he was at her side, taking her arm to assist her to the Grand Tier Box reserved for them.

All Suzette's songs had settings of *grand luxe*, circumstances familiar to her listeners. She sang for women who wore diamonds and rubies, emeralds and sapphires, who wore full-length sable coats. She sang for men who could buy these expensive tokens of esteem for their girlfriends. Men of importance who arrived in long limousines with chauffeurs in uniform and lived in vast and expensive apartments that overlooked the Bois de Boulogne, tended by swarms of servants. At least, they gave the impression they lived in that style. Suzette's songs flattered their pride and they adored her for it.

They also adored her, of course, because she was beautiful and they wanted to take her to bed. In the ordinary course of events this could be expected to make their girlfriends jealous, but Suzette managed to avoid that. The girlfriends applauded her songs because they too were flattered, they all took it for granted her songs were about themselves.

Yes, that's me in the limousine wearing the Dior gown and the diamond necklace, each one of them thought as she listened, *I'm so very sexy the men are panting to kiss my hand. She is clever this chanteuse, she understands me, how I live.*

Suzette's songs were uniquely her own. The words were written by Michel Radiguet, a twenty-year-old student who fell hopelessly in love with her the first time he saw her. That was in a cheap and sordid bar up in Montmartre, on the night of her debut as a singer, when she was singing the old favourites everyone knew like '*J'attendrai*' and '*La vie en rose*'. He was a poet, this Michel and a romantic too. He had abandoned his studies without a second thought to devote himself to writing poems for Suzette.

She liked Michel's verses and she had persuaded another friend to set them to music for her. This was Jacques-Charles Delise, bar pianist **and drunk**, the man who had taught her to sing when she was a nude show-girl at the Folies Bergère. Naturally, he too was in love with her.

She remembered now where she had met the man sitting alone at a table near the dance floor. It was at the film premiere where she had been taken by Antoine Ducasse. He was someone important in film-making and he had been waiting in the foyer to welcome the stars when they arrived.

He had suggested to Suzette that he would like to discuss her career in movies – in a whisper, of course, as his wife was standing next to him at the time. Needless to say, Suzette had not believed a word of it, the only career he envisaged for her involved lying on her back with her legs apart, she was sure of that.

It was his party after the premiere, that's how important he was. But he hadn't tried to approach her again when she arrived there with Antoine, after their diversion in front of the big mirror. It was possible Madame had been keeping a close eye on him with so many young women about, ever so slightly drunk and eager to interest him in their talents. As actresses, perhaps.

His name was Brocq, Suzette remembered now, Julien Brocq. *Ring me at my office*, he had said that evening in the cinema foyer, but she had not troubled herself to do so.

Monsieur Brocq seemed especially to like the Opera song – it had a very catchy tune Jacques-Charles had provided. It was original, of course, but the type of originality that evoked half-memories of other tunes. It was Jacques-Charles' talent, using well-known material in a different way. Suzette had learned much from him and she owed him a debt of gratitude she meant eventually to repay.

Would she have let him make love to her during their singing lessons together? It had never been established, maybe because he had never really tried.

For the best part of a year she had gone for regular singing lessons to Jacques-Charles' dingy room in Montmartre, never less than twice a week, sometimes more often. At first, when she did not know him well, she paid him for lessons. And when it became evident that he had fallen in love with her to the extreme edge of desperation, she decided to reward him otherwise. At the end of each lesson, she stripped naked and let him look his fill at her beautiful body.

Suzette was without qualms about being seen naked. Her career on stage at the Folies Bergère had rid her of inhibitions – she had learned to cope with hot male eyes staring at her body, her bare *nichons*, her superb thighs, her delicious belly . . . she was there on stage to be admired.

And that was all Jacques-Charles ever dared do – admire her! Some weakness in his character held him back from touching her. Perhaps it was the fact that she was so young and beautiful, so perfect, and he was much older, lanky and balding, a failure in his own estimation and not often sober after five in the afternoon.

He was so frantically in love with Suzette he did not believe himself worthy enough to embrace her. He looked, he admired, he sighed, he wrote music for her, he drank himself unconscious on cheap *pastis* thinking about her, he dreamed of her. He thought about her when he lay on top of other women and pretended that he was making love to her. But when she stripped naked for him, he dared not push her legs apart and pierce her with his male part.

In the very exclusive night club on the Avenue George-Cinq, Suzette leaned gracefully against the small white grand piano, her raven-black hair shining in an overhead spotlight. She was wearing matt black chiffon, cut low in front to display the deep cleavage between her breasts and contrasting delightfully with her skin. She preferred black for public appearances, she thought it added a touch of elegance to her performance.

The three-man band played marvellously well for her. Without even trying she had captivated their hearts, all three of them, and they responded perfectly. When the last ripple of applause for '*Palais Garnier*' had faded away, they paused for only an instant before beginning her next song.

This one was called '*Avenue Foch*' and was about a woman walking her fluffy little white dog, pausing at a lamppost and under a tree. Her lover was waiting eagerly for her, he would make love to her all afternoon. He was young and handsome. And rich.

Yes, the women listening said silently to themselves, *a young and handsome lover who adores me, yes, that is what I want, she is absolutely right, this singer*.

For the most part, the men who brought them to the club were not very handsome and not young. In truth, some were decidedly middle-aged. Or even older. It is a universally observed fact that men in their twenties choose girlfriends of their own age, and men between thirty and forty choose girlfriends who are younger, twenty-five at the most.

There is an arithmetic progression involved here. It confirms that, in proportion to the increase in a man's age, his girlfriends become younger, so that by the time he reaches his late fifties or early sixties, he chooses a girlfriend eighteen years old.

Nevertheless, though the facts are as they are, uncomfortable perhaps, a little make-believe can be very consoling. The women hearing Suzette's song could dream that the ardent young man in the luxurious apartment was waiting for each of them alone. And as for the men who heard Suzette, they naturally saw themselves as the lover, awaiting the beautiful woman with the little dog. They knew they deserved no less because they were important.

Suzette smiled at Julien Brocq, sitting there in the club on his own, a bottle of champagne in a silver bucket on his table. He was distinguished in appearance, no one would deny that, and he was important in movie-making and he evidently had a great deal of money. But she had no wish to be a film star, she wanted to be a great cabaret singer, like Mistinguett only better.

She saved for last the song she liked best. It had become

the most popular song in her repertoire, it was the very first poem that Michel wrote about her, when he was still a student.

> *In the Place Vendôme, a jewellery shop,*
> *A bracelet of ice and fire,*
> *Diamonds cut square, heart's-blood rubies,*
> *The tall man at her side*
> *Clasps it on her wrist,*
> *His love, he says, will last as long*

When she had finished, everyone applauded and Julien Brocq rose to his feet to give her a standing ovation. Naturally, it would have been impolite not to acknowledge him after that and so she paused at his table. At once she realised that he was even more important than she had imagined – while he was kissing her hand a waiter held a chair for her, while another rushed over with a fresh bottle of vintage champagne and poured her a glass.

'Mademoiselle Bernard,' said Brocq suavely, 'what a pleasure to meet you again. I am sure you have forgotten me, I am Julien Brocq. We met at the film premiere.'

'I assure you I have not forgotten you,' said Suzette, who of course had entirely forgotten him until a moment or two ago.

He told her how immensely impressed he was by her singing, by the charm of her songs, by the elegance of her delivery. And it went without saying, he was careful to say, that she was by far the most beautiful woman present in the club. In fact, now that he gave it more consideration, he was certain she was the most beautiful woman he had met for a very long time – and he passed his days in the company of world-famous film stars. Surely she must realise that a career in movies lay in readiness for her?

Suzette gave him her smile that made men go weak at the knees and told him she did not want to be a movie star, she wanted to be a famous singer.

'But you can be both!' he exclaimed and his hand touched her hand lightly. 'There is no one like you, I know this, it is my profession to know such things. You can become an international star, believe me, with proper guidance and good friends to help you achieve your true potential.'

Even in the darkness of the night club, his eyes glowed with passionate intensity while he told her these flattering things. But Suzette had learned her childhood lessons about men and the emotions that drove them – and not in a comfortable and secure family *milieu* but in the poverty and squalor and brutality of the rue Belleville. There the men were unshaven, they smelled of garlic and sweat, they were always out of work and usually half-drunk on cheap wine.

They promised girls as young as thirteen they would care for them, they sweet-talked them into standing with their backs against a wall and their clothes up round their belly. They beat their women, these types, they back-handed them across the face, they threw them down on their backs across the musty bed they shared, they took their brief pleasure and told the women they were lucky to have a strong man to look after them!

Belleville or Champs-Elysées, men are the same everywhere and have the same desires. Roughneck or company director, they all wish to get their hand up a pretty girl's skirt, all the world knows that. Julien Brocq was more accomplished, he approached matters with skill and calm. He had achieved as useful an understanding of women as any man is ever likely to. That said, his ambition was to get his hand into Suzette's knickers. She knew this, and Julien knew that she knew it.

'I adore all your songs,' he said, 'and in particular the one about the Place Vendôme and the jewellery shop. I find the tune especially pleasing. And the sentiment is amusing.'

So saying, he amazed Suzette by taking from his pocket a flat square leather case and opened it to reveal a bracelet of sparkling diamonds set in platinum. At least she assumed it was platinum because it was too pale to be gold and she believed it improbable anyone would set diamonds in silver. The glittering stones were small, it was true, but undeniably diamonds.

Julien took the bracelet from its velvet-lined box, smiled at Suzette and clasped it around her wrist.

'*Voilà!*' he said. 'The next time you sing that song you will be wearing the bracelet it speaks of.'

He leaned over to kiss Suzette on the cheek, very lightly. He is charming, she told herself, he understands how to do things. She returned his kiss, her perfect lips touching his cheek for a moment. A trace of her expensively subtle perfume reached his senses and caused him to sigh in silent delight.

'It is beautiful,' she said, twisting her wrist so the stones caught the little light there was in the club and shone bright, 'but it is impossible for me to accept it.'

This took Julien by surprise. He had been confident that his completely open and frank approach was sure to succeed. Who ever heard of a night-club *chanteuse* refusing a genuine diamond bracelet? He was struck silent for a moment while Suzette took it off and put it back in the jeweller's box. There was a name on the lid in gold script, he truly had bought the bracelet at a shop opposite the

Hotel Ritz in the Place Vendôme.

He recovered from his surprise and explained very pleasantly that Suzette should not misunderstand his gesture, this was not a blatant attempt to insinuate himself into her affections – no no no! It was a mark of his respect and also a small token of his absolute conviction she would shortly be a star, it was his way of paying homage to her success to come.

While he was saying all this he put the bracelet back on her wrist and kissed her hand so very charmingly she relented a little, just enough to ask him why he thought she could become a film star. His answer was lengthy and flattering, he spoke of her beauty of face and figure, he mentioned her delightful way of putting across her lovely little songs, her evident talent, her this and her that . . .

Suzette was only half-listening to him. There was a smile of encouragement on her face, the sort of expression that made men go to extraordinary lengths to please her. But in truth she was looking at Julien with careful eyes, her shrewd mind at work as she tried to reach a conclusion about him.

The diamond bracelet was very beautiful. Apart from that, to wear it would be a sign of early success. She would like to own it very much. But she knew what the price was. There was a decision to be made.

She guessed Julien Brocq's age at fifty. He was a heavy-set man, thick-shouldered and solid. His hair was dark brown with not a trace of grey, from which she concluded it was tinted. A clear sign of vanity, that, which was a good sign in Suzette's view, vanity being an excellent motive for a man to preserve the ardour of youth.

His grey suit was from a very good hand, his blue-striped tie was of silk and his shirt looked to be hand-sewn specially for him. He had a heavy gold wristwatch, no doubt the finest the diligent Swiss could provide and a thick gold wedding-ring. A man of substance – a man of significance. And influence. An interesting face, in a heavy sort of way, thick eyebrows, a determined chin.

The decision had made itself. Julien looked as if he would be a strong and vigorous lover, that was the most important thing. The diamond bracelet was a trinket, a part of the arrangement, but not the essence of it. If he had been sixty, baldheaded, ugly and dull, not even a shopful of bracelets would have persuaded Suzette to give serious consideration to his unspoken proposal. But as a man he was acceptable.

Naturally, accepting his overture by taking his bracelet was nothing to do with the type of arrangement blonde Zoe and plump-bosomed Regine entered into. For those two it was a question of making a living, they had no particular talents beyond parting their legs. At that they were very skilled, or so they claimed. Over a drink at the bar, in relaxed woman-talk when there were no club members about, Regine maintained it was worth a fortune of anybody's money to play with either of her *nichons* – with a discount of thirty per cent to handle the pair of them. And a price to be negotiated for the use of her other *agréablements*.

Zoe was less well-endowed up top and sneered cheerfully when Regine tried to claim an advantage. *Quality, not quantity*, said she, and she would explain how by exercise she had strengthened and trained her inner muscles so expertly that she could do it all for any *Jean*, however drunk or tired or feeble. All she had to do was lie on top of him, slot him into her *belle chose* and give him a squeeze massage with her belly muscles.

33

For that a *Jean* would pay a lot of money, she said, her pride in her ability very evident. And when she'd done it to them two or three times in a row without getting off, a bonus was always forthcoming.

Amusing, yes, but this had nothing at all to do with Suzette or her decision about Julien. She was not in the same business as Zoe and Regine, she was a singer, that made a difference. No one with any glimmering of intelligence could fail to see that.

Not that it played any important part in her decision, but no doubt there would be other trinkets from Julien after they were good friends. Tributes to her desirability, naturally, and very appropriate tributes, from a man who was to be so favoured. And if he wished, later, to discuss a possible career in movies for her, there was no harm in listening to him.

She still did not believe her future lay in film-making. That was for actors proud of their profile and for women with little but their face and figure to recommend them. And from what Suzette knew, it took ages to become a star, months of sitting about on film sets while technicians fiddled with lights and cameras and argued. Then nothing would happen for a long time until the studio released the film. Then would come a long spell of waiting until they were ready to make another film.

Suzette was not by nature patient enough for all that. It was her determination to make her own career and not be dependent upon others, particularly not on men. She had known all there was to know about men and their ways by the time she was sixteen. They were unreliable. But it would be interesting to hear what Julien had to say about appearing in a movie for him.

Not that she knew what Julien did in the world of

cinema. Did he direct movies or did he produce them? Did he design them? Or write scripts for them? No, that seemed too unimportant for a man of Julien's bearing. Was he a backer, a financier?

When the bottle of vintage champagne was finished at about two in the morning, Julien suggested they should leave. He knew she was going with him and he glowed with pride and pleasure to think what lay ahead. Suzette nodded and excused herself for a moment to collect her belongings, so she said, from the dressing-room. Julien would have been greatly surprised if he had been able to accompany her. Pleasantly surprised, of course.

The truth was that Suzette sang bare-bottomed. Every evening before she left the cramped little dressing-room, after making up her flawless face, checking there were no runs in her black silk stockings and running a brush over her glossy jet-black hair, her very last action before she went out to sing with the band was to hoist up her elegant frock and take off her knickers.

She did this because she was convinced it brought good luck. Her little superstition dated back to the night of her debut as a singer, at a sordid cellar-bar in a part of Montmartre that tourists never see. Drunks and layabouts, tarts and their pimps were her first audience – an audience far from appreciative of her singing. She had almost despaired and given up her ambition to be a singer.

But a turning-point came in her life when she went up the cellar steps and out into the semi-deserted street for a brief respite in the night air. Whereupon an unknown young man in a roll-top sweater followed her to kiss her hand and praise her singing – and he took her knickers down in a doorway. To be sure, it was a miserable and desolate place, more suitable for down-and-outs to sleep in than for an act of passion. There was a metal sign on the wall that said *Defense d'uriner*.

Nevertheless, this stranger's adoration revitalised Suzette and she recovered her will to succeed – she returned to the squalid cellar to sing with new enthusiasm.

The young man in the sweater was a student and he had fallen in love with Suzette. He was Michel Radiguet, the poet who had turned up one day and thrust his verses into her hand. Since that night in Montmartre Suzette's path had been upwards. In a year she had become an established *chanteuse*, sought-after and moderately well-paid. And wearing no knickers when she sang had brought good fortune, she was sure of it.

Julien Brocq had not tried to put a hand up her clothes while they were chatting about diamond bracelets and other symbols of regard and affection. Perhaps he was too polite a man or too respectful to indulge in this act of male superiority, although Suzette doubted that. Men were men – they all wanted to do the same thing. And thank the Good God for that! It may be he felt their acquaintance needed to develop a little further before he permitted himself such acts of intimate friendship.

If he had been minded to slip a hand under her black chiffon frock, to caress her bare thigh above her stocking-top . . . well, why not, now she had accepted the terms of his arrangement? She liked to have her thighs stroked by distinguished-looking men. And if his perfectly manicured hand had strayed a little higher yet, then he would have become aware of an interesting state of affairs – an exciting state of affairs. It was his loss that he hadn't been adventurous.

In the privacy of her dressing-room Suzette raised her frock and stepped into her black silk knickers. They were elegant in the extreme, and they concealed remarkably little of her. As it should be, she thought, glancing at herself in the full-length mirror, we must make use of the advantages we have been given.

Julien had a taxi waiting for him outside by the kerb in the Avenue George-Cinq and Henri, the club doorman, standing by with his hand out for a tip. Suzette got in and turned to Julien to tell him her address – she preferred to entertain new friends in her own apartment rather than go off into the unknown with them. In fact she insisted on it, until they were better acquainted. And there was no reason for them to demur, the girlfriend with whom she shared the apartment was away on tour.

But Julien had already instructed the cabbie where to take them.

'The Hotel Ritz?' said Suzette, her perfect eyebrows rising a little. 'You are staying there, Julien?'

'I have a permanent suite there,' he said, 'for meetings and business, you understand. And if dinners with stars or foreign distributors or others go on too late, I stay overnight to save myself the journey home. Do you like the Ritz?'

He didn't wait for an answer, he assumed that everyone was in complete agreement with him about everything he said. And if by some extraordinary mischance it proved otherwise, their opinion could be ignored. He chatted on about the advantages of keeping a suite on a permanent basis and Suzette concluded that he was not spending his own money – the suite was paid for by whatever company he owned or partly owned or worked for. It was possible the bracelet had been paid for in the same manner.

The taxi sped down the Avenue des Champs-Elysées and it was a relief to Suzette when Julien put his arm round her and kissed her properly. She still recalled with a feeling of mild outrage her chaste taxi journey with Antoine Ducasse, who had only held her hand. But Julien was no soft narcissist of an actor, he was a man accustomed to action, to decisions, to enforcing his will many times a day. His free hand was stroking Suzette's breasts while he kissed her, he was making an appreciative little noise in his throat.

At least, she thought, her hand cupping the bulge she could feel in his trousers, he won't have to be coaxed to make love, this one. He will need no reflection of himself in a mirror to arouse him. It is *my* body he will adore, as he should.

The suite was suitably magnificent, furnished in elegant nineteenth century style. In the sitting-room Julien took Suzette into his arms, held her tightly against his body and kissed her. After a few seconds she felt his stiff part pressing against her belly, through their clothes, a strong steady pressure, promising well for his competence as a lover.

Suzette was tall, it was necessary for a show-girl, and Julien was of average height for a man. When they stood in an embrace their eyes were on the same level and their mouths met in the kiss without any need for him to bend his head. And as the kiss went on, his hands slipped down her long back, gliding delicately on the chiffon of her frock, to stroke the superbly rounded cheeks of her bottom.

Men could be impossibly impetuous about love-making, she said to herself, wriggling her bottom sensuously under his stroking. Left to their own foolish devices, they were capable of bending you over an armchair or sitting you on a polished table or even pulling you down on the floor! When all the time a comfortable bed was available!

But then, men were by nature absurd creatures. Even the

best of them needed to be steered in the right direction by a woman. Suzette caressed the nape of Julien's neck and the back of his head and murmured in his ear a suggestion.

'Yes,' he said breathlessly, 'through here,' and with an arm round her waist he led her into an impressive bedroom. The bed itself was very large, it was formed of a beautifully patterned wood, highly polished.

He threw off his jacket and tie and addressed himself with an eager attention to the delicious task of undressing Suzette. He removed her frock, her shoes and her silk stockings. He placed at least a score of kisses on each part of her body he uncovered and two or three times that number on her bare breasts. Suzette found it most enjoyable and she let him direct proceedings in his own way this first time together. Later on he would find she was by no means a passive partner in bed, she had her own little caprices to satisfy, her own thoughts on amusement. But for now, Julien was King.

She was standing by the magnificent bed, naked except for her little silk knickers and her diamond bracelet. That was going to stay on her wrist forever, she had decided, it was her trophy. Julien was on his knees on the oriental carpet, his big hands clasping the cheeks of her bottom through the thin silk. He was kissing her bare belly and thrusting his wet tongue into her dimple of a belly button.

'Take them off, *chéri*,' she murmured, wanting to feel his hot mouth kiss between her thighs.

'Yes!' he said, a boyish eagerness in his voice.

But he didn't hook his fingers into the waistband to slip the knickers down her superb thighs. Nothing so very ordinary! He pressed his face close to her belly and with his teeth he began to tear at the flimsy little garment. His hands stayed where they were – tightly clenched on her bottom.

Suzette's knickers were edged prettily with lace at waist and leg. Julien had the lace banding of a leg between his teeth and was worrying at it, he shook his head from side to side like a hunting dog with a hare, ripping at it most cruelly.

'*Ah, mon Dieu!*' she exclaimed in pleasant shock, twining her fingers into the curly brown hair above his ears. He was fierce and strong. She heard a thin tearing sound as the silk ripped and she felt the fine material part across her belly.

'Julien!' she cried, and from his violence she was warm and moist between the thighs, her knees were trembling, her hold on his hair was insistent.

He was a wolf savaging a helpless fawn. His fingernails sank into the tender flesh of her bottom. He was growling furiously deep down in his throat as his teeth bit at the ruined silk and ripped it again, till he laid bare her palpitating belly all up to the waistband.

Suzette had surrendered to his brutality, she was deliciously moist and trembling. She stood with her thighs apart for him – those beautiful long thighs for which thousands had sighed and grown hard in their trousers in her days at the Folies Bergère. She heard Julien gasp as he saw the tender lips between her thighs, smooth-shaven and bare.

He did what was expected of him, he pressed his mouth to that eminently kissable spot and paid due homage to her beauty with his tongue. She felt the torn remnants of silk sliding down her legs. She was naked now, except for the glittering bracelet.

He stood up to rip off all his clothes. Suzette saw him naked for the first time – his thick-set muscular body was covered in a pelt of brown hair, from his shoulders down to his belly and his thighs. She stared at him, surprised by his hairiness, then she smiled when her gaze dropped below his waist. A stiff shaft of flesh stood at a sharp angle from a thick and curly bush of dark-brown hair. There was not even a hint of grey, obviously he went to the trouble of tinting the lower curls as well as those on his head.

She lay on the bed waiting for him, her limbs spread out on the pale blue satin bedspread, her enchanting body displayed for his delight. He scrambled on to the bed and covered her at once with his bulk, his weight supported on his elbows while he settled his hairy belly on hers. She waited almost breathlessly for the feel of his stiffness sliding up into her. But not yet, his face was at her breasts, his tongue was licking their warm fleshiness, his lips sucking at their firm buds.

Suzette spread her legs wide and drew them up, opening herself wide for him. His hand was between their bodies, he was guiding the purple head of his stiff part to where she wanted it to be. *Yes* . . . she murmured and she held her breath when his hard flesh slid into her. She could feel her body opening itself to take him in.

He gave a long push and the entire length slipped up into her and she sighed *Yes* again. The part of her mind still capable of rational thought insisted she didn't truly like big and brutal men, hairy apes who crushed her beneath their weight . . . but she was immensely aroused by what Julien had done to her, was doing to her . . . there was no place for rational thought as the moment of orgasm approached!

'Ah, Suzette!' he moaned. She wrapped her legs round him and gripped his waist hard with her thighs. He thrust into her with strong remorseless strokes, his heavy rump thumping up and down in a rhythm as relentless as the

41

pistons of a steam locomotive.

She felt the hairiness of his chest and belly rubbing against her tender flesh, the rough kiss of his hairiness against the insides of her thighs as she gripped him between them. She was overcome by his maleness and she submitted absolutely to him. Her body was afire with wild sensation, her mind ablaze with hunger to reach the furthest limit of sexual delight.

The curls between his thighs were harsh and bristly, the dark brown nest from which arose his hard and penetrating flesh. She sighed to feel the rough touch of his thicket against the soft bareness between her legs, it aroused her to a frenzy.

Oh, what a man! the thought ran through her pleasure-drugged mind. *Ah, what a beast! he is a wild animal from a forest! What is he doing to me? He will drive me insane! It is marvellous, this that he is doing to me! I want it to go on forever! He's made me so wet and hot – oh my God, I can feel it starting to happen! Yes, this is it – my belly is being turned inside out – ah, so violent . . . so exquisite . . . yes, yes, yes!*

She panted and twisted under him, her fingernails scoring his hairy back as she felt her climax arriving. His own excitement was intense, he responded to the writhing of the beautiful body beneath him with faster and more powerful thrusts, ravaging her belly with all his might. And a moment later they both reached the crisis in a great flurry of cries and groans, shudders and throbbing spasms, that seemed to go on and on forever.

ANTOINE AND
AN ACTRESS

To claim that Leonie Laplace was Antoine's mistress would be to mislead. A man so utterly self-absorbed as Antoine Ducasse had no great need for devotion from one particular woman, nor could he spare the time necessary to keep a woman content. Yet Leonie had been the most important and influential person in his life since he first met her. And that was almost ten years ago, when he was a struggling young beginner in the theatre.

Leonie was very famous then, of course, one of the celebrated actresses of the Paris stage. And, naturally, she was much older than Antoine, very nearly twenty years older if it is necessary to be precise in so delicate a matter. As all the world knows, she had divorced her third husband and vowed in public never to put herself at the mercy of another man.

She was tall and slender, her hair a rich dark chestnut tint, elegant and with a touch of hauteur in her manner, as was to be expected of so important a person. To Antoine she seemed almost a goddess, a great lady of the theatre, respected and admired. He fell in love with her at first sight. Or at least, he would have done so if he had the capacity to fall in love with anyone other than himself.

And Madame Laplace smiled graciously at this

ravishingly handsome young man when he was introduced to her, she talked to him for a few moments and she took to him. It was all very well to declare to the newspapers that she had suffered too much at the hands of cruel, insensitive and stupid men and would never allow herself to fall in love again. But, on the other hand, her self-esteem required her to have a suitable man on his knees at her feet. It was expected of her in her elevated position, her public demanded it. And her friends would gossip unkindly about her *fading charms* if she was seen too much alone.

Yet her years of experience in many beds had convinced Leonie that lovers were tricky creatures. A middle-aged man might well be tender and understanding, but that was of no use to her. She must have a *young* lover, it was necessary for her public image. Through her art and by means of three marriages Leonie was very well-to-do. It went without saying that young men had no money, anyone she admitted to her intimate friendship would expect her to be generous to him. That was not to her liking at all.

It was easy for her to guess Antoine's secret nature for she too had more than a touch of self-love – who in the theatre didn't? It seemed to her that he could be transformed without any great difficulty into the type of lover she required.

She suggested he might call upon her the next afternoon when she would be happy to give him whatever advice she could to assist his struggling career on the stage. Nineteen-year-old Antoine was totally overwhelmed, he couldn't believe his good fortune! The great Leonie Laplace had recognised his talent and was she taking an interest in him!

The next afternoon revealed how very intimate an interest she intended to take. This surprised him at first, but he accepted it as his right. *I am, after all,* he said to himself, *extremely good-looking, as well as highly talented.*

At the time Antoine lived in a cheap and not very comfortable room in a small hotel. Leonie had an apartment on the Left Bank in a modern building on the Boulevard du Montparnasse, not far from the Carrefour Vavin and within easy strolling distance of the intellectual haunts where she liked to be seen drinking and eating and talking, *Le Dome* and *La Coupole*. And in fact it was on the terrace of *Le Dome* that Antoine first met her. There she was with an entourage of theatrical friends one afternoon when he arrived alone for a cup of coffee, all he could afford.

He recognised the great Leonie Laplace at once, as who would not. She was at the very top of the profession he was at the bottom of. That close-cut cap of rich chestnut hair, her trade-mark, so to speak! That long intelligent face, that thrilling voice from two tables away! The great Leonie!

A beneficent Fate had even arranged that one of the attentive entourage sitting with Madame Laplace was known very slightly to Antoine. He was a director named Lanette he had auditioned for once without getting the part.

L'audace, et encore de l'audace, et toujours de l'audace! as that ill-fated politician Georges Danton declaimed on some long forgotten revolutionary occasion or other. Perhaps audacity was not a large part of Antoine's nature but this was too great an opportunity to miss. In a moment he was on his feet and across the terrace to shake the surprised Lanette's hand with all the warmth of an old and trusted friend.

Leonie's eye fell on the handsome young stranger, she smiled graciously at him. And since it was clear that Lanette couldn't remember his name, Antoine introduced himself and expressed his unsurpassed admiration for Madame Laplace, and so on and so on.

The next afternoon found him in her elegant apartment, in a drawing-room done in Second Empire style. In this, as in other ways, Leonie was a traditionalist. She had, after all, launched her career on the enduring classics of the theatre, the glories of French literature. Namely, the tragic plays of Corneille and Racine, those dramas which every cultured person holds in high esteem and which no sensible person after leaving school ever wants to be troubled with again.

Madame Laplace kindly invited Antoine to sit beside her on a yellow striped sofa with spindly legs. They talked for half an hour, or rather she talked and he listened, merely making tiny sounds of agreement or appreciation of her intelligence and wit from time to time. When Leonie saw she had him completely under her spell, she advanced the proceedings skilfully. Antoine was so delighted to be in her company, and to be taken seriously by her, that he was unaware exactly when she took his hand. Or how she had got so very close to him on the sofa without apparently moving at all.

When she kissed him, he accepted the situation and kissed her gently back. The kisses continued, between Leonie's flattering murmur of how very good-looking he was, what fine eyes he had!

To be courted in this way by a great lady of the theatre was so utterly overwhelming that Antoine was convinced he had died and was in paradise. Her thin hand was inside his jacket, caressing his chest, and little shivers of delight ran through him.

Second Empire style furniture was not made to be sprawled on. Ladies and gentlemen of that era sat straight-back-upright and conversed politely; exchanges on any more intimate topics were reserved for the privacy and comfort of the bedchamber. Social customs have changed – here was Antoine lolling languidly, head on the padded sofa back, his legs sprawling over a red and gold Aubusson carpet. Leonie bent over him and he stared up at her with intense eyes.

'I think I love you,' he said softly.

She put her hand flat on his grey-trousered thigh and drew it slowly upwards, up to where a heavy stiffness within caused the thin material to bulge out.

'But of course you do,' she said with a little smile, and her fingertips caressed his bulge.

She felt the hard flesh under the cloth jerk, an uncontrolled and uncontrollable throb, a movement that spoke more eloquently than words ever could of the intensity of his passion.

His mouth opened a little but he said nothing more. He sighed in gentle disbelief when she opened his trousers wide to slip a hand in and take hold of his hot and jumping flesh.

Naturally, Leonie had no intention of making love here in her drawing-room, not when her comfortable bedroom was only a step or two away. She was merely making certain this handsome young stranger was in an appropriately passionate mood before she led him to the bedside and bestowed upon him the inestimable favour of allowing him to remove her clothes and kiss her naked body.

But in this she underestimated the devastating effect she had on Antoine. He was so aroused he didn't last a minute. As soon as she held his jumping maleness in her hand – it was enough to bring on his crisis! There was no need for caresses, there was no time. His flesh had a will all of its own.

His awestruck admiration of the great actress together with the touch of her hand on his throbbing pride, this did for him. His eyes turned opaque, he gasped, and his passion spurted into her hand.

'Yes, you certainly do love me,' she said, her smile thin and surprised, 'but are you always so absurdly fast?'

His face reddened at the implied rebuke. He sat up and wiped his wet belly with his shirt, then took Leonie's hand, the hand that had inflicted so unexpected an ecstasy on him, and kissed it with respect.

He told her he was overwhelmed by her attentions to him, and he reeled out the usual nonsense men do at inconvenient moments of this type – he had lost control of himself in the turbulent and divine emotions her graciousness had inspired in his heart – he would respond from this moment on to her amiability with a due sense of worshipful obligation and passionate duty. And so on.

There was a half-smile on Leonie's face as she listened, even a touch of cynicism if the whole truth were told. Had it been any other man who had presumed to take advantage of her well-known good nature she would not hesitate to kick him downstairs – her apartment being one floor up. But she felt there was something special about Antoine so she listened intently to his words. And to the unspoken words behind the words, those being more important.

Leonie adored being praised, being set on a tall pedestal and worshipped as a superior being, particularly by good-looking young men. Most especially when they indicated their respect by kissing her feet, as this one now proceeded to do, down on his knees on her Aubusson carpet.

He was even more submissive than she, marvellous as

she was, had the right to expect! He kissed her feet, he took her high-heeled shoes off and kissed her long narrow feet, her toes, her arch, her heel, her instep, all through her silk stockings.

This was extremely gratifying to Leonie's self-esteem but it did not go far towards inducing satisfaction in other ways. She had to urge him on to higher things from his display of abject submission.

After the foot-kissing and various declarations by Antoine of his undying devotion to her and his endless regard, and other assurances in this vein of high-flown nonsense, Leonie gave him her most gracious smile, stood up and drew him to his feet, and led him into her bedroom.

Leonie's bedroom was not so much a place to sleep as a shrine to love-making. The bed was almost an altar to her divinity, a huge four-poster with thick gold-inlaid columns that supported a gilt-encrusted wooden canopy with swags of pale gold silk all round and golden cords with big tassels. To make love to Leonie Laplace on that bed was an act of worship – the fortunate lover allowed to mount her on it left next day in a state of grace.

Or so it should have been. But human nature being as contrary as it is, matters did not always turn out to Leonie's complete satisfaction. It had been known for lovers to take the fullest advantage of her most intimate favours and go away grinning, in foolish male pride of achievement, not realising what an honour had been extended to them. These ingrates and insensitives were not invited back, needless to say.

Neither were those whose sensual efforts on her behalf could go no further than one single penetration of her graceful body. They were sent packing very smartly. There was no such thing as a banquet with only one course.

Leonie expected to be served an interesting hors-d'oeuvre, then a substantial main course that was satisfying yet not sating, followed by a light and tasteful dessert course.

And if the man of the moment was up to it, a small savoury to round off the banquet, a little *croque-monsieur*, perhaps.

If time was pressing and the lover was of particular interest to her, Leonie would from time to time content herself with two courses, a snack-meal, as it were. But she regarded this as not very good for her, a mere stopgap, certainly not to be thought of as her regular diet.

Alas, not many get what they want in this imperfect world and sometimes when they do get what they want they find they do not like it. Leonie's third and final husband, Matthieu Le Vey, was a man of large appetite and strength, he could provide her with three courses nightly, four or even five if he was in the right mood. But unfortunately, as it was his nature to be violent in bed, he was a veritable cannibal in this respect.

His sensual brutality was so new to Leonie that she found it enchanting before they were married, when they were simply lovers. She thought it hugely arousing to be gripped tight and used like a doll with convenient apertures. Matthieu's rough handling threw her into repeated ecstasies. He did not restrict his banquet to four courses, he was no gourmet but he was certainly a glutton, he went on and on until he was sated, then rolled over and fell instantly asleep. After a night with him Leonie slept till noon the next day and woke up feeling wrung-out like a dish-rag, but very, very contented.

Then they married and he carried on in exactly the same way. This ought not to have surprised her – he had been her lover for six months – but it did. They went to Egypt for their honeymoon – Leonie wished to see those sites of antiquity where Cleopatra the imperious and tragic queen had played out her high destiny. And it began well enough, Matthieu never missed a night. Leonie awoke each day as happy as a dewy-eyed eighteen-year old bride on her first morning. But three weeks of this brought her to the edge of total exhaustion. Never in her wildest dreams had it occurred to her it was possible for a man to wear her out in bed!

Back in Paris it became a matter of fending Matthieu off – at least on alternate nights. In her mirror Leonie could see dark shadows under her eyes, she had lost four kilos in weight and she walked a little bowlegged. There was nothing in the world she wanted more than to go to bed alone and sleep for a week.

Matthieu was killing her off with his brutal love. Yet he was astonished when this was pointed out to him. He was hurt, then angry. He demanded to be told whether or not a husband had any natural rights. His own understanding on this matter was clear. He insisted these rights must not be withheld from him, not for a single night. Or even an afternoon, if he so desired. Leonie claimed the right of refusal and kept her legs close together. Matthieu eventually became surly. He had to be got rid of.

Other men had disappointed Leonie in other ways. But that did not discourage her, except briefly. She was always ready to try again, her expectations remained high. And she was conscious of a certain potential in Antoine Ducasse, it might be possible to mould him into the lover she wanted. That is to say, attentive and adoring, properly grateful and anxious to please her, never demanding of her time or attention except when it suited her.

While Antoine was gaping at his first sight of her

enchanting bedroom, Leonie sat him on the side of the canopied bed with his trousers round his ankles, his jacket and tie discarded on the floor. She stood in front of him and removed her primrose silk blouse and the brassiere beneath, letting him see her small pear-shaped breasts. Naturally, he sighed deeply when he saw how very elegant they were, but he did not reach out to touch them as any other man would.

It was as she thought, he would be passive and it was for her to control what happened between them. If she could control him as she wished, she would have an extraordinarily handsome young lover to show off to her friends and use as she pleased in the bedroom. This would suit her well. She pulled her knickers down to expose the curls between her slender thighs, wanting him to admire the rich chestnut tint.

Antoine babbled broken little words of praise, enraptured by what he saw, but his hands remained flat on the bed at either side of him. Leonie moved in closer until her silk-stockinged legs touched his knees. His upstanding part throbbed, thrusting out from his underwear, and Leonie began to wonder if the sight of her lean pale belly and chestnut tuft might cause it to spurt again! That would be too ridiculous. Once she could just bring herself to forgive, twice would be an impossible insult!

To prevent any such emotional catastrophe, she bent her knees and moved in closer yet, straddling Antoine's thighs, lowering herself slowly – until the moist lips between her legs touched his hard and out-thrust flesh. He gasped aloud when she slid it into her, her bejewelled fingers guiding the purple head into its destination. She reached down to take his wrists and place his hands on the cheeks of her bare bottom.

'Kiss me, Antoine,' she said firmly, bowing her neck to bring her mouth to his. And during that kiss, fierce and demanding on her part, tremulous and willing on his, she completed her slow descent to sit across his thighs and so force his stiffness all the way up into her belly.

'Leonie . . .' he murmured, daring to use her name for the first time, 'Leonie . . . *je t'adore* . . .'

'Naturally,' she exclaimed, her long intelligent face flushed with emotion as sensations of delight spread through her body. She bounced up and down on his lap, using him for her pleasure, then heard him cry out in sudden climax. She felt him explode wetly inside her and redoubled her efforts.

While he spurted into her shaking belly, her tempo increased and her lunging became more furious. She knew he had finished but he was not yet limp and soft, his stiff flesh was still capable of gratifying her. Her pear-shaped little breasts bobbed up and down to the rhythm of her movement, her sliding thrust him into her, five, ten, twenty times more. Then the moment arrived! She bent her neck and bit Antoine's bare shoulder, gave a long melodious wail and dissolved into ecstasy.

That was their first meeting, more than nine years ago. Since then much had changed. Antoine was now twenty-eight and well-established in the acting profession, thanks mainly to Leonie's advice and influence. He was not a leading actor, perhaps, but that would come with time. His good looks had improved, if that was at all possible. He dressed well now, he was more sure of himself.

Leonie Laplace was still at the pinnacle of her profession at forty-six, or so the reference books said, but the age of actresses is at best a matter of conjecture. In one respect nothing had changed at all, Antoine remained her devoted attendant, to all intents and purposes her official lover though that was hardly the relationship between them. She was seen in public with him, at first nights, at important parties, in pictures in magazines and newspapers.

When the mood took her, rarely more than two or three times a week now she was older, she summoned Antoine to her apartment, took him into the bedroom and undressed him. It was always that way round, never at Antoine's instigation. Years of familiarity had improved his staying power, he no longer spurted into her hand the instant she clasped his hard part.

In fact, on the second and third time, he was able to contain himself until Leonie achieved her climax, as long as she didn't take *too* long about it.

Ten days after his attendance at the film premiere there was a message for Antoine – to the effect that Madame Laplace wished to see him at five that afternoon. He thought it odd she didn't phone him herself, the message was brought up to him by the concierge of the building on the rue des Beaux-Arts where he now resided. Someone had telephoned on behalf of Madame, said the concierge, and asked her to pass on the message.

Her errand done, she stood waiting for Antoine to give her a few francs as reward for dragging her well-fed asthmatical body up a flight of stairs to convey Madame's wishes.

He arrived at Leonie's apartment punctually at five – she became distraught if anyone kept her waiting, though her own record of being on time was notoriously imperfect. He rang and after a delay the door swung open. What happened next had the dimensions of a hideous nightmare.

Leonie was dressed in black, a lustreless black unrelieved by jewellery of any kind, nor any touch of colour. Her face seemed whiter than any living human face could be and her short chestnut hair was somehow pulled back tightly and bound. Before Antoine could utter a word to the terrifying apparition that confronted him, she seized him by his necktie and dragged him inside the apartment, slammed the door hard and slapped his face with both hands in turn. Several times.

'But ... but ... but ...' he stammered, throwing up his hands to protect his face from her repeated blows.

'Ah, you raise your hand to me!' she screeched, her face was so suffused with rage and hatred that he hardly recognised her as the woman he had known for so long.

'Yes, strike me, knock me down and trample on my defenceless body!' she cried. 'Break my bones, bruise my flesh as you have bruised my heart, you ingrate!'

She swung open-handed at his head again and he backed off warily – in his mind was the thought that Leonie had gone raving mad. He retreated before her onslaught until he found himself in the drawing-room, backing across it until his legs were against one of her Second Empire armchairs. She struck at his face again and he fell backwards into the chair.

Instantly she was at his throat like a tiger, her hands round his neck in a death grip, her knee grinding painfully into the vulnerable soft parts between his legs.

She called him a great many unpleasant names as her fingernails dug into the soft flesh of his neck and alarmed him greatly. He begged her to stop, she retaliated with a long bitter harangue about betrayal, perfidy and deception.

Some of the phrases she hurled at him had a familiar ring. It occurred to Antoine that she was playing a part from one of the dramas that had made her famous, she was being Phedre or Medea or Cleopatra or some other tragic heroine. The vital word was *tragic*, this intense emotion would surely end in doom and death if allowed to continue. His own death, unless he could get her hands off his throat soon!

With sickening clarity he understood the reason for her rage. On the sofa lay the latest edition of a famous news magazine, a publication everyone with any claim to significance must read. It lay as if it had been discarded in fury, open and face-up, and a page had been torn right across. Antoine had seen the magazine the day before, it had big photographs of Jean Gabin and Simone Signoret arriving for the film premiere.

There were shots of some of the other important people, stars and just-good-friends accompanying them to the premiere. And a picture of Antoine and Suzette Bernard. Not because either she or he were stars, that was understood, but what cameraman could resist taking Suzette's photo when she wore a low-cut frock? And what picture editor could resist printing it? When all was said, she was much sexier than most of the starlets present.

'Leonie!' Antoine gasped. 'Let me speak – I can explain!'

'Speak?' she said furiously. 'Speak what, lies? Why did you take that woman to the premiere? Who is she?'

'Nobody – a nightclub *chanteuse*. Emile wanted me to take her, I never met her before then, I swear it!'

'Lies, lies! Why should your agent, drunk and incompetent as he is, suggest you take a nobody to this function when he knows you could have taken me!'

Naturally, that was not a question Antoine had any intention of answering. To even hint that a young unknown singer might be more beautiful or glamorous than the great Leonie Laplace would be to invite instant annihilation.

'Emile did explain it to me,' he said, 'but I'm not certain I understood him properly. He is almost your keenest admirer, of course, but it was something about film people not appreciating serious talent. Your artistry is too far over their head, their shallow little minds are more impressed by low-cut dresses and half-naked breasts. I let Emile persuade me to take this woman with me because I rely on his judgment. Was I wrong?'

'They took *me* seriously when I appeared in a movie,' Leonie said icily.

In his nervous haste to defend himself Antoine had forgotten for a moment she had starred in a movie, ten or more years ago. It was the screen version of a classic French novel, of course. Leonie could not be tempted away from the stage for anything less than the best. As Madame Bovary she had committed adultery with high passion, drunk the arsenic and died most effectively in remorseful agony. Intelligent critics pronounced the film a resounding success, though the queues outside the cinemas where it was shown were somewhat short.

'No one could fail to give you the respect and admiration you deserve!' said Antoine hurriedly. 'But as you know, a premiere has no connection at all with high art. It is only a publicity occasion, all smiles and press photographs.'

'At the premiere of *my* film the Minister of Culture sat at my side,' said she, crushing Antoine with her words. He thought it best to say nothing.

'And after the premiere,' she continued relentlessly, 'there was a party? You took this woman to it? What is her name?'

'Mademoiselle Bernard,' he said, sounding as off-hand as he could manage in such trying circumstances. 'It was necessary to go to Brocq's party. Emile insisted I show myself there, it was necessary for my career.'

'And after the party, you took this slut to your apartment?' Leonie hissed, her tone very dangerous, her fingernails digging hard into the flesh of Antoine's throat.

'I gave her a lift to her apartment,' he said. He knew he was walking on a knife-edge.

'Ha! You went in with her! She took her clothes off and you threw her on the bed! Confess it, you animal, you betrayed my love and trust with this ... this hat-check girl!'

'No, no, no!' Antoine gasped. 'It isn't true, Leonie. I said goodnight to her on the pavement. I went on to my own apartment alone, I got into bed alone and slept all night alone!'

And, indeed, he was telling the truth. He had taken Suzette to Brocq's party after making love to her naked against the mirror on his bedroom wall. At about two in the morning he dropped her off by taxi at her door and headed for the Left Bank alone.

Evidently some trace of sincerity in his voice got through to Leonie. She loosened her murderous grip on his throat a little and stared down into his frightened eyes.

'Can I believe this?' she demanded.

'It is the simple truth, I swear it! You must surely know by now it is you I adore, Leonie, no one else.'

'Men are deceivers,' she declared, her face doubtful, 'no one understands that better than I – the way I have suffered at the hands of brutal men has taught me a bitter lesson. My trust is betrayed, I am mocked and derided by those I give my heart to.'

Antoine had enough sense to know that whatever it was she had given him in the past years, it was not her heart. But did that matter, when she had given him so much else? What did he want with her heart, anyway?

'Leonie, *je t'adore*,' he said huskily, '*je t'adore, chérie.*'

He was, after all, a moderately capable actor. Leonie's eyes softened, her face lost the lines of anger and outrage.

'Truly?' she murmured, taking her hands away from his throat to stroke his hair. 'Perhaps you do.'

'Only touch me, and you will understand,' he cajoled her. He took her hand and eased it under his waistband, down into his trousers, where his male part had been stiff ever since she had first smacked his face. To his infinite relief, she removed her knee from between his legs. She sat on his lap and put the palm of her hand where the knee had been, clasping him between the thighs. She kissed his mouth, her wet tongue flicking over his parted lips.

'I forgive you, Antoine. For all the grief and heartbreak you have caused me, I forgive you.'

He murmured his devotion and gratitude, his adoration and his respectful homage, while her knowing fingers stroked the length of his male part, urging it to grow even harder and thicker. He moaned slightly in pleasure when, with a slashing gesture of her hand, she ripped open his trousers. He moaned again when he felt her fingernails glide over his stiff flesh.

'This nonsense of wanting to become a film actor,' she said, 'I want you to drop it, Antoine. Your career lies on the stage, film acting will ruin your talent. You said it yourself not two minutes ago, film people do not understand acting, they do not take it seriously. All that they look for is a handsome face or a big bosom. Such people are not worthy of our consideration.'

She pushed him with a hand against his chest and he fell back in the armchair, his legs spread wide, his quivering part standing up stiff and ready. He had survived her murderous jealousy with no worse injury than scratches on his throat, he was very happy now to let her make use of his body to comfort herself and attain a suitable mood to take him out to dinner somewhere expensive.

Leonie slid to her knees on the carpet, her head down between his thighs. Her wet tongue was ravishing him in the manner her experience had shown he found irresistible.

As Antoine's excitement grew he writhed, as if already in the throes of ecstasy, his head rolling from side to side along the chair back. He was panting hard, his hands were clenched tight. Then he straightened his arms and reached down until he touched Leonie's face with a delicacy that thrilled her.

His fingertips played over her flushed cheeks and the corners of her mouth, while she plied her tongue skilfully.

She paused in her ministrations to take his hand and suck his middle finger into her mouth. Her breath was hot on his hand, her tongue velvet and slippery.

In another moment he would be gasping in climactic sensation, he knew, he could feel the sensual pressure deep in his belly soaring to an unsurpassable level. He stared blindly up at the drawing-room ceiling, all his senses submerged into the single sense of *feeling*. He could hear nothing, see nothing, his whole body had become immensely sensitive and Leonie's least touch sent waves of delight through him.

He felt her clasp his leaping part in her hand again and he sighed to feel her palm was wet to the touch, she had licked it to intensify his sensation. His loins jerked up from the chair cushion, he had reached the very limit of endurance.

'Now!' he moaned. 'Leonie – now!'

'You don't escape me that easily,' she said, though her words were lost on him.

She squeezed him so tightly his eyes bulged and became round and his threatened convulsion was arrested. She grasped him behind the knees with both hands and hauled him off the chair. He slid heavily to the floor and Leonie had him helpless on his back on her handsome carpet.

She was up on her knees, arms crossed to hoist her dull black frock up her body and over her head. Antoine was so far lost in sensation that he failed to observe she wore nothing under the frock, no stockings, no underwear, nothing. Her elegant breasts were bare, so too her slender thighs and her lean belly; her triangle of chestnut curls was proudly shown.

If he had seen this, he might have asked himself why. Was her drab frock a type of mourning for what she had called her grief and heartbreak at his infidelity with Suzette? Was it a way to make him feel guilty? The answer was obviously *yes*. Leonie was being excessively dramatic.

But no underwear? If Antoine had been capable at that moment of logical thought, he would not have been able to remember any previous occasion when she had worn nothing under her frock. So what could be her purpose now? Was it possible that Leonie had decided the outcome of their stormy meeting *before* he arrived at her apartment to be greeted with blows and abuse? Had she determined how far to revile him before she forgave him?

The logic of the situation was simplicity itself. When Leonie put on that ghastly black frock, she took off her knickers. There was only one possible reason for that and it was purest comedy. It was to make sure, when the correct moment arrived, there was no obstacle in the way of receiving Antoine.

Antoine moaned as he waited while she pulled her frock

over her head and threw it aside. His eyes stared blindly upwards at her drawing-room ceiling. He had no idea what she was doing. He was desperate for release from the overwhelming sensations that her caresses had aroused in him.

In two seconds more she was astride him, her thin hand down between her thighs to part the wet lips there while she steered him inside. Then he knew what she meant to do to him, she meant to ride him till she achieved total gratification. He responded at once as he always did for her. With a nervous thrust he was up inside her belly, gasping and crying out to feel his moment of climax arrive in urgent delight.

He panted and babbled in release. He jerked and throbbed from head to toe as he spurted his passion into Leonie's enveloping flesh. Three times, four, five, six, he squealed and convulsed under her, then with a last spasmodic heave he collapsed.

Leonie's hands were on his shoulders gripping tight. She rode him fast, her eyes wide open, staring down at his handsome face with an expression that might be described as calculating. Then at last she reached her peak and screamed shrilly.

When she was calm again it was as if there had never been any face-smacking or angry words. The tempest was over, the sun was shining in a bright blue sky.

'Now I know you love me,' she murmured, spacing her words out between rapid little kisses on Antoine's closed eyes.

'*Je t'adore*,' he sighed and his arms slid round her waist as she lay down flat on him, her belly on his, her pear-shaped breasts flattened on his chest.

'And because you do,' she went on lovingly, 'I know

you will stop trying to get into films – it causes me so much grief.'

'Yes, *chérie*,' Antoine sighed, '*je t'adore.*'

In the afterglow of passion fulfilled he was not listening to her words. He was waiting for an appropriate moment to suggest they went for dinner to the Brasserie Lipp that evening. Later, of course, after they had been to bed for a couple of hours for Leonie to complete her satisfaction on his willing body. Almost everyone who mattered would be there from nine o'clock to dine.

Leonie always paid when they went out together and he liked this because he could choose the most expensive things on the menu. But while poor Antoine was thinking of food and letting Leonie kiss his face in her possessive way, he had no idea what he was agreeing to.

GABY RETURNS
WITH A BOYFRIEND

The friend with whom Suzette shared the apartment in the rue de Rome was Gabrielle Demaine, a dancer. She was exactly as old as Suzette, tall and long-legged. They were about same height, but their figures were different – Suzette was sumptuously fleshed, Gaby had the supple body of one who high-kicks twice-nightly on stage for a living.

But the most striking difference was their colouring, Suzette was raven black of hair, Gaby's was silvery blonde both above and below – as her boyfriends discovered to their delight.

Gaby's dance troupe had had a long run at the Cabaret-Mouchard, a tourist type of establishment on the Grands Boulevards. During this time they had presented themselves as South American rumba dancers, Hungarian gipsy dancers, Lebanese exotic dancers, Cossack sword dancers, even as English Bluebell dancers.

The dancing remained much the same, of course, however it was named. The music was different, though not much, and regardless of whichever nationality they were supposed to represent, the girls high-kicked to show off their legs and bottoms, like a French Can-Can. Though the costumes were different, all were designed to display a perfect view of thighs and belly buttons.

The dancers were not as naked as the show-girls at the Folies Bergère. Gaby and her colleagues were performers after all, not merely a living back-drop. But customers of the Cabaret-Mouchard expected to see attractive young female bodies for their money, dancing or not, and so that is what they were shown.

When that engagement came to an end, the troupe went on tour: Amiens, Bordeaux, Clermont-Ferrand, Dieppe, Marseilles, Nantes, Nice, Reims, Toulouse, Lyon – in fact anywhere a theatre and audience could be found for young long-legged Parisian dancers wearing exotic costumes that concealed little of their pretty bodies.

When Gaby came back to Paris at the end of the tour she had a new boyfriend with her. They had met in Lyon, the final stop on the tour. His name was Tristan Villette and he was very well-to-do. And young, which was a big advantage. In general, young men had no money and older men who had were not very exciting in bed, with some notable exceptions as Suzette explained to Gaby. For example a certain film mogul, an important person named Julien Brocq.

At this point she flashed her diamond bracelet to demonstrate what she meant. And Gaby retaliated by flicking back her blonde hair with both hands to show off her new diamond ear-studs. The two women laughed, hugged each other and kissed cheeks.

This Tristan was a Parisian. He had gone to visit a cousin in Lyon, he said – there was some difficulty at home, it appeared, that had driven him to seek a temporary refuge. He had not been too specific in describing the annoyances of his daily life to Gaby, not at first. Later on, when he trusted her, he explained his problems to her in great detail.

She found it amusing and this made him sulk.

He wore a stylish brown suit and a striped bow-tie when he came to the apartment and met Suzette. He was twenty-four or twenty-five, slender of build, averagely good-looking and he had charming manners. He didn't do anything in particular for a living – there was no need, his family had money. When he had first seen Gaby dancing, he was so overcome by tender emotion for her that he sent huge armfuls of flowers to her backstage, and he bribed the manager to arrange an introduction in a bar near the theatre.

In short, he made himself so very pleasant that she went with him to a hotel. What happened that night was bizarrely amusing. Next morning he was so enchanted with her that he moved out of his cousin's apartment and into the hotel to stay – and begged Gaby to join him there for the rest of her time in Lyon. Though she didn't know what to make of his performance in bed she was delighted to have the opportunity to live in one of the best hotels, instead of the cheap theatrical establishment the dance-troupe had to put up with.

At the end of the tour Tristan decided to accompany Gaby back to Paris, family annoyances or not. He gave every appearance of being devastatingly in love with Gaby. Perhaps he would suggest a permanent arrangement, that was the thought in Suzette's mind when she heard the extent of Tristan's devotion.

'Perhaps,' said Gaby, shaking her head, her pale blonde hair floating lightly, 'but the truth is that he is quite mad.'

The two women were talking over breakfast of *café au lait* and sweet rolls with apricot preserve. Whether they slept alone or brought a boyfriend back to the apartment neither got up before eleven and they never went out before midday. Suzette wore a white silk dressing-gown, a gift from Julien; Gaby was in a kimono of pale pink with a mauve chrysanthemum embroidered on the breast, a present from Tristan.

'How is he mad?' Suzette asked. 'He seemed polite enough.'

'The thing is this,' said Gaby, 'I know it sounds ridiculous, but he can only make love properly in public. All the nights we spent in a hotel room, it took hours to make him go stiff. Even then he couldn't manage much.'

'Get rid of him,' Suzette said at once. 'Men like that are no use to anyone, whether they buy you presents or not.'

'But,' said Gaby, 'in public he's a different man. He met me every night at the stage-door after the performance, to take me to dinner in the nicest restaurants. And afterwards – *mon Dieu!* After a stroll along the river embankment in the dark he'd have me with my back against a wall three times in half an hour. In the daytime, *oh la la!* The things he made me do! In parks and up alleys, afternoons in the cinema. And in the hotel.'

'You said he was no good in the hotel,' Suzette reminded her, a tiny frown on her superb forehead.

'No good in bed in the hotel room, I said. He'd lie there all limp and useless, while I was crawling stark naked all over him to rouse his interest. One night we went back to the hotel after he'd made love to me a couple of times up against a tree in the square near the theatre. Going up the big staircase to our room he got the urge again, there on the first landing. Before I knew what was going on, he'd got me over the banister, staring down into the hotel lobby below, bare-bottomed with my clothes round my waist.'

'No! Was there anybody about?'

'It was after midnight and the lobby was empty, except for a night porter dozing behind his counter. I was terrified someone would come in late and look up – and see what Tristan was doing to me.'

Terrified or not, the truth was that Gaby had not resisted in any way the poorly timed advances of her strange new boyfriend. On the contrary, she had slid her feet apart on the thick carpet to let him feel between her thighs. He had taken her knickers off the first time he made love to her that evening, under a plane tree, and put them in his pocket. Gaby was proud of her bottom, the cheeks were small and taut, beautifully rounded. She loved having them stroked, she was very well inclined towards men who praised the elegance of her bottom.

He touched the soft lips between her thighs for only a moment – they were already loose and open to the touch after the repeated episode under the tree. He moved in very close behind her, she put her arms flat on the broad polished banister and braced herself on well-spread legs.

In another moment he had his trousers open and presented his stiffness to her awaiting flesh – there was no uncertainty, no inconvenient limpness about him tonight! He pushed in till his loins were pressed against her bare bottom and wound his arms about her waist to hold her while he rode fast and hard. And in spite of her nervousness about being discovered, it took little enough to bring on her sexual crisis.

Her silver-blonde head jerked up at the climactic moment, her eyes stared down the stair well and she tried not to shriek as Tristan spurted hotly into her. But the sensations were strong, the pleasure too fierce. Her faint cry went echoing down to the lobby and disturbed the sleeping night porter. The man stirred in his chair and looked around in a puzzled way, but fortunately not upwards.

By then Tristan had pulled out wetly and flipped her clothes down. He took her hand and hurried her into the room they were sharing, grinning broadly at his success.

'After that,' said Gaby, 'he had me over the banisters every night when we got back to the hotel, even when he'd already had me two or three times round the town in the open air. I didn't complain, although it wasn't the most comfortable place to make love, lying over a hard wooden banister. And he wanted to do it again in the early mornings, most days. He'd wake me about six, carry me out on the landing and drape me over the banister!'

'What a time to wake up!' said Suzette. 'I'd be furious!'

'At that time of day I'm too sleepy to lose my temper,' Gaby said with a smile of remembered pleasure. 'I just let it happen – there I was, stark naked, and Tristan in his pyjamas standing behind me and thumping away. After which he'd carry me back to bed and let me sleep till eleven or twelve.'

'And you never got caught?'

'Once,' Gaby confessed, the faintest pink blush touching her cheek. 'A chambermaid with a mop and bucket found us at it one morning. She let out a scream that must have woken everybody in the hotel, Tristan immediately started to squeal – and went off inside me like a bomb!'

'It is obvious what excites him,' Suzette concluded. 'The fear of being seen stiffens his resolve. You are right, *chérie*, he's insane.'

'No doubt of that,' Gaby sighed, 'but nicely insane. I rushed back into our room while he calmed the chambermaid and gave her a colossal bribe to say she'd screamed because she saw a mouse. Then after lunch he bought me these gorgeous diamond ear-studs, to console me for the shock I'd suffered, he said.'

'You seem to attract the wrong type of man, I can't think why – this one sounds even worse than that pervert Lucien you went with before he left Paris with the police after him,' Suzette said with a shrug.

She knew how scatterbrained her dear friend Gaby was – and always had been – and always would be. Sometimes she did things which were foolish and even infuriating, but what of it? That was part of her charm.

'Lucien was a very charming man,' Gaby said with a smile, 'he was kind and generous. And what is a little perversity between friends? At least making love never becomes boring. And as for dear Tristan, he too is charming. And generous. He is much more cultivated than Lucien. I like him.'

'Evidently. Have you asked why he can only make love where he can be discovered at any moment and mocked? For most men this would be a fearful thought that would keep them limp and unable to do anything. Has this Tristan always been this way?'

'No, something unfortunate happened to give him this complex, only a year or two ago. Before that he was as normal as any other man, he says.'

'Normal as any other man!' said Suzette with mild derision. 'That is to claim very little, they are all slightly warped in different ways. What was this unfortunate event?'

'He was making love to his fiancée and her mother came in and caught them right in the middle of it. The shock to his nervous system was so profound that he has never completely recovered. Ordinary love-making leaves him limp – the danger of possible discovery excites him. Isn't that odd?'

'A fiancée?' said Suzette. 'The more I hear of this man the less I trust him.'

To say that Tristan had undergone a most distressing shock at being found on top of his young fiancée by her mother sounds as if it was a comic event, laughable and not to be taken seriously. It does nothing to explain why the effect on him was so utterly catastrophic. For that, a little more background is required.

Tristan had become engaged to be married very young – he was only twenty years old at the time. This was with the blessing of both his parents and also with their urging. They were serious-minded people, Monsieur and Madame Villette. Their private view was that their youngest son was a little too handsome and much too flighty for his own good.

Evidently he needed the anchor of a wife and a family to keep him steady and sensible. The mother of the young lady he became engaged to was also of a mind that early marriage would benefit her daughter, a pretty eighteen-year-old who had alarmed her mother by showing signs of having a mind of her own.

Tristan loved Lucile Champlain passionately. She was a brunette with hair the colour of sandalwood and small round breasts. As Lucile loved him with an equal fervour it seemed that all was for the best in the best of all possible worlds. But, naturally, nothing is ever that perfect. Madame Champlain was a widow, her husband had perished in the war, and for that reason or another she held staunch moral views.

She herself had been untouched by any male hand, her body and mind were pure and virginal when she had married Monsieur Champlain twenty years before. A kiss on the cheek was the most that he was permitted before they married. Madame Champlain was firmly resolved that Lucile also should go virgin to her marriage bed.

Needless to say, it was too late for that. Tristan was young, vigorous and hot-blooded. He had had his hand up Lucile's clothes the second time they met and she had surrendered herself entirely to him when they had known each other for a week. Which apparently was long enough for the pair of them to decide they were in love, desperately and eternally.

If it were left to them to arrange their affairs, they would have trotted round to the Hotel de Ville for the Mayor to marry them that afternoon, then go to bed together. Naturally, things are always more complicated than that, even lovers are required to comply with various social arrangements.

Madame Champlain was pleased when Tristan declared his intent to marry her daughter, he was of a good family and well provided for. But she insisted that things should be done in proper order and at a respectable pace. They must be engaged for six months, there was so much to be arranged, so many members of the family to be told. And so on, and so on.

Which was all very well and ought to have caused the lovers no great annoyance. Except that Madame Champlain redoubled her vigilance over Lucile. It seems she had been warned by a friend of similar views to her own that, in the deplorable collapse of moral standards since the war, engaged couples assumed all the privileges of marriage. Unless prevented – for their own good, of course! How shameful if dear Lucile went to the altar with the swell of pregnancy visible under her wedding-dress! What would the parish priest say to that!

As a result of all this, it became very difficult for Tristan to be alone with Lucile long enough even to kiss her and stroke her breasts for a moment. And as for anything more, the bliss they were both dying for every hour of the day was almost impossible to arrange. There were sighs and frowns, meaningful glances and deep frustration, snatched kisses, a quick feel of her breasts, and Tristan would go home by Metro with his male part stiff and lonely in his trousers.

But there came an evening when something unexpected happened to change this unsatisfactory state of affairs. It was Lucile's Saint's day, a Church festival her religiously inclined mother regarded as worthy of celebration. Tristan was invited to dine *chez Champlain*. To insinuate himself into Madame's good graces he took with him four bottles of excellent wine.

The meal was superb, the wine a great success, and Madame drank a glass or two with pleasure. In effect, she drank more than she knew, Tristan keeping her glass well-filled. By the end of the meal three of the four bottles were empty. In the sitting-room after dinner, Madame, who had consumed as much wine as the two others together, insisted they take a little glass of cognac.

As might be expected, after a while Madame Champlain started to doze, her head on the back of her armchair and her eye-lids slowly descending, her mouth just a little open. The two lovers were sitting side by side on the sofa facing her, half a metre of space between them.

As Madame's watchfulness become ever laxer, they moved on the sofa toward each other, they murmured words of love and desire, they leaned close until their thighs brushed lightly.

Although Tristan had deliberately planned this

opportunity to embrace his beloved, he was a little hesitant at first. But all seemed well. With a nervous glance or two at the dozing mother, he slipped his hand under Lucile's skirt and let it rest on her thigh, just above the knee. She smiled at him, a most charming little smile that encouraged him to go further. Another glance at Madame Champlain and he slid his hand up higher, moving his palm gently over the silk stocking until it rested on the warm bare flesh between stockings and underwear.

'*Chéri, chéri,*' she murmured as she slowly moved her feet apart on the floor to part her thighs for him.

Tristan's fingers found their way with ease into the open leg of her knickers, past the little edging of lace and up into the warmth of her groin. She sighed at the touch, in another moment he had found her bush of soft curls.

'Lucile,' he sighed faintly, 'come outside with me.'

'Shh . . .' she whispered, 'if we move she will wake up . . .'

Tristan's fingertips were stroking the tenderness between her parted thighs. His cheek touched her cheek, his mouth was close to her ear, the tip of his tongue probed gently into it for an instant and he began to murmur *Lucile, je t'adore, je t'adore* . . . over and over again. Banal words, of course, but appropriate to the situation. Only a complete idiot makes great speeches to a girl when he has his hand up her knickers.

Tristan was far from being a fool. While he was murmuring his incantation to still Lucile's fears and arouse her, his middle finger probed into her moist warmth to caress her little bud so very gently that she could almost think the wing of a brightly coloured butterfly was touching her.

More than two weeks had passed since the last time they

had been able to enjoy the touch of each other's body. And that had been a hasty affair. They had been to the Luxembourg Gardens, Madame Champlain with them to make sure they didn't lie down upon the grass together and do something she didn't approve of. On their return to the Champlain apartment, Madame had paused to have words with the concierge, a person with whom she had a long-standing and incomprehensible quarrel.

Lucile and Tristan had continued on up the stairs, leaving her to give the concierge a piece of her mind. The same thought struck them both at the same instant, they hurried into the apartment, closed the door – and at once he had her against the wall with his mouth on hers in a passionate kiss, his hand under her skirt.

They knew they had only a moment before Madame came hurrying up to make sure nothing unseemly was taking place. And in those very few moments they delighted each other. Tristan's nimble fingers aroused her to sighing ecstasy, her busy hand flicked open his trousers and stroked him until he spurted into his underwear. A moment later they heard Madame's heavy step on the landing and broke away from each other with a hasty kiss and a grin.

Since then, nothing. So it was not to be wondered at that Lucile after dinner on her Saint's day became aroused so easily and quickly. She pressed close to Tristan on the sofa, kissing him lovingly – at the same time trying to keep her eye on her dozing mother. Her hand lay over the long upright bulge in his trousers, squeezing it against his belly.

Through the fine material she could feel it throbbing at her touch, and in another second she threw caution to the winds and ripped his trousers open wide. His stiffness jumped out and she gasped to see its strength, she seized it in her hand.

'Lucile!' he whispered sharply. 'Let's go into the next room. Your mother is asleep, she won't wake up if we're careful.'

His fingertip had aroused Lucile immensely, between her well-parted thighs she was very slippery. She wanted to go with him, wanted it with all her heart. She was on fire to feel her belly penetrated with the hard flesh she held in her hand. She wanted to feel it slide into her softness. She sighed as she squeezed it and the way it jumped in her grasp perhaps decided her.

Together they rose silently to their feet, eyes fixed warily on Madame Champlain. Lucile was nearest to the door, she turned slowly and carefully and led the way, moving soundlessly and hardly daring to breathe. Tristan followed close behind, holding his jutting part in his hand to stop it swaying up and down to his steps.

They were out in the passage. Tristan glanced back and pulled the door gently shut. What he saw was reassuring to him, Madame Champlain was fast asleep, breathing through her mouth, which was open to show a gleam of teeth between rouged lips. He dared not close the door completely in case the lock clicked.

On silent feet he followed Lucile along the passage and into her bedroom. Once inside, she clung round his neck, thrusting her belly and thighs against him, kissing his face frantically. She had hold of his straining part again, her hand flicking up and down.

There was no time to remove clothes and with her mother only lightly asleep in the apartment it would have been foolhardy to do so. He walked Lucile backwards to the bed, the rub of her close-pressed loins against him produced sensations so exciting that he was convinced he was going to spurt into his underwear long before he reached the tender haven between her thighs.

She let him press her down on the bed, spreading her legs as she settled on her back. He flipped the skirt of her rose-pink frock up above her waist and his hard-risen part jerked mightily at the sight of bare flesh above silk stocking-tops.

Lucile was staring into his flushed face, her eyes gleaming and the tip of her pink tongue showing between her lips.

'Tristan – be quick,' she murmured. 'Quick, *chéri*, before she wakes up!'

Her thumbs were hooked in the waist of her knickers, to push them down and bare herself for him. Tristan seized the delicate little garment and jerked it down her thighs, uncovering her handsome light-brown bush of curls and the gentle lips that had parted slightly under his stroking. He was aroused almost to the point of climax, the sight of Lucile's body bared for him pushed his emotions right to the very edge.

He hurled himself on her, his belly hot on hers. Her knickers were around her knees, it was impossible for her to spread her legs wide. Tristan was too excited to care and so was Lucile – she took hold of his wildly throbbing part to thrust it between her closed thighs and into the slippery lips. With two pushes he was deep into her and his climax was at hand. He felt his belly clenching for the first spurt.

As for Lucile, she was so very aroused that ecstasy overtook her at the instant she felt Tristan slide into her. Her bottom bucked upwards from the bed, her hands seized his shoulders and she began to gasp rhythmically.

At this critical moment the bedroom door was flung wide open and there stood Madame Champlain, an expression of outrage and loathing on her face at what she saw taking place. Her daughter was underneath a man, clothes up round her waist, thighs exposed! A long wailing moan indicated that her daughter was in the very throes of the sexual climax!

Tristan heard the door crash against the wall and turned his head in horror, to see his future mother-in-law glaring at him. She was biting her knuckles to prevent herself from screaming, her eyes were bulging out of her head like a madwoman. Tristan was caught, found out, exposed, at the most intimate of moments – and by the person in the world he feared the most!

The effect was bizarre. The realisation of his plight did not inhibit his natural function, quite the reverse – it pushed him straight over the edge into urgent sexual release. While he was staring open-mouthed and thunderstruck at Madame Champlain, his heart ceased its beating for some moments and his breathing was suspended, but down below the waist – ah, that was a different reaction! His stiff part jumped angrily, his belly clenched in a knot of sensation – and his passion spurted into darling Lucile.

'Stop it, stop it, stop it!' Madame Champlain was crying out hoarsely, her eyes fixed on his in a deadly glare.

Tristan was past speaking. *I'm sorry, I'm sorry*, he wanted to say, but no words came out of his mouth. His belly continued to throb and flood Lucile with his desire.

'This fiancée of his,' said Suzette, 'is he still engaged to her? Or did the mother make him marry her at once?'

'It's all very strange,' Gaby said. 'The mother hasn't spoken to Tristan since that day. It's four years, would you believe it? The engagement is still on and the mother doesn't try to stop them being alone together, not since she found out her darling girl wasn't a virgin any more. But she's against her marrying Tristan – she doesn't think he's worthy of being her son-in-law.'

'And the girl goes along with this? She must be as crazy as her mother. Why does Tristan stay engaged if his nervous system was totally ruined so he can't make love to the girl, even with no interference from the mother? He's mad too.'

'That's why he fell for me,' said Gaby. 'I'm adventurous and I enjoy the lunatic escapades he arranges to experience a dread of discovery at the magical moment. Lucile's as conventional as her mother in many ways, she wants to make love in bed with the door firmly shut. Which is not much use to Tristan. And why are you being so prim, *chérie*? Your singing career really started when Michel had your knickers down in a doorway in Montmartre.'

'That was Destiny,' Suzette answered fervently. 'It was not a casual event by night – it was written in the stars!'

'What is your horoscope sign, I've forgotten,' Gaby said with a grin, 'Virgo, perhaps?'

'Laugh if you will,' Suzette retorted, 'but keep in mind that it is summer now – standing under a tree with your knickers off for this man may be amusing. But come winter and the icy winds are blowing along the boulevards, you won't be so interested in alfresco love-making.'

Gaby giggled and shrugged her slim shoulders.

'Who said it has to be in the open air every time? I haven't told you what he got up to when we got back to Paris on the train.'

'Not standing up in a train corridor!' Suzette exclaimed.

'No, it was too crowded for that. And besides, I was with the troupe. Tristan travelled in the Third Class with us, although he always goes First. He didn't complain about the hard seats – he was charming. He paid for coffee and sandwiches and snacks for everybody, they were impressed and they thought he was a marvel. When he wasn't listening they all kept telling me how lucky I'd been to catch a man as good-hearted as him. In fact Marie Boussin got so jealous that I thought she was going to scratch my eyes out!'

As the tale of Tristan unfolded, Suzette listened to her dear friend's ridiculous story with growing amusement. There was no doubt in her mind that Gaby's latest acquaintance was off his head. Though in the nicest possible way. It seemed he was able to turn a simple taxi ride into an adventure in eroticism.

By the time the train arrived at the Gare de Lyon he was high in the esteem of her dance-troupe colleagues, this dashing and handsome young man. The train came to a noisy standstill at the platform and immediately he found porters to take charge of all their baggage, kissed their hands and waved them *au revoir*. He had his own belongings and Gaby's put in a taxi while the rest of the dancers headed for the Metro.

Gaby had already suggested he come home with her for a drink or a cup of strong coffee to reinvigorate him after the journey. He was reluctant to go to his parent's apartment, it seemed, he being on difficult terms with them over the endlessly postponed marriage to Lucile Champlain. He asked Gaby where she lived and told the driver to take them to the rue de Rome.

It was evening and dark already, street lamps were brightly shining. When the taxi got as far as the Place de la Bastille, Tristan decided on a change of plan. Without explaining himself to Gaby he leaned forward to tap the driver's shoulder and tell him to forget the rue de Rome and take them back to the railway station

'But why?' Gaby asked. Not that she minded much where he was going to take her. His right arm was round her waist, holding her close to him, his other hand was inside her rust-red jacket and caressing her pointed breasts through the thin silk of her blouse. She was fond of her elegant red tweed costume, it had come from the Chanel sale. She turned her face to Tristan and kissed him, the wet tip of her tongue sliding between his lips.

The taxi-driver shrugged and grumbled under his breath at the change of plan. He drove right round the Place de la Bastille, ignoring the evening traffic, threatening the lives and safety of everyone else on the road, then headed back to the Gare de Lyon the way he had come.

Before he could pull up in the forecourt, Tristan pointed to a narrow road running down the side of the station. The driver grunted in the exasperated and disobliging way of taxi-men and followed it some way before he asked over his shoulder where he should stop.

Tristan had his hand up the skirt of Gaby's two-piece and he was stroking the insides of her thighs, up above her stocking-tops. At the driver's question he glanced out of the window to see just where they were. He told the man to take the next turn to the right. Gaby looked out over Tristan's shoulder, her body trembling to the insidious touch of his fingers up between her slender thighs.

It was a part of Paris she had not seen before and would not want to revisit, a shabby old district where the railway tracks ran, a semi-derelict area more than ready for knocking down and redeveloping. They were driving along a narrow and dismal road between anonymous buildings and anyone who was about was hiding in a doorway or up an alley. Halfway between lampposts Tristan instructed the driver to stop.

'Why are we stopping here?' Gaby asked, knowing exactly why. In truth she was not at all pleased by the location Tristan had chosen for a further demonstration of his ability to make love in impossible circumstances. Like her friend Suzette, Gaby had grown up in the poverty of Belleville and had no wish to find herself in the same sort of surroundings.

Instead of answering her pointless question, he took his hand from under her skirt long enough to extract a banknote of large denomination from an ostrich-leather wallet and reached across the seat to give it to the taxi-driver.

'We shall stay here for twenty minutes,' he said, 'then on to the rue de Rome. Just sit quiet and stare out of the windscreen and pay no attention to what goes on in the back. Understand?'

The size of the tip persuaded the driver to go along with the outrageous idea. In the surly manner of his trade he indicated his agreement.

'Tristan!' said Gaby. 'You cannot possibly suppose that I am going to make love in the back of a taxi while the driver sits half a metre away and listens! Are you out of your mind?'

He had her jacket open and her blouse, he stroked her breasts while he fastened his mouth on hers in a kiss so thrilling that it swept away her sensible objections. He took her hand in his and steered it to the join of his thighs. She had his trousers open in an instant and delved in his underwear to find his hard and throbbing part. Now his hands were up her skirt, both hands easing her knickers down her legs, his fingers touching the soft lips he had bared.

'This is ridiculous . . .' Gaby murmured weakly, 'it is shameful and impossible . . .'

He smelt of lavender after-shave, his skin was smooth, he was well-tended in all ways, exciting, masculine, attractive – and his fingers were driving her out of her mind with sensations of delight. Without waiting for him to do any more, Gaby got up on the taxi seat and straddled him, her skirt round her hips, her knees clasping him tight.

His hands were down between their bellies, bringing his stiff part to the tender opening between her thighs. The touch sent a wave of wild emotion through her, she trembled and sighed, avid for more. He edged inside slowly, she was murmuring and shaking as she almost begged him to push hard. *Impatiente*, he whispered, then with a long push he slid the whole length into her and she gave a little scream. The taxi-driver hunched down in the front seat grunted as if in disapproval, but kept his bargain and did not look round.

Tristan had his hands on Gaby's hips and was moving strongly in and out of her – it took very little of this before she lost all control. She felt herself swamped with sensual pleasure – she was giddy from it. Her arms were around Tristan's neck to pull his face close, her lips were on his, her tongue flicking in his mouth.

It was impossible to let him continue like this, she began to bounce up and down on him, to wiggle her hips, slithering along his stiffness. He retaliated at once, stabbing up into her with brute force. She sat boldly upright astride him, her movements teasing him with devastating sensation. And before long her sly assault was more than his jangling nervous system could endure. He moaned and fell back against the taxi seat, his body jerking like a marionette on strings while he spurted his passion into her.

He gasped that he adored her beyond belief, that she was the only woman for him, that he would never, never let her go – and similar protestations men make in the sexual frenzy which are of no great importance thirty seconds later.

His thrusting outburst brought on Gaby's own climax. Her head went sharply back, her silvery-blonde hair straying loose from under her little hat. She felt Tristan's spurting in her belly as the ecstasy of those moments coursed through her, from her loins to her heart, making it pound and leap, into her breasts, their tips as hard as acorns, up as far as her throat, to make her pant and sob, then up into her mind, where it erased every conscious thought.

The taxi-driver had a bottle of cheap red wine hidden beneath his seat. While the lovers in the back sighed and moaned their passion, he uncorked his bottle and upended it for a long swig. In his expert opinion, three-quarters of the people who rode in his taxi were crazy and the rest were mean.

LUCILE AT
LONGCHAMP

During his intimate friendship with Gaby, Tristan had
conveyed the impression that he had lost interest in his
fiancée and did not see her very often. Not that Gaby gave
the matter much real consideration, she did not want to
marry Tristan, though she liked him and wanted to enjoy
his company. Outside that, what he did was his own
concern. He never actually said Lucile was reluctant to
indulge his need for risky love-making but in some
intangible way he had planted the thought in Gaby's mind.

None of this was true. He saw Lucile most days for an
hour or two and he often took her out to dinner and to
entertainments. He was alternating his attentions to Lucile
with his attentions to Gaby, each of the women unaware of
his duplicity. As for his vague suggestion that Lucile was
unwilling to oblige his urgent need, the truth was he
continued to stand her against walls and trees and behind
parked trucks and down on the Seine quays and anywhere
else that occurred to him. And she had no objection to any
of it, though she became a little anxious on deserted Metro
platforms in the middle of the afternoon.

Why she went along with Tristan's endless postponement
of the marriage is not easy to say. Perhaps she thought she
was better off as she was, free for much of the time to do

what she chose. Perhaps she was too passive by nature to assert herself against his wishes. Perhaps she had become accustomed to her in-between way of life. Whatever she thought in her secret heart, she gave no sign that she was discontented with things as they were.

She uttered no word of complaint when Tristan dashed off to Lyon after a quarrel with his parents. She phoned him and wrote him little notes and he arranged to have flowers delivered to her twice a week. He was gone for three weeks without any word of reproach from Lucile. Then he came back and resumed exactly as before. He said nothing about the beautiful blonde dancer he'd met in Lyon. And never gave a hint that he was still meeting her now in Paris.

Happy man, fortunate Tristan, to have two charming and ardent women at his disposal, enough money to indulge them and himself, no dull daily occupation to take up his time, good looks and robust health! But, as every sensible person knows, there is a flaw in the organisation of human affairs, an imperfection of a kind that makes for instability. Even the best arrangements are shakily based and will collapse if the wind blows hard from an unexpected quarter.

This unpleasant truth was demonstrated to Tristan on the last Sunday in June, not long after his return from Lyon. It was the day of the Grand Prix de Paris at Longchamp. Tristan was mildly interested in horse-racing and he took his fiancée there. They enjoyed a good lunch in the track restaurant, that was at least as important as the racing, and as the time approached for the big race, Tristan left Lucile in the grandstand while he went to place a bet. It was a considerable bet – he was convinced he knew the winner.

Lucile did not share this interest in race horses and which of them could run faster than the other. When

Tristan had been away for ten minutes she became bored, she quitted the grandstand and strolled among the crowd, looking for him. It was a sunny day, warm and clear, the people were good-natured and, for the most part, well-dressed. And in the Parisian way of things, here and there a man raised his hat to Lucile and smiled hopefully. And where the crowd was thickest, nimble fingers pinched her bottom affectionately.

Tristan was nowhere to be seen, the start of the big race was only minutes off. Lucile sighed in exasperation and let herself be carried along by the crowd – going against the stream needed more determination than she thought worthwhile at that moment. These people were going somewhere, she would go along with them and see what was so interesting.

She found herself at the railings, opposite the winning post, that was where the crowd about her wanted to be, right there at the finish to see the winner cross the line. She was soon aware of an air of anticipation and excitement, the people round her were talking and jostling. She was pressed up against the rail with men to her right and left, crowding in close, staring down the course, waiting for the race to begin.

Lucile felt someone press against her back, not a hand but a body, moulding itself to the curve of her waist and bottom. And at first the pressure was light, as if by chance, much like the touch of a man's hand brushing against a woman's bottom in a crowded Metro carriage. Then the touch became a little firmer, a little insistent, a little more suggestive.

Lucile made no effort to escape this close contact. Tristan had caught up with her at last, she realised. After placing his bet he couldn't find her in the grandstand and came looking for her by the winning post. He loved playing his little games with her, this was the one he'd invented for the Metro. They'd get into a carriage separately, in the rush hour, and stand at opposite ends. Gradually he'd slide through the crowd until he was next to her, then start pressing his body against her back.

Sometimes the travellers nearest would notice what he was up to but no one ever said anything, mostly they grinned and looked away. After all, Tristan was not the only man in the carriage who was rubbing himself surreptitiously against a girl. But he took it further than the average commuter dare – when the carriage was very tightly packed, he'd slip a hand under Lucile's frock and feel between her thighs. Once or twice he'd undone his trousers and rubbed his upright bare part against her leg.

The crowd pressing up against the race-course railings seemed very suitable for his Metro game. But at times he took too much for granted, this Tristan, he forced his will on Lucile whether she was in a mood for his open-air caprices or not. She decided to punish him a little, she would make his over-developed self-esteem suffer – she would pretend it was not him standing close behind her.

When he declared himself, she would pretend to be surprised – let him believe she would allow another man, a stranger, to put his belly and loins against the round, thinly clad cheeks under her silk frock. That would certainly make dear Tristan jealous and disturb his sleep at nights!

And he deserved to have a few uneasy nights. Now her mother had no more objections to him he sometimes stayed with Lucile all night but these occasions were futile and discouraging. Lucile did all she could to arouse him. She massaged his body with her own naked body, she handled him, caressed him, sank her nails into his flesh – but whatever she did, gentle or brutal, nothing was of the slightest use to bring him up hard. Unless, at two in the morning, she put on a raincoat over her nakedness and he put on trousers and jacket, and they went out into the street for her to lean on a lamppost for his attentions.

Draughty, risky, uncomfortable, but the only way. He deserved to be made to suffer a little emotionally for subjecting her to these inconveniences!

Meanwhile, of course, there at Longchamp, against the railing near the winning post, the continuing touch of his body against her was agreeable. His thighs pressed against the back of her thighs, through her pale blue silk frock, his loins pressed to her bottom. She sighed when his hands encircled her waist. She felt his breathing on her neck, soon she was almost dizzy with mounting sensation.

She did not turn her head to murmur *Tristan chéri* or give any other sign of acknowledgement. That would destroy the delicious pretence that it was a stranger doing these intimate things to her. The crowd of race-goers around her surged suddenly forward and cheered, the big race had started, the horses were pounding round the track towards them.

He was raising her frock at the back, hoisting it stealthily, centimetre by centimetre, until he could slide both hands under it. His fingertips smoothed up the back of her silk stockings, they touched the tender flesh of her thighs and the warm bare part between her stocking-tops and her lace-edged knickers.

It was so exciting, so distastefully exciting to be handled and abused by Tristan in public, Lucile was thinking. It was so very bizarre, yet so delicious! Although she grumbled a little to herself after the episodes under a streetlamp, her raincoat open to expose her bare body to him, in truth she found them to be immensely exciting.

The crowd waved race cards, betting tickets and newspapers in their mounting fervour, men on both sides of Lucile shouted and jostled, paying her no attention. And all the time those knowing fingers were sliding up her thighs, then inwards, slipping into her loose knickers, feeling the warm lips between her legs and stroking them softly, to and fro.

But that was only one hand manipulating her so expertly! The other hand was behind her, also up in her knickers and the fingertips lay in the crease between the cheeks of her bottom. There they stroked tenderly, as lovers do.

Lucile stared straight ahead, her red-painted mouth open a little, her breathing becoming very uneven. The hands that were playing with her so delightfully were enchanted hands, she told herself, they were not joined by arms to a man's shoulders – to Tristan's shoulders. On a man's shoulders there was a neck and head – it was what swirled about inside the head that gave rise to complications. Not the hands or fingers, they gave pleasure. Only the head could bring pain, when the thoughts inside it became expressed in words and then in actions which could be contrary to her own desires.

There was no such annoyance with enchanted hands – they lived a life of their own, alone and apart, they were not instruments of male desire, of Tristan's desire. They had one purpose only, to caress between Lucile's thighs, to make gentle love to her, to arouse exquisite sensations in her.

She was the Sleeping Princess, she told herself dreamily, she was lying on her swan's-down bed, in the round chamber up at the top of the tall and slender stone tower, held there by a magic spell. But the Prince had arrived, the

Prince who was promised to her. He had fought his way through the dense thicket that grew round the foot of the tower during her bewitched hundred-year sleep.

He climbed the tall smooth tower, gripping it with his hands, his arms outstretched to cling on and his body pressed close to it. He gained the top at last, the domed top of the tower where the enchantment held the Princess a prisoner. His quest was to arouse her, he had come for this alone, on his long and arduous journey. She lay limply upon the swan's-down bed, her eyes still closed, but she was beginning to stir as he leaned over her.

In the fairytale for children, the Prince kissed the Sleeping Princess awake, but that was said only for the sake of decency. In truth, it was the gentle touch of his fingers in between her parted legs that roused her, the caress between moistly parted lips. Those skilful fingers that sent throbs of delight through Lucile's quivering belly, how shamelessly clever they were!

There was nothing clumsy or maladroit in their touch. They caressed her so very precisely, yet so insistently, they raised breathtaking sensations in her, they pestered her delicately – ah, so very delicately!

Through the haze of delight that was overwhelming her, Lucile realised with a shock that it could not be Tristan doing this to her! It wasn't possible, he was hasty when he made love, he had neither the skilfullness nor the patience to pleasure her so marvellously – to torment her so exquisitely!

It must be a stranger with his hands in her knickers! A red flush spread over Lucile's face as she realised that a complete stranger was taking advantage of her!

She was caught in a trap of her own making, her own illusion had taken on a disastrous reality! She must put an end to this shameful episode at once – at the very least she must slap the molester's face! He would surely be grinning, monster that he was! She would wipe the grin from his face with a heavy smack and she would scream *Rape* and frighten him.

But shameful though it was, what he was doing to her, Lucile could not help but be amazed at the gentle skill of his fingers – she adored the manner in which he was touching her body, even while she detested how he had taken possession of her without her permission. Monster he surely was, but a masterful monster, one who knew how to bring women under his control and use them for his pleasure.

If he could give her such fantastic pleasure with his fingers – a pleasure so intense she wanted to laugh and cry at the same time – then to what unattainable ecstasies could he cause her to soar if he used another and more robust part of his body? Ah, it was too late to think of resisting him now, the race was almost over, thrills of passion were ravishing her belly.

About her the crowd waved and shouted in encouragement and in anxiety as the horses galloped towards the finishing post. The favourite was a good length out in front, its scarlet-and-green-clad jockey flailing at its rump with his whip.

It thundered past the winning post only a moment after Lucile reached and passed her own private winning post – her unwilling little cries of ecstasy drowned out by the triumphant shouting of the crowd round her.

Now that those shameless fingers had forced the supreme pleasure on Lucile they withdrew slowly from her groins and then from her knickers. The loins that had pressed so close to the warm cheeks of Lucile's bottom eased away from her. She felt no more hot sweet breath on her neck. The crowd about her was beginning to disperse as holders of winning tickets made for the pay-out, there was room to move at last.

Lucile was still dazed from the intensity of her climax, her face was flushed and her breathing not yet back to normal. But she had to know who had done this to her, she had to know if he was young or old, if he was handsome or plain, a Frenchman or a foreigner. She was a little unsteady on her feet as she turned to confront whoever it was, this rapist who had dared to molest her in broad daylight – and in so very public a place.

Within arm's reach stood a dark-haired woman in a picture hat and an elegant orange and white frock! A woman of thirty-five or thirty-six, a woman with a long thin nose and a smooth olive tinted complexion, a woman with dark eyes, red painted lips and a knowing smile on her face. *A woman!*

Lucile was stunned by the sudden revelation. *Mais non, mais non!* she cried out in disbelief. Then her knees trembled, her mouth hung open for a moment. She stared into the woman's dark eyes, into their velvet depths, battling to understand why this stranger had ravished her so boldly. She could discern no evil gleam in those eyes, no perverse glitter, only the tiniest hint of amusement at her own mortification.

The woman reached out to put a hand on Lucile's shaking arm. Her fingernails were painted a bright scarlet and beautifully shaped, the hand of a person of means and leisure. Lucile could only stare in astonishment at the fingers touching her bare arm – those long thin fingers that only moments ago had exploited her sexuality in so incredible a manner, fingers that had raised her to a tremendous climax of sensation. The thought was so strange to Lucile that she was speechless.

She wanted to seize those fingers and bend them backward till they broke and the dark-haired woman screamed in pain! And she also wanted to raise the scarlet-nailed fingers to her lips and kiss them for what they had done. She wanted to bite them hard, to draw blood with her teeth and savagely punish their owner's wicked presumption! And she also wanted to press those fingers to the join of her thighs, against the moistness underneath her frock!

Lucile's conflicting emotions were plain to see on her face. The other woman smiled faintly and introduced herself.

'I'm Nicole Gruchy,' said the woman in orange and white silk. 'You seem to be a little hot and disturbed, it's the noise and this crowd and the heat. Come to my box and we will have a cool drink.'

Without staying for a answer she tucked Lucile's arm under her own and led her leisurely away from the white-painted rail and toward the grandstand and the private boxes. For Lucile it seemed all this was happening in a dream, none of it could ever possibly be real.

'Tell me your name,' said Nicole Gruchy.

'Lucile Champlain.'

There were eight or nine people in Nicole's box, standing and talking, sipping champagne – elegantly dressed men, women in big brimmed summer-hats and couture-house frocks. A white-jacketed waiter brought tall glasses on a silver tray for Nicole and her new guest. Nicole insisted Lucile should sit down for a moment. She smiled as she said Lucile looked just slightly fatigued – a short rest and a glass of champagne would put that right.

'I cannot stay,' Lucile said breathlessly, 'my fiancé will be looking everywhere for me. He will be frantic if he cannot find me, madame.'

Nicole's head leaned close to Lucile's, her long and wicked fingertips touched the inside of Lucile's wrist, a thrilling little touch that made Lucile's hand tremble.

'Not madame,' she said, 'Nicole. This fiancé – suppose you go and find him, what then?'

'What do you mean?'

When Nicole replied, her voice was as soft as a caress.

'I mean this – the fiancé will take you to his apartment or to yours, I do not know of your arrangements. He will kiss you and stroke your breasts and get your clothes off. Of this I can be certain, because it is what men always do with pretty women. I despise them.'

'And you?' Lucile said staunchly. 'You are different? Can I believe that, after what happened down there in the crowd?'

'What is his name?' Nicole asked, as if she hadn't heard the question at all.

'Tristan Villette.'

'And when he has stripped you completely naked, this Tristan, this missing fiancé of yours,' Nicole continued, 'he will force you to lie down on your back, with your legs wide open, and he will lie on top of you and push his stiff thing into you.'

'He is not like that,' Lucile protested, more accustomed with Tristan to leaning against walls in the dark or bending over a park bench behind a hedge, than to lying on her back on a bed.

'At heart they are all the same,' Nicole insisted. 'With some few variations they all do the same thing to you. They are very boring when they do it! It is tedious beyond words, this lying on your back while they ram away and moan and pant.'

'Ah no!' Lucile objected, feeling obliged to defend herself. 'You make love sound more like a martyrdom than a delight.'

'Martyrdom!' Nicole scoffed. 'If only it were so thrilling! Ah, to be stripped naked by a masked executioner before a crowd of shouting onlookers, pegged out on the hot and dusty ground with arms and legs spread wide, the cruel whip slashing breasts and belly and thighs! Then dragged to a wooden block and forced to kneel, bent over it, bare bottom on show to spectators – and waiting in utmost terror for the gleaming axe to fall and sever head from neck! That must be the excitement of martyrdom! But I fear dullness and dreariness is all one can expect from men.'

Her description of public martyrdom shocked Lucile, who found herself blushing faintly at the idea of being stripped naked in public and tortured.

'Such words!' she said. 'What a thing to say! But tell me, do you include your husband in your denunciation of men?'

To emphasise her point she tapped with an admonishing finger the gold ring on Nicole's hand.

'But of course! He is the worst offender of all!'

There was little that Lucile could say to that. She shrugged her shoulders and remained silent.

'You look perfectly recovered,' Nicole said cheerfully. 'Come with me for a little stroll in the fresh air, the atmosphere of this box is vile with the smoke of cigars and cigarettes.'

Lucile found herself unable to refuse – Nicole's presence and personality were very persuasive. Outside the box Nicole put an arm round her waist in the friendliest manner and guided her in the direction she intended, which was to her waiting limousine.

Lucile stared at it in admiration and awe. This was no modern post-war factory-made pressed-steel affair. It evidently dated back to the great days when luxury cars were built by hand and designed to last forever. It was long and sleek with two-toned bodywork, the huge curving wings and top were shiny black, the sides and bonnet were a gleaming cream.

Beside it stood a chauffeur in black uniform and with a thick black moustache. He bowed to Madame Gruchy and opened the rear door for the ladies – a discreet hand under the elbow assisted them inside. Lucile sank on to the broad seat of soft burgundy leather, marvelling at the magnificence of the veteran vehicle.

Nicole gave the chauffeur no instructions, nor did he ask for any. He slid into the driving seat, switched on the engine and drove smoothly away.

Lucile saw with surprise the rear windows had curtains, held back by silver fittings, pale grey curtains, damask by the look of them. A flick of Nicole's finger freed them from the clasps, they swung across to cover the windows and impede the curiosity of anyone outside. Inside, in the sudden intimacy of the closed car, the leather seat was wide but Nicole chose to sit close to Lucile, the trace of a smile on her face in the shadow.

She leaned over gracefully to press her lips to Lucile's in a long and fervent kiss.

'But this is impossible!' Lucile protested faintly when she at last could break away. 'Stop the car at once and let me out, I cannot endure any more of it!'

'But why do you want to get out – don't you like me?' Nicole asked. She was smoothing Lucile's light-brown hair with a hand that trembled a little, 'Surely you're not still worried about your boyfriend – I've forgotten his name already, what did you say it was?'

'Tristan. He will be worried about me when he can't find me, he will think I've been carried off, kidnapped.'

'And so you have, *chérie*,' Nicole murmured, her long fingers caressing Lucile's cheek, 'I am carrying you off.'

'Ah no,' Lucile sighed as the questing fingertips touched her lips lightly, the same fingers that only half an hour ago had taken the unspeakable liberty of caressing the other lips under her frock, those soft warm lips between her legs.

'You can't escape from me,' Nicole murmured, 'I won't let you go until I have made you fall in love with me.'

She pulled off her hat with the wide brim and threw it to the richly carpeted car floor at their feet. She put her arms about Lucile and made her lean back against the burgundy leather.

'Why so tense?' she whispered into Lucile's ear. 'There is no point in resisting me, *chérie*, I mean to have you again. Let your body go loose, just as it was when I first caressed you by the railing.'

Her hands pressed against Lucile's thighs, tracing the smooth outline through the thin silk of her dress and stockings – she pushed Lucile's knees apart. Her mouth was hot on Lucile's, her kiss was so very intense it destroyed the will to resist her. A gasp escaped Lucile when she felt her knickers being taken down and Nicole's hand between her thighs, stroking with slow little movements.

'But you are adorable, little Lucile,' she murmured, raising her head to stare into her eyes. 'The instant I saw you I loved you – it was a thunderstroke out of a clear blue sky. I knew at once I must have you for my own.'

'No, it is impossible,' Lucile sighed, hardly able to speak, so enchanting were the throbs of pleasure through her body from the caress of Nicole's fingers. 'I love Tristan.'

'What nonsense! He has imposed his will on you, that is all. Men are selfish and beastly, they use pretty girls like you for their coarse pleasures and call it love. But tonight you shall stay with me and I will show you what real passion is and how it is expressed in truth and delight between lovers. And before tomorrow's sun comes up, you will realise you love me.'

Ecstasy gripped Lucile's belly, she moaned and jerked in the firm grip of her abductor. And this time the throes of pleasure were brief but extraordinarily intense, racking Lucile till she almost lost consciousness.

When she came to herself again and became slowly aware of her surroundings, she found her hand had been guided under Nicole's silk frock and into her underwear. Her palm lay over silky-soft hair and warm flesh, her wrist was caught between strong thighs to keep her hand in place.

Her head rested on Nicole's breast, whose arm lay around her shoulders to keep her close. Nicole had opened the front of her own frock and her brassiere was undone to expose her breasts. Bare warm flesh lay under Lucile's cheek, a little bud between her lips felt tender and yet firm.

Lucile gave a slight moan, she was bewildered by all that had happened to her in so short a time – from standing by a railing to being carried off in a limousine to the sensations of delight she had experienced at the hands of another woman! The events of the afternoon were so outrageous it was impossible to make any sense of them.

She had been seduced and debauched in public, carried off and misused again. And by a woman! A fine-looking woman, it was true, who wore elegant clothes and owned a limousine – but still a woman!

To comfort herself in this bizarre predicament, Lucile drew the tender fleshy bud into her mouth and her eyes closed while she sucked at it. *Ah!* she heard Nicole gasp, *Lucile chérie!*

Lucile's hand seemed to have a will of its own, without her intention it was stroking the soft curls between Nicole's legs. Her fingers caressed soft smooth lips, they probed between and felt how moist and warm Nicole was.

Ah! Nicole sighed again and she spread her legs to let Lucile find her secret bud and touch it.

Lucile had never touched another woman's body before in this way. She was hardly aware she was doing so now, her mind was a haze of gentle pleasure from the warm breast she sucked at. Her fingers moved as if in a dream and caused throbs of pleasure to shake Nicole. She, predatory Nicole, had now cast herself as an offering to another – with a feverish hand she pulled her dress up to her hips and flung her legs as widely apart as possible.

'Take me!' she moaned. 'I am yours, *chérie*!'

In her climax she flung her legs up higher than her head and screamed loudly.

Nicole lived in the Avenue Victor-Hugo, a very grand building not far from the Etoile. A maidservant opened the door, smiling to see the two women arm-in-arm, pink-cheeked and just a little dishevelled from their pleasant exertions in the shady interior of the curtained limousine. Nicole nodded to her as she passed, then another maidservant appeared to enquire if Madame required anything. Nicole said she would ring for a light meal later, a meal for two in her room, when she was ready. She swept Lucile straight through the apartment without pause, into a large and elegantly furnished bedroom.

No sooner was the door closed than she flung her arms tightly about Lucile, rubbing their bellies together smoothly while she kissed her.

'No,' said Lucile, trying to disengage herself. 'Suppose your husband comes in – I would die of shame!'

'There's no fear of that,' Nicole soothed her, caressing her bottom gently. 'He is not permitted to set foot in my room – it is clearly understood between us.'

She removed Lucile's frock, slipping it up over her head, and casting it casually aside. She took off Lucile's brassiere and her knickers, she stooped to kiss the light-brown curls before she rolled her stockings down her legs. When Lucile was naked Nicole bent her backward over the bed and lay upon her to kiss her mouth, her hands roaming sensually over her breasts.

Lucile was dismayed to think she was letting herself be used in this way by a woman, yet her excitement was rising furiously and it would not be denied by minor considerations about gender or other matters that seemed irrelevant at that moment.

She put her arms round Nicole's neck and clung to her eagerly and longingly, she sighed into Nicole's open mouth, she parted her legs widely for Nicole to touch her and make her melt into ecstasy. But Nicole pulled away from her slowly, smiling at her desire, and stood upright while she undressed herself.

They lay naked on the bed together, the satin counterpane was turned down to the foot, out of the way. Nicole's hands roamed over Lucile expertly, stroking every part of her, in the hollows under her arms, between her small pert breasts, along the inside of her thighs, between the cheeks of her bottom.

The prolonged sensations threw Lucile into a frenzy of sexual arousal but Nicole did not put her hand between her thighs and give her the *coup de grâce*.

'We have all evening and all night,' she murmured in Lucile's ear. 'You are a prisoner of love here in my room until you fall in love with me, Lucile.'

Lucile moaned and raised her head to press her avid mouth to the pink bud of Nicole's right breast – it was as firm as a nut between her lips. She sucked at it hard, making Nicole gasp and sigh, she put her fingers between Nicole's legs and probed into her moist softness, feeling for the slippery secret bud. Never in all her life had Lucile imagined touching another woman like this, of wanting to be touched by her. Yet at this moment there was nothing she wanted more in the whole world!

'No, you don't, *chérie*!' Nicole sighed, 'not yet! First you must tell me you love me.'

She did not wait for any response, she jerked her breast away from Lucile's mouth. *Je t'aime*, Lucile moaned, so highly aroused she would say anything, anything at all, to solicit the actions that could bring on her crisis. Nicole laughed, she didn't for an instant believe her.

'Not yet,' she said, 'but you will, that I promise you!'

She kissed Lucile's palpitating belly and spread her flat on her back. She pushed her legs well apart and lay between them, her pink-flushed face smiling at Lucile over her little bush of light-brown curls. Lucile's slender body bucked on the bed, she squealed when Nicole's hot tongue slid wetly into her.

'Yes, yes!' Lucile moaned. '*Je t'aime, Nicole, je t'aime!*'

The tongue flickered, Lucile writhed and panted, trembled and sighed. She reached her climax quickly – her body arched up off the bed and she cried out shrilly, *Je t'aime* . . .

'Perhaps,' said Nicole, when Nicole lay limp, 'but time will tell. If you say it after I have made love to you all night, I may believe you, and then you shall make love to me.'

'But I have,' Lucile whispered, 'in the car – you screamed so loud! You can't have forgotten.'

'That doesn't count, *chérie*, we didn't know each other then – any pretty woman I picked up in an all-girls' bar would do that much for me. It was an introduction, almost like shaking hands. But by morning we shall know each other well. And then you will have the right to roll me on my back and demand my surrender to you, as I demand your love.'

For Lucile this talk of love was a dream, yet not a dream. In a way it was a dream come true, yet it was so strange she could hardly understand how she had got here, on a satin-sheeted bed in a superb apartment. She turned on her side to look at Nicole and touch her face.

She trailed a finger down that knowing face, from forehead to chin, that face with the thin aristocratic nose and the shining eyes that were as soft as brown velvet. She ran her palm slowly down Nicole's long arms, down her long slender body with small pointed breasts. She touched her delicately rounded belly, then the thick and curly brown hair between her thighs.

Ah yes, Nicole was *very* attractive, she was superbly groomed, wonderfully experienced . . .

Yes, thought Lucile, *yes* – no more leaning on brick walls in the dark, clothes up round my hips and a draught blowing round my bottom while Tristan pants and jerks.

No more lying on damp grass in the Bois de Boulogne behind a tree while he climbs on top, with people strolling past only five metres away!

Lucile had made up her mind. From this day onward love-making would be upon this comfortable bed, in this luxurious bedroom, warm, dry and secure from prying eyes. She glanced round it in approval, taking in the slender-legged white settee over by the window, the elegant dressing-table with its tinted mirror – and in a tall porcelain vase a delicate sprig of roses, three green leaves and two pink buds not yet open.

Yes, it would be easy to fall in love with Nicole!

AT THE
FOLIES BERGERE

No formidable decisions were necessary – it was never going to last very long, the *affaire* between Suzette and Julien Brocq. A woman so intent on making a career as a singer has no desire to acquire friendships that require too much of her attention. And a man so immersed in the world of movie-making finds it hard to focus on other interests.

If Suzette had complied with his wish to put her in films, it would have created a bond between them. But she was solidly set against any kind of dependence on a man, any man – however much she liked him. She wanted to be a success on her own terms, not a star because a man had assisted her. In short, when the first excitements of love-making had run their course, there remained little between her and Julien beyond a mild esteem.

She knew the *affaire* had started wrongly. His unexpected gift of a beautiful diamond bracelet when they had known each other only a quarter of an hour was absurd. And insidious. She should have refused it. He insisted it wasn't just a bribe to get her into bed – a mark of respect, he said. Neither of them believed that – they, knew it was to get her to open her legs. She'd been singing her '*Place Vendôme*' song and the bracelet fitted in well with the words. Otherwise she'd have laughed in his face.

Giving and accepting something of this value had set the tone for what was to follow. It had become evident Julien preferred girlfriends of a less independent mind. Young and beautiful, of course, and not exactly stupid. Assuredly not the dumb blonde type brought to the world's attention by Hollywood movies – the type who finds her way to stardom by removing her knickers and lying down on the casting-director's office couch.

Or so Julien maintained when she mentioned it to him. He was most indignant at the thought – perhaps American men found such compliant women attractive but a Frenchman required more in an intimate friend than a beautiful body and big breasts, he said. She must have a mind and be able to talk amusingly, over dinner and at other sophisticated places of public entertainment.

But not too intelligent, Suzette thought wryly. No man wants a high-brow lecture when he is whispering *les petits riens* in a girl's ear and has a hand on her knee. In these moments it is necessary for her to be entirely feminine.

Julien believed that he knew precisely what he looked for in a woman but anyone else would have found his requirements confusing. And many women would have found them offensive. One thing was clear – although Suzette was the most beautiful woman he knew, she did not meet his specification in other ways. And this was an irritation because he liked her a lot. But she was too independent of spirit.

She refused all his offers of parts in movies – singing parts even, though she was so set on becoming a singing star. He was sailing for America soon, where he had business to discuss in Hollywood. He made his mind up that when he went, that would be the end of their *affaire*. No fuss, no angry words, just a final gentle parting. When he told her of his impending long journey, and of the six or eight weeks he might be away, she understood.

Their last outing together was memorable. Julien learned that Suzette had not been back to the Folies Bergère since she had left to launch her career as a singer. Her engagement at the night club in the Avenue George-Cinq had ended and she had some time free before starting at another club. Julien asked if she would like to revisit the Folies Bergère, she laughed and said yes.

He arrived early to collect her – he always arrived early for appointments – and she was still dressing. This promptness was meant to impress and perhaps in business it did. Suzette found it to be one of the minor annoyances of his personality.

She was in her bedroom, wearing her orchid-pink silk kimono, leaning toward the mirror to darken her long eyelashes when she heard him at the door. She had bathed in perfumed water, washed and dried and brushed her raven-black hair, polished her fingernails and lacquered her toenails. In short, she looked marvellous. She let Julien into the apartment, kissed him on the cheek and suggested he sat down for a minute while she finished dressing. Needless to say, he followed her straight into the bedroom, put his arms round her from behind and fondled her breasts through the thin kimono while he nuzzled her neck.

'Such enchanting perfume!' he murmured as his hands found their way into the top of the kimono to feel her bare breasts, 'and your skin is like satin.'

'All over me,' she said, leaning back against him.

'Ah!' he sighed, understanding the reference. He pulled open the kimono and his hand slid down her body, caressed her belly and found what it was seeking – the delicate smooth-shaven lips between her thighs.

'Enchanting!' he said and his voice trembled a little. 'I think you have paid special attention to this.'

'Oh yes,' she agreed softly, 'always, when I am to meet you.'

What absurd creatures men are, she was thinking, he is here to take me to dinner and to a show, then to the suite at the Ritz to make love all night. Yet here he is, panting, hot and stiff in his trousers, just because I tell him that!

'Let me see!' Julien babbled. He was more like an adolescent feeling a girl for the first time than a movie mogul of mature years with a wife and grown-up children.

He was down on his knees in front of her, hands on her thighs while he stared greedily at the long beautifully shaped lips of her *jouet*. He kissed them ardently.

'I have never seen one more beautiful than yours,' he said in delight. 'I shall miss you terribly when I am in America, I can see now that I shall suffer.'

Suzette spread her thighs a little wider and laughed at him.

'What nonsense! You will have all those blonde-haired little American starlets to make love to,' she said.

'They are made of plastic, American women,' he said, pressing his fingertip between the soft lips. 'They are not created from flesh and blood, like you. To lie on them and make love is the same as doing it to a mechanical doll. I know – I have visited America before. The movements and sounds they make are correct, but there is no *soul* inside, they have nothing to give except a few moments of physical pleasure.'

'How sad!' Suzette said. He sounded so serious she was glad he couldn't see the smile on her face, now that he was clasping the bare cheeks of her bottom and kissing her hotly.

His tongue forced its way in between the soft lips, spreading them to reach her hidden bud. She sighed while he lapped at it, her hands on his shoulders to support herself. He was an expert with his tongue, this Julien Brocq, evidently he had developed his ability on a large number of young women in the film world. At this particular moment, it must be said, his attentions were not tremendously welcome – Suzette was hungry, she would prefer to finish dressing and go out to eat.

Nevertheless, these intimacies aroused her very quickly. She closed her eyes and smiled secretly to herself, feeling throbs of pleasure in her belly. Julien had one most endearing trait which compensated for his many failings. His admiration for her body was extravagant, he truly adored her. This made an impact of considerable importance on Suzette. She adored her own body and was well-disposed to any man who truly shared that emotion.

Julien was so enthusiastic and so skilful that he brought her to a climax before he even realised how excited she had become. He gripped her bottom hard to steady her when she squirmed and moaned. Her loins jerked, her belly quaked, her knees trembled. It delighted him to do this to her, it gave him a strong sense of power. He felt he was in total command – that she was his to dispose of.

Of course, it made him highly excited too. When her delicious tremors had passed, Suzette pushed him on to the bed and opened his trousers wide. His stiff flesh jutted out, quivering with passion. He reached for her with eager hands to roll her on her back but she was able to elude his grasp. Something important had occurred to her – she had not replaced her diaphragm after her bath. She pushed Julien down on his back and there he lay, formally dressed for the evening, in an expensive suit of midnight blue, a white silk shirt and a blue striped tie. And fifteen centimetres of hard pink flesh thrusting upwards in blind eagerness.

She sat on the bed at his side, her pink kimono open wide to reveal her beautiful naked body to his bright-eyed stare. She didn't clasp his upstanding part in her hand, not at first. She circled it with her fingertips, sliding up over the taut flesh, up from the thicket of dark-brown curls on his belly, up to the purple tip. She felt she was touching his innermost nerves now, reaching to his secret core, pushing him towards a pleasure that was so intense it was almost an agony.

Julien sighed and moaned, his legs twitched and his hand lay on her bare thigh, the fingertips just touching those soft lips he had made slippery with his tongue. With a fixed expression he gazed up at her naked breasts, at the fullness and roundness of them as they swung above him to the movements of her hands on him.

His body was shaking, he had reached the furthermost point of his ascent to ecstasy, in a moment she would see him spurt. Now she held him full-handed and stroked firmly, her other hand was reaching for the carefully pleated linen handkerchief tucked in the breast pocket of his elegant Jacket.

'Oh!' he gasped. 'Suzette!' while she caught the outpouring of his pleasure in the fine linen.

From when he entered the apartment to this moment less than ten minutes had passed! Briskly businesslike, it could be said, as if such commercial virtues have any place in the conduct of intimate pleasures between dear friends! *Perhaps we can go and eat now that's out of the way,* Suzette thought, planting a tiny kiss on his cheek.

But no, there was still another consideration of importance to be attended to. Julien rearranged his clothes and waited for her to complete her *toilette*. She wore a short evening frock, black satin with a thin edging of gold at the hem. Now Julien rose to his feet and kissed her on both cheeks, as if he were a general on parade awarding the Croix de Guerre to a soldier who had risked all. From his jacket pocket he produced a jeweller's flat box.

It was a diamond brooch, expensive, ostentatious. And Suzette realised at once it was his farewell gift. He pinned it on her bosom and took a step back to admire the effect. He nodded with satisfaction, stepped forward again and took her in his arms to kiss her properly. She kissed him warmly and went to the mirror to see the effect – the glittering diamonds on black satin were stunning!

For dinner before the show Julien insisted that only the very best would do, it being a special evening for them before his departure. He insisted on taking her to the celebrated Chez Drouant. It goes without saying the food was beyond criticism and virtually beyond praise. Julien decided what they were to eat, to make certain there would be no mistakes. This way he had of making all decisions and ignoring anyone else's wishes was a trait of character Suzette found less than endearing.

He chose the Beluga caviare first, to be followed by lobster Thermidor. For the main course, roast duck with blueberries. It was utterly delicious and afterward Suzette could manage only a tiny morsel of Brie, though Julien ordered *banane flambée* for himself. Needless to say, with this feast he ordered a superb Meursault and then a Chambertin and finally a sweet Sauternes.

In truth, Suzette was becoming a little surfeited, even bored perhaps, with Julien's expense-account life style. It seemed to be cost alone that guided his choice and won his praise – food, restaurants, clothes, hotels. And jewellery, though that seemed more reasonable. His method of choice simplified all matters of taste, to be sure, but to one of Suzette's robust outlook there was something unsatisfactory in this. On the other hand, Julien took such honest pleasure in spending money – company money, of course – that it would be ungracious not to go along with him.

For herself, Suzette would have been content with a meal less elaborate: a farmhouse cassoulet, a glass of village wine, then a slice of crumbly Roquefort. And no more.

Julien could afford to grow thick in the middle – it was not expected of a man over forty that he remain slim and athletic. But Suzette dare not permit her gorgeous body to become broader or thicker. She shuddered at the mere thought that her superbly rounded bottom might spread and her marvellous thighs become plump!

True, to be beautiful was no longer her main profession but she did not flatter herself her singing was so wonderful that she could afford to let herself become plain and still hope to reach the top. She almost convinced herself that love-making was the best possible exercise to keep her body in excellent shape. But this was not as reassuring as it might be, frequent and vigorous as her escapades in bed were.

In a women's magazine she had read with interest that one act of love was the equivalent for a woman of climbing two flights of stairs, or of walking a kilometre at a brisk pace. But then, medical experts are unconvincing and confusing as philosophers. Theory proved one thing, evidence demonstrated another. For in the apartment above Suzette's there lived Madame Arlette Saumur, a blonde-dyed widow of forty or thereabouts. She entertained men regularly by way of making a living.

Suzette and Gaby were on friendly terms with her. She dropped in for a cup of coffee and a chat sometimes and they went up to her apartment now and then for a tiny glass of cognac. Arlette was not a street-walker. She had a fixed circle of men friends, ten or a dozen, whom she obliged. They were middle-aged and boring of appearance but decent, well-established men – civil servants, shop-keepers, lycée teachers – the sort who form the traditional *bon bourgeois*.

Suzette had seen them on the stairs, some going up earnestly, some returning with a more relaxed gait. They smiled at her – the Frenchman was not yet born who could pass so very beautiful a woman without smiling and raising his hat. One even enquired if he might call upon her, touching his chest over his wallet to indicate he had money to spend.

With so many friends to entertain, Arlette spent more time on her back than any six average married women. And if it was true that doing it once exercised the body as much as ascending two flights of stairs, as the magazine article stated, then it was evident Arlette performed the equivalent of running right up to the very top of the Eiffel Tower twice weekly!

Yet for all that, Arlette was decidedly plump. She claimed to be *comfortably* shaped, she said her men friends adored her like that – there was something solid for them to get hold of!

Suzette's show-girl standards allowed for a certain amount of female flesh in the right places. Patrons of the Folies Bergère were not admirers of flat-chested girls with no bottoms. But even by these standards Arlette was seriously overweight. And to Gaby's dancer's eye, she was gross! She had a pair of *nichons* as big as Charenton melons, Gaby declared they rolled about under her clothes like fruit on a barrow. And her bottom was podgy – it stuck out when she walked, the cheeks wobbling up and down.

Alas, though Arlette was a thoroughly pleasant woman to know, she was living proof that the love-making theory was incorrect.

After dinner, Julien tucked Suzette's arm in his and together they strolled at the leisurely pace necessary to a well-filled stomach to the avenue de l'Opéra and a taxi stand. In the taxi, on the way to the rue Richer and the Folies Bergère, Julien laid his hand lightly on Suzette's knee and stroked a little through her fine silk stocking. But he was too somnolent from the rich food inside him to attempt any further intimacies.

The show was wonderfully well-staged, as was to be expected. The sets were imaginative, the music was lively, the costumes glamorous and amusing. There were dancers and singers, acrobats, illusionists, comedians, jugglers and, above all , the show-girls – superb young bodies very nearly naked, adorned with plumes of feathers, satin, spangles, golden paint, silver lamé, shiny black leather . . .

'And you, Suzette,' Julien murmured his admiration, 'you were one of these enchanting young ladies in ostrich plumes and gold spangles, posing in front of a coloured waterfall, in the days before you became a singer? I find that charming.'

In the dark she ran a hand affectionately up inside his thigh and found a telltale stiffness. Evidently, seeing the show-girls had aroused his interest. The typical male urges were asserting themselves again, after being lulled for a while by the little episode in her apartment.

After the show she took Julien to a bar she knew not far

away which was popular with members of the cast. Old friends kissed her cheek and admired with open envy the shining diamond brooch pinned to her frock. They were introduced to Julien, completely recovered now from his after-dinner torpor. He adored being the centre of attraction of a crowd of pretty perfumed women. They were now clothed but clearly the memory of their nakedness on stage was fresh in his memory.

Two of Suzette's good friends from the line-up were there and in high spirits, Angelique and Jasmin. Angelique had a new boyfriend with her, evidently she had rid herself at last of Jean-Pierre Buffon. He used to meet her here every night and he was an unsympathetic type but well-off.

Julien seemed especially taken by Jasmin Bonaventure. He said she looked extremely photogenic and asked if she had ever taken a screen test. Jasmin said no, looking warily at Suzette to see if she was jealous of this interest in her. Suzette shrugged.

Jasmin had a boyfriend in tow, in a vague sort of way. He was a member of the cast, a handsome chocolate-skinned man who said he was from Gaboon, whichever part of Africa that was. On stage he juggled with golden balls that reflected light in darting flashes at the audience. At first he stood upright and juggled, then he balanced upside down on one hand, using his feet to aid his free hand. He balanced on his head alone on top of a large golden sphere to juggle upside down – so fast it was impossible to count how many balls he kept in motion.

He performed other marvels of dexterity and skill, and he did it all barefoot and naked except for a tight little *cache-sexe* made of dazzling white leather. It appeared to be so very full, his *cache-sexe*, that many women in the audience were moist between the legs at the end of his act.

Jasmin had been interested enough to find out for herself if the reality lived up to the promise. The eye of desire promised twenty centimetres and as thick as a cucumber. But men could not be trusted in so personal a question – it was possible the juggler stuffed a pair of discarded silk stockings down the front of his *cache-sexe* before he went on stage.

Suzette winked briefly at Jasmin, put on a quizzical look and gave a tiny nod in the direction of the juggler's now trousered loins. *Any good?* she was asking.

Between women matters of this sort need no words spoken, each understands the other perfectly. Jasmin made a small gesture of her hand, an almost imperceptible movement. She turned her palm quickly over and back again, only Suzette saw the gesture that clearly said, *Comme ci, comme ca!*

Then it was Jasmin's privilege to ask the same question about Julien, standing there among the show-girls, well-dressed, self-assured, wealthy, powerful, the giver of diamond bracelets and brooches. Jasmin was not exceptionally tactful, she posed the question by closing her hand so only the smallest finger stood out and even that curved downward.

Suzette grinned at her and flicked three fingers up for just an instant to indicate Julien was a lover who did not roll over and fall asleep after just one bout. Jasmin pouted in disappointment and envy.

Angelique said she had heard Suzette singing on the radio. It was a record they played, Suzette explained, they didn't want her to sing live. Though she did not mention it, this she owed also to Julien, who knew people in the record industry and was able to arrange a deal with Polydor. Dear fat red-nosed Emile, Suzette's agent, had rubbed his hands gleefully and ordered another drink – he insisted he'd known all along that sending her to the film premiere with Antoine Ducasse would be a turning-point in her career.

Suzette shrugged and said there was a little more to it than that. Emile allowed himself to be prised away from the zinc-top bar long enough to represent her interests and ensure the terms of the deal were favourable.

That settled, she persuaded Michel, who needed little coaxing because he loved her to distraction, to compose a new song for her to record. '*Rue de la Paix*'. She had no problem at all to get her singing-master Jacques-Charles Delise to agree to devise a pretty tune for Michel's words – but holding him to his promise was harder, in competition with the bottles of *pastis* beckoning to him from every bar in Montmartre.

On the other side of the record, she sang her very favourite song – '*Place Vendôme*'.

If Julien was taken by Jasmin, she thought, he would know where to find her when he returned to Paris. The juggler from Gaboon was no great obstacle, Jasmin was merely using him to tide herself over a dull patch. She would drop him without a second thought if an important person like Julien Brocq put his hand on her knee and made her an offer. And it was very possible she was more fitted to suit Julien's needs. She was the type he seemed to prefer – very sensual, not too bright, easily led. And there was a surprise in store for him if he did get Jasmin's clothes off – something Suzette knew from sharing the same dressing-room at the Folies Bergère.

Jasmin's magnificent breasts had buds of a very dark red, almost umber. Before appearing on stage she toned them down, so as not to be too different from the other show-girls. She overdid this some nights and coloured them a little-girl pale pink. Outside work she was proud of her difference. She had confided one night to Suzette in this very bar that she found it ravishing beyond all belief for a lover to smear her dark buds with honey – and lick it off. Suzette thought it was a trick she could teach Julien.

How strange, Suzette thought, I am making arrangements in my mind for him with another woman! He hasn't given any sign that he wants to end it between us. But she knew in her heart it was finished for her, as much as for him – perhaps more so. If he tried to take up with her again when he came back, she would tell him she didn't want to.

She asked Angelique if she knew what had become of Francine – a nude dancer at the Folies Bergère in Suzette's time there. An unforgettable incident had taken place backstage one night when the show-girls combined to save poor Francine from a beating by her jealous and ill-humoured partner. They had advanced on him like an army of Amazons, most of them dressed to appear on stage in the opening number. They were superbly proportioned women, almost naked, but determined to stop Francine being abused.

The partner, Gilles, was lean and muscular, more than a match for the embattled show-girls if it came to exchanging blows. But he was also left-handed, as they say, and the sight of so much naked female flesh adorned with sequins and rhinestones was too much for his susceptibilities. He fled, cursing, and soon after that Francine left him.

She was only eighteen years old, a pretty brunette with a slim body and dancer's legs. She moved in with the Magnificent Magyars, a trio of Hungarian jugglers. They said they were cousins, but as they had only four words of French between them it was hard to know what they meant.

They shared little Francine between them, Sandor, Lazlo and Janos, large men with glossy blue-black hair, expressive hands and fiery eyes. She adored them all equally.

'She's in London with the Hungarians,' said Angelique, 'I had a postcard from her not long ago – a picture of an obelisk they call Cleopatra's Sewing-needle.'

Francine and the Magyars had merged their acts – they juggled her now instead of knives and torches and hoops and the usual clutter that jugglers throw about a stage. She posed gracefully in nothing much but a feather or two and gold sequins while the cousins hurled her from hand to hand.

'She wrote they are appearing at the London Palladium,' said Angelique. 'This obelisk in London looks the same as the one in the Place de la Concorde. What can have been in Francine's mind when she chose this postcard, instead of Buckingham Palace?'

She said it with a grin and Suzette grinned back, they could both guess what Francine had been thinking of. It was a wonder she had any time for sight-seeing in London, being on stage all evening and keeping her three lovers content in the daytime.

Naturally, Julien paid for all the drinks Suzette's friends ordered and for this reason they all stayed longer in the bar than they otherwise would. But eventually the *au revoirs* were spoken and the cheeks were kissed and Julien found a taxi to take him and Suzette to the Hotel Ritz. He was in a very good mood after his hour among the show-girls and he talked about films and his forthcoming visit to Hollywood.

In the bedroom of his suite he removed his jacket and put his arms about Suzette. She was balancing precariously on one high heel while she took the other shoe off. The sudden embrace very nearly tipped her over but Julien held her and she grasped his shirt front to save herself. The buttons pulled away to reveal his thickly haired chest. She laughed and trailed a hand over the dark-brown pelt that covered his body.

'You have mistaken your vocation in movies, *chéri*,' she said, 'instead of making them, you should be performing in them.'

'I? What part could I possibly play – a gangster?'

'You would be perfect as King Kong,' she said with a giggle.

The thought amused Julien highly. There was a certain aptness in the suggestion. When he glanced over Suzette's shoulder into the mirror his reflection showed a thick-shouldered, heavy-set man, broad of jaw, his chest a mass of hair where his shirt was torn open.

'Yes!' he exclaimed. 'Yes, by God – it is true! I shall be King Kong and you are the white woman the tribe has offered me as a sacrifice!'

His hands closed on Suzette and lifted her from her feet. He took three strides toward the bed and placed her on it on all fours.

'I shall scream!' she cried. 'You will kill me!'

Julien threw himself to his knees behind her, inspired by her readiness to fall in with his game. He flipped up the skirt of her black evening frock and jerked her shiny black satin knickers down her thighs to bare her bottom. He handled the round cheeks she was offering, licking and biting them.

'My gorilla!' said Suzette. 'So huge and hairy!'

Julien slipped his hand between her open legs from behind and fingered the slim bare folds of flesh, searching between them for the tender little bud. He was all gorilla now and showed no gentleness or finesse. He was brutally strong, intent only on his own satisfaction . . .

Suzette wriggled her bottom to his warm licking and then felt him climbing over her back. He had ripped his shirt off and opened his trousers wide and his hairy chest and belly slid over her smooth skin. He began to make ape noises, he was snuffling and grunting. She almost laughed but restrained herself.

How very bristly his chest was against the skin of her back! The feel of it aroused her. His hands were under her belly and he stroked it hard. His fingers moved down to feel her bare-shaven nakedness, already moist, and opened it. From behind, his stiff flesh touched the inside of her thigh and moved against it. He was making little jabbing movements against her with his loins, his hardness prodding her.

His fingers found her secret bud and tickled it, making her sigh and squirm with pleasure. She pushed her bottom towards him and raised it as high as she could, her face down on the satin bed-cover. His ape noises became louder and fiercer as his stiff part penetrated her from behind, sliding strongly into her slippery warmth. She felt him burrowing deeper with a twitchy to and fro movement.

He was clinging to her shoulders with his hands, smacking his belly against her beautifully round bottom. Was this, she asked herself, the manner in which gorillas mated in the dark African jungle? Perhaps Jasmin's juggler from Gaboon would know. Jean-Marc Borongo, he said his name was. What a pity for poor Jasmin he failed to live up to his advance publicity, so to speak.

But surely *some* part of the massive bulge in Jean-Marc's soft white leather loin-cloth must be solid flesh? It was possible Jasmin had not aroused him to the limit, he might have been no more than half-stiff for her. Men needed properly handling to get the best out of them . . .

Suzette was bent over under Julien's weight, her breasts and belly lay flat on the bed to stop herself collapsing under him – especially when he began his final run, short sharp jabs, to the noisy accompaniment of huffing and puffing and jungle-style howls.

It had ceased to be merely humorous, at least to Suzette, but any other observer of what was taking place would have found it extremely comical. Suzette had become aroused by the way Julien handled her body and the force of his thrusting – and naturally by the rub of his bristly pelt on her satin-smooth skin. It was formidable to be seized by this giant ape and held a helpless captive in his mighty arms, while he satisfied his bestial lust – ah, how extraordinary a Fate, how insanely exciting!

Suzette was hot and wet, ready for him in every way. And when he gave a triumphant cry worthy of King Ape himself and spurted into her, she shook in tremors of ecstasy, her muscles squeezing tight about his leaping flesh. He was so highly aroused by his own game that he was like a fountain, hurling his passion into her.

'Ah, ah, ah!' Suzette gasped in her pleasurable throes.

'Huh, huh, huh!' Julien howled in ape-like delight.

In this manner it continued, *ah, huh, ah, huh!* until at last the spasms subsided, the thrusting and heaving slowed gently to a stop. The jungle-couple fell on to the bed, side by side, and lay grinning at each other.

Later on that night, when they lay naked in each other's arms, Julien privately reached the conclusion he would never find a woman as beautiful, as sensual, or as enthusiastic about love-making as Suzette. By now it was almost the middle of the night and dark in the room. He surprised her by begging her to accompany him to Hollywood.

'But Julien, I don't want to be a film star, you know that,' she said, 'and I can't be a singer in America, they don't speak French.'

'We will arrange something,' he said ardently, 'I promise it. Listen to me, I adore you, I cannot go away and leave you. Come with me!'

Suzette kissed him and slid her hand down his hairy belly and between his thighs, to stroke him a little and calm his nervous chatter of not being able to live and work unless she went with him to bring happiness into his days. And many another similar declarations of eternal passion, more suitable to a younger man.

MICHEL IN THE
LATIN QUARTER

Since the day Michel Radiguet had met Suzette, every poem he wrote was about her, every one! For '*Place Vendôme*' he pictured her in a jewellery shop, her lover buying her a diamond necklace as a token of his complete devotion. Michel saw himself as the lover though he'd never had more than fifty francs in his pocket at one time in his life.

It was Suzette he imagined arriving at the opera by limousine, wearing a sumptuous Dior ballgown. The man escorting her to a box on the grand tier was, yet again, Michel himself, though he personally preferred jazz.

And so with all his other poems – the verses Jacques-Charles set to music, the songs which created Suzette's reputation as a night-club singer. In justice, it must be confessed her beauty played a large part in her success. A plain singer could never have made the same impact with such tenuous little songs.

For her recording with Polydor Michel composed a new poem for her. This was the famous '*Rue de la Paix*', the song which became an instant hit when the record was released and took her from night-club *chanteuse* to stardom.

It was a simple little poem that Michel wrote – all his poems were simple and lucid of emotion. A woman strolled alone along the elegant rue de la Paix, in high heels and a silk frock, and a pale mink wrap about her shoulders. She looked into the shop windows as she walked, the boutiques and the jewellers, she saw pretty silk underwear, beautiful frocks, diamond-studded wristwatches. There was sadness in her heart, because her lover was not with her.

Naturally, Suzette ought to have listened to the words rather more carefully than she did at the time. But her thoughts were elsewhere, on the recording session only ten days away, and the absolute necessity of persuading Jacques-Charles Delise to stay sober long enough to compose a tune for Michel's words. So far he had done very well, but there existed always a nagging doubt about the reliability of the alcoholically inclined.

Sometimes the sombre hopelessness of Jacques-Charles' adoring love for her made him so melancholy he became reeling drunk and stayed that way for two or three days. After which he would lie in bed, sick and weak for several more days, to recover.

Merde alors! she said to herself, *why is it that inadequates are attracted to me? Is this my destiny?*

The reason was not hard to find. It was strength of character and determination to succeed that drew the defeated to her. Her ambition was a beacon in their darkness. Take Jacques-Charles – he had thrown away a promising career as a concert pianist for no reason Suzette could discern. But she liked him and she knew he had great talent when he could trouble himself to make use of it.

And Michel was another in the same mould! He was only a year or two younger than Suzette, yet he sometimes gave the impression he was still a child. He was a university student when Suzette first met him, on her debut as a singer in a Montmartre cellar. He gave up his studies because he decided he was in love with her so devastatingly that he could do no other than devote his thoughts and his life to her – or so he said. What idiocy! She tried hard to discourage him from this excessively romantic and futile gesture, but he had made up his mind.

No more books or lectures. *Adieu* examinations. From now on he dedicated himself to an intense and continuous contemplation of Suzette. True love demanded no less!

Needless to say, he did not inform his parents in Fecamp that he had abandoned his studies – it would be too inconvenient if his father stopped sending him money to live on. Suzette tried to give him money, a sort of payment for the songs, but this he refused to accept – he said proudly that the poems were written for her, they were hers to use as she pleased.

This was all very well in its way but it posed problems. How did a beloved go about encouraging an admirer to produce a poem on demand? These things are supposed to flow from the heart, not from the pressure of a career.

He came to Suzette's apartment mostly in the afternoons. She suspected he came every day, but often she and Gaby were out so she was never wholly certain. When the recording contract was arranged and set down in writing, she asked Michel forthrightly to compose a special poem for her. She told him what it was for – by nature she was less given to deception than most women.

He came back with it two days later, a dozen lines scribbled on a crumpled piece of paper, with crossings-out, words put in, lines transposed. Suzette read it with difficulty and told him it was marvellous, a beautiful lyric, the best he'd written. In secret she was hoping Jacques-

Charles could make more sense of it and put it into a better shape for a song.

Michel's face lit up with pleasure at the praise. When Suzette first met him he always wore a shabby brown jacket, frayed trousers and a roll-top black sweater. These were the only clothes he owned – he looked a typically scruffy Left Bank student. She insisted on buying new clothes for him – not a suit, of course, it was impossible in his world to wear so bourgeois a badge of servitude! But he accepted a new jacket of corduroy, a pair of good grey flannel trousers and a few shirts. No tie, that would be to betray his high moral principles.

He was a good-looking young man, that goes without saying, or Suzette would not have been interested in him. He was twenty years old, dark-haired and very slender, as if he didn't eat enough. His eyes were large and dark, his face sensitive, his eyelashes as long as a girl's and though he was by nature shy, he was very masculine – impressively so – in the way that mattered most.

Gaby was out somewhere with Tristan, no doubt risking arrest by letting him make love to her in a public park or some other inappropriate place. Suzette was dressed casually in a blue and white shirt with a grey linen skirt, for an afternoon at home. Michel was sitting on the sofa, she was standing nearby to read his new poem, holding the paper up towards the window to catch the light.

He preened to hear her praise his work and when she stroked his face he almost burst with joy and pride. He reached out and put a hand on her leg, very unsure of himself still, even after making love to her for almost a year now. She smiled at him and he grew more confident. She ran her fingers through his mop of thick dark hair and he slid his hand under her skirt and up her thigh.

Poor Michel, would he ever achieve a degree of self-esteem to enable him to cope with this rough and ready world? It seemed most unlikely. Left to himself he was destined for life in the shadows, just like Jacques-Charles. Even while his hand stroked the satin-smooth skin of Suzette's thigh above her stocking, his expression was almost embarrassed, though his luminous dark eyes never wavered from her face.

Suzette waited for him to become aroused, he would be bolder then. And after a while he sighed and slipped his hand into her knickers and touched the warm bareness between her thighs.

Poets have always had many names for this cherished part of a woman's body – *rose* and *rosebud*, for example. The short little word used in the streets is too brutal when lovers caress each other intimately. Michel called it her *orchid*.

He adored it, he dreamed of it every night, or so he said. He woke in the mornings stiff and perspiring with her *orchid* occupying his thoughts and wishes. Since that never-to-be-forgotten night he first touched it, in a dark doorway in Montmartre, he couldn't look at any other woman, much less touch her.

Suzette shrugged and tried not to smile whenever he told her this rigmarole. To her, love-making was as natural as breathing and this idealisation of a simple pleasure seemed to her unhealthy.

But at least Michel had advanced as far as pulling her skirt up and her knickers down, to kiss her *pink orchid* lovingly. He pressed his face to the smooth-skinned lips, he murmured little words of adoration. He could have been in a church, down on his knees before a painted picture of a Saint, praying for grace!

The idea was ridiculous, it made Suzette smile. Impossible to imagine herself as a chaste Saint! Or her *orchid* as an object of religious veneration! But it *was* very exciting, the way men adored it!

Michel lifted his face from his devotions, starry-eyed and enraptured. Suzette sat on his knee and his hand went up between her legs without hesitation now. Her little silk knickers were at half-mast, his caress was firm between her thighs. He kissed her mouth while he stroked her, his fingertip easing within to touch her bud. He stroked delicately and yet so very thoroughly she almost reached a climax sitting on his lap.

She kissed his ear and stood up to lead him into the bedroom. He followed her hastily, shedding his jacket on the way, his stiffness bulging out the front of his fine grey flannel trousers. A step or two inside the door he stopped and stared at Suzette, lost in his poetic rapture. Though perhaps it was not precisely poetry that filled his mind just then – some other emotion may have been responsible for the pink flush on his cheeks and the irregularity of his breathing.

In effect, the picture presented to him when he went into the bedroom was one to stir the blood of any man below eighty years of age! Suzette lay crossways on the bed, looking up at him. Her blue and white shirt was fully unbuttoned, her brassiere undone and her beautiful round breasts uncovered. Her skirt was up to her hips, her little knickers down around her thighs, her belly bare. Michel stared in awe, hardly breathing, as if struck dumb by a vision of paradise manifesting itself to him. In one sense it had, of course.

Suzette broke the magic spell by raising a knee sinuously and pushing her shiny black shoes off with her silk-stockinged toes and letting them drop on the floor. At once, Michel's power of movement was restored to him, he leaped on the bed with her and slid her knickers all the way down her legs.

Suzette sat up quickly to open his trousers and pull out his straining male part. He was handsomely endowed in this respect, not too big, not too small, fourteen centimetres of smooth hard flesh superbly shaped for its natural purpose.

As soon as it was on show, Suzette lay down on her back again and threw her legs up and open – her smooth-petalled *orchid* his for the plucking. He crouched between her legs, he licked her belly, he bit at the satin-skinned insides of her thighs. She squirmed in delight, she gasped, her thighs clamped round his head, and her *orchid* was pressed close to his mouth. What could he do but lie flat and push his tongue into it?

He was so enthusiastic in this that he brought her to a first climax before he realised how very excited he had made her. She moaned and writhed on her back, her loins jerking and her belly shaking in ecstasy. And when Michel understood, his emotion was so overwhelming that he uttered a long wail against her wet and slippery flesh and spurted his passion into his underpants.

His pleasure was noisy but short. He wailed and twitched, his hands clenched very tight round Suzette's hips. And then it was finished and he lay still, his cheek resting on her warm thigh. Even in the throes of her own orgasm, Suzette guessed what had happened to Michel – his adoration had overwhelmed the ordinary responses of his body.

She breathed in deeply, smiling to herself, her hand on his head to smooth his dark and ruffled hair.

She was calmer now, her heart beating slower as the final tremors of pleasure faded away. And he too became tranquil, his legs against hers had stopped twitching. In a little while she would undress him completely and kiss him and tell him she was flattered by the intensity of his devotion to her. Men liked to be told that sort of thing, it flattered their ludicrous pride and made them feel like giants.

From their love-making in the past she knew it would be about ten or fifteen minutes before he recovered his powers and grew hard again in her hand. Then she would spread herself comfortably on her back and have him lie on her. She wanted to feel his stiff flesh slide into her, to ravish her beautiful body. Not only for her own pleasure, though that was of importance, but because he deserved no less than the greatest delight she could offer for the poem he had written.

It was a long, delicious afternoon. Michel's appearance might be girlishly sensitive to some eyes, but in bed he was all man. He demonstrated this four times by five o'clock. Suzette asked him to come out for dinner with her to a bistro she knew not far away where the food was good and wholesome and plentiful. She didn't say so, of course, but it seemed a good idea to make him eat a hearty meal. He was too thin, his belly was flat and his thighs lean, and when his male part stood up stiff and hard the contrast with the rest of his body gave it a semblance of being much larger than it truly was.

But he said he couldn't stay, there were things he had to do. Another time, perhaps, he did adore her so. And so on. He dressed and she went to the apartment door naked for a final kiss before he left. He pressed her warm body close to him while he kissed her twenty or more times, his eyes dark and shining with some inexpressible emotion. His sensitive hands played over her bare bottom, he whispered over and over again that he loved her to distraction. Then he departed.

Although he had given up being a student, Michel kept on with his student ways. He lived in the same dingy room in a lodging-house in a crumbling part of the Left Bank. He passed his days and his nights with the students he knew in the Quartier Latin. He hung about the Saint-Michel fountain with a vaguely intellectual crowd of his own age. He ate, when he thought about it, the cheap but indifferent food of the little bistros close to Boul'Mich.

None of his friends had any money, what student ever has? It was possible to live on a few francs a week – nothing cost very much. There were the flea-pit cinemas that showed experimental art films worthy of endless serious-minded discussion on their significance. There were clubs where amateurs played jazz and the price of a glass of cheap wine was enough for admission. There was free entertainment when you knew where to look – and where better than the Place de la Contrescarpe with its clock?

Tramps huddled on the ground under the trees here and street-singers and fire-eaters performed, in the hope of collecting a few francs from the hard-up watchers.

Above all, there were the existentialist cellars, where pale-faced and underfed young *artistes* accompanied themselves on the guitar, while they sang their mournful songs of despairing love, meaningless life, Marxist politics and the death of the old world that had failed them. And endless variations on the same theme, greatly appealing to idealistic and half-baked youth.

It was here, in one of these cellars, that Michel met

Solange Barbot late one night, only a few days after delivering his new poem to Suzette. The cellar was as dark as the Pit and filled with the pungent smoke of ten thousand Gauloise cigarettes. Under a dim spotlight two men in identical check shirts were singing of who-knew-what. The tables were close-packed and full, the wine atrocious, the beer worse. In short, it was a typical student dive.

Ever since Professor Jean-Paul Sartre announced to the world the meaninglessness of human existence, Sorbonne students had taken to calling themselves existentialists. Doubtless one main attraction of this philosophy was its insistence that bourgeois duty and morality were myths for grandmothers. Everyone had the responsibility to do whatever pleased him, or her, best. There was nothing else worthy of consideration in human existence.

For Paris students this naturally meant they should get drunk and sleep with as many girls as possible. Or, if they were left-handed, as many men as possible.

Michel became acquainted with Solange by chance, it could be said. It came about because she had a shouting quarrel with the young man sitting with her, a boyfriend perhaps. When the angry shouting reached a deafening pitch, neither giving a centimetre to the other, she jumped up and smacked her boyfriend's face, a stinging slap that could be heard from one end of the cellar to the other.

She turned on her heel and strode away. But not all men defer to women, the boyfriend – ex-boyfriend now – came after her. He dropped a hand on her shoulder, spun her round and returned her smack. It was the hearty smack of a man whose patience has been tried to breaking point. She screamed as the blow sent her reeling backwards until she crashed into the table where Michel sat with friends. Over went the glasses, spilling the red wine, and she fell backwards to sprawl across Michel's lap.

She was dressed in a style that had come to be the recognised uniform of *Quartier Latin* existentialists: black stockings, black skirt and black roll-top pullover. It is unnecessary to say that her hair was long and straight and lanky – and very dark. Her complexion was pale, her eyes were made up with some blue-black cosmetic. In brief, she looked as if stricken by an incurable wasting disease. This was thought highly *chic*.

She stared up at Michel's face, summed him up in a moment and said, 'Save me, save me! Don't let him murder me!'

This posed a problem for Michel. He had no desire to involve himself in a fist-fight with a man he had never seen before and didn't want to see again. A much heavier man than himself, what's more. On the other hand, it was mortifying to appear fearful when appealed to by a girl in distress.

Happily, the problem resolved itself without the need for any intervention by Michel. The ex-boyfriend stalked away, content that he had made his feelings clear, and left the smoky cellar. When Michel saw this, he smiled down at the girl.

'You are perfectly safe, mademoiselle, I assure you,' he said with his most charming smile. Normally he was exceptionally shy with women, with this one he felt at ease – perhaps the unusual introduction was responsible.

Naturally, he had grabbed at her when she fell across his lap to prevent her slipping to the cigarette-end-littered floor. He was holding her closely and only now did he realise he had one hand under her shoulders and the other over a breast. The blush that suffused his cheeks went unnoticed in the dismal lighting but personally he could not help but be aware of the round breast under his palm, warm and soft to the touch through the thin woollen pullover. It was apparent to him that she was wearing nothing under the roll-top.

He withdrew his hand with a quick word of apology and helped her right herself. And even then, his hands on her waist to raise her to a sitting position, he found she wore nothing much under her skirt either.

Now it was her turn to apologise for disturbing him, this she did so very nicely that Michel persuaded her to take the chair next to him and accept a glass of wine. He had been sitting with two friends, both students, one of them with money to spend, having that very day sold a valuable scientific volume to a dealer in second-hand books, of whom there were hundreds in the *Quartier*. He judged it unnecessary in the transaction to inform the buyer that the volume had been lifted earlier in the day from a book shop only two streets away.

The friends, Albert and Marc, were as intrigued as Michel by the lovers' tiff they had witnessed. But all Solange would tell them was that Jules Dufour was a pig and a brute and she hoped he'd be run over in the street by a truck and die slowly in agony in the gutter.

An hour passed, several glasses of wine were drunk and it became evident to Michel's friends that Solange was interested in him, not them. That being so, when the cellar closed at about two in the morning they said *au revoir* up on the pavement outside and took themselves off. Despite the deafening noise in the cellar, Michel and Solange had exchanged views on nearly everything to be found under the sun and agreed with each other on most items of significance.

They strolled arm-in-arm along the Boulevard St-

Germain, the pavement still thick with home-going crowds. They were not going anywhere in particular, Michel and Solange, they were drifting and talking. She told him his assumption she was a student was wrong, she was an eighteen-year-old runaway who hung around students and she had been in love with Jules Dufour, the pig, the brute, the madman, the woman-beater, etcetera.

Jules was an artist, or he was going to be an artist when he finished at the Beaux-Arts. Michel asked if she was his model but the very thought astonished her. She laughed the thought to scorn. Jules never used models – all that nineteenth century academic painting was *merde*, Jules said so. Only third-raters like Dali clung to realism now, or even the distorted version they called Surrealism.

Jules refused to paint the everyday things anyone could see – nude women, landscapes, whatever. Jules had power to see beyond the commonplace, his vision embraced a wholly *other* dimension of *being*. This he expressed in whorls and slashes and blobs of colour – huge, awesome, manic. He was a genius, this Jules, but she never wanted to see him again, never! She would be happy if he fell out of his attic window when he was drunk and smashed all his bones on the courtyard below!

She did not mention it directly but Michel realised she had nowhere to sleep now she had quarrelled with the artist. After some hesitation he suggested she came to his room for the night – he assured her he had no ulterior motive. She thanked him and accepted his offer right away on the understanding that he did not attempt to take advantage of her unfortunate situation.

Michel guided their footsteps away from the main thoroughfare and down toward the Seine and the lodging-house where he lived. His room was at the very top of the rickety old building under the roof, sweaty-hot in summer and shivery-cold in winter. The floorboards were bare, the walls unpainted for a generation and a cold-water tap dripped into a cracked sink. Three hooks on the wall for hanging clothes, a narrow iron-frame bed, a rush-bottom chair – *et voilà tout!*

He had never let Suzette see it, the comparison with her own comfortable apartment would have put him to shame. Even that wasn't nearly good enough for her – one of his best poems set her in a fabulous apartment on the Avenue Foch, walking her little white dog under the trees. Not that she had such a dog, but it seemed appropriate to Michel for those who could afford to live in the Avenue Foch.

But Solange took in his room in one quick glance and appeared to find it satisfactory. And from that he concluded the painter Jules Dufour lived in not very different circumstances.

It was very late, almost three in the morning. Michel did not own a watch but he knew what time the cellar club closed and he guessed how long he had been strolling about with Solange, deep in conversation. He was tired and so was she by the look of her.

He indicated the narrow bed and hoped she had no objection to sharing it as it was impossible to sleep on the chair.

Solange had no objection but she reminded him briefly he had given his word there would be no *funny business*. She hated and despised men and she wanted nothing more to do with them. So if Michel had brought her to his room with any sneaking idea about getting her on her back, he could forget it!

'But of course not!' said Michel, aghast that anyone could think him capable of an act of infidelity toward the only woman he had ever loved – the only one he would ever love if he lived to be a hundred – Suzette! He said nothing to Solange about Suzette. He was not that simple!

Solange yawned and stretched and pulled her roll-top pullover up over her head, indifferent to whether he watched her or not. Her flesh was very pale, Michel saw, and he had been correct in thinking she had nothing under the roll-top, no brassiere even. Her breasts were small, already a little slack, perhaps she was not telling the truth when she claimed to be eighteen. Or perhaps too much vigorous handling had caused them to droop just a little.

Not that it mattered how young or how old she was, or whether her breasts were perfect or sagging. Michel had no interest in her body, his motives toward her were purely charitable. It was important to him to keep that clearly in mind.

She had a thin silver chain round her neck and a medallion on it, dangling between her breasts.

'Is it St-Christophe?' Michel asked, reaching out to take it between his fingers and lift it for a closer look.

Entirely by chance his fingers brushed the warm skin between her breasts just for the briefest of moments. His hand shook at the unexpected contact – his wrist almost touched the dark red bud of her left breast.

'Yes, St-Christophe,' she agreed, 'he protects me. Of late he has not been very helpful, but all that will change soon.'

Michel dropped the medallion and stood back. Without turning away, Solange unfastened her waistband and let her black skirt drop to the floorboards. Again Michel was proved correct – she had nothing on under it, no underwear, no stockings, nothing at all, except herself. Between her legs there was a patch of very dark curls she made no effort to conceal. Michel stared in astonishment, it was so unlike what he had become accustomed to with Suzette.

Solange noted the direction of his stare. She gave no sign of being embarrassed by a man looking at her secret. It was more than possible she had modelled for Dufour, or some other artist less contemptuous of *everyday* subjects such as naked women.

'I've a good thick fur coat,' she said, in a matter-of-fact way, 'it keeps me warm in the winter.'

She moved her feet a little apart to open her thighs and give Michel a better look. She did this not in a provocative manner, as might be thought of a woman exhibiting the charm between her thighs to a man, but with the air of one showing herself to an artist for his opinion.

'Very useful,' Michel said, not wishing to continue with this topic of conversation.

Really, it was most unattractive, this tuft of curls between her legs, he thought, unaesthetic and unpleasing when compared to the satin-smooth flesh he had kissed so ardently and so many times between Suzette's thighs. Thank Heaven he had no sexual interest in Solange!

She turned away from him indifferently, giving him a view of the small round cheeks of her bottom, and pulled back the sheet to get into bed naked. What else could she do? She had no other clothes than the ones she had taken off. All else must still be at Dufour's place.

After a moment's reflection, Michel followed her example and undressed. He removed his brown corduroy jacket and shirt, then he blushed and turned away from the bed to take off the rest of his clothes. He put out the light and got into bed beside her – he tried to stay as near the edge as he could without actually falling out. It would be unfortunate if she got the impression he wanted to cuddle up to her.

'Goodnight, Solange,' he said, his back to her to prevent any suspicion of *funny business*, as she called it.

'Goodnight,' said she, and turned over to present her back to his back.

The street outside was quiet, even in the daytime it carried almost no traffic, only those who lived there going on foot about their business. And at three in the morning nothing stirred, even the neighbourhood cats prowling the rooftops were silent. In five minutes Solange was asleep and Michel listened to her tranquil and regular breathing.

Time passed. Michel could not go to sleep. He turned over in bed again and again, but carefully so as not to disturb Solange by his restlessness. The pillow was hot under his cheek, it was impossible to get comfortable. The bed was very narrow and the ancient mattress had a sag in the middle. However carefully he moved, he found himself sliding down until his hip touched her bare bottom, or his thigh lay against hers.

His male part was stiff and demanding. It was understood that he had not the slightest wish to make love to this stranger who shared his bed. He was in love with Suzette Bernard and there was no other woman in the entire world who could tempt him. Yet to his amazement he was holding his stiff part tightly, just as if he was afraid it might commit an act of treachery by itself, against his will.

In his restlessness he had rolled over on to his side, facing inwards. Solange faced away as she slept – his throbbing pride was within three or four centimetres of her naked bottom!

No, no, no – it was utterly impossible he could even consider relieving his urgent emotions in this shameful way just because a humanitarian act placed a naked woman in his bed. Perhaps if he thought hard enough about his adored Suzette, the temptation would pass. But even while he comforted himself with this vague prospect, his hand was stroking his hard flesh up and down.

How simple it would be to slide it in between Solange's legs from behind and let her warm thighs clasp it . . . and reach round to hold her soft breasts . . . while he gave the last few thrusts now needed to release his urgent passion! He edged toward her a little, his clasping hand busy.

Some vibration through the mattress must have reached Solange in her sleep and alerted her to what was going on. She moaned a little and rolled over to face Michel, so close her naked belly brushed against his hand and his straining part.

'What are you doing?' she asked, only half-awake. 'Why won't you let me sleep?'

Her hand found his hand, which now was very still. Michel was in a sort of horrified paralysis at being discovered.

'Ah, that's it, is it!' she said, her tone empty of emotion. 'I might have guessed! You men are all the same!'

She pushed his hand away, then seized his stiff part and slid her hand up and down it furiously. Evidently she was accustomed to being awoken in the night by the demands of the artist Jules Dufour. Michel twitched in mortification and wanted to make her stop – it was demeaning to be treated so very casually – and by a woman who had known only kindness from him!

However clear his intention, his body betrayed him. Solange's hot palm jerked up and down the smooth skin of his hard flesh until his already over-stretched nerves could tolerate no more. After only nine or ten strokes he gasped, his feet drummed upon the mattress and his belly convulsed as his passion spurted wetly.

In four more quick strokes she drained him completely and let go, leaving him panting, trembling, and shamefaced.

'Now go to sleep,' she said, not the least trace of interest in her voice. She yawned and turned her back on him again.

But poor Michel lay awake for a long time, suffering pangs of conscience and agonies of despair. However he tried to explain things to himself, the fearful truth was he had been unfaithful to the beautiful woman he loved with all his heart. And to make matters worse, he knew if he told Suzette what had happened she would only laugh and pat his face.

What could one say? She said she adored him, she acted as if she did whenever he was with her. But as for faithfulness, it was of no importance to her – she did not offer it, nor did she expect it.

But Michel *wanted* Suzette to demand his fidelity to her, as a proof of his true love! Her *laissez-faire* attitude dismayed so ardent a worshipper as Michel – how could she be sure he loved her if she didn't insist he stayed away from other women? Why wasn't she jealous in the normal way? Perhaps her indifference to what he did when he was not with her signified his love was of little importance to her?

He was trying to resolve this difficult metaphysical question when he fell asleep. He woke up with a start in broad daylight, confused and hot, feeling he was being smothered.

He found he was pinned on his back to the bed and Solange was sitting on his chest, her knees bearing down on his upper arms, her thighs splayed wide. He stared at her naked body in sleepy surprise, up past her small hanging breasts where St-Christophe dangled, up to her face. Her cheeks were red, her eyes bright.

'You tried it on last night while I was asleep,' she said. 'Even when you'd promised you wouldn't. And this morning I wake up to find your hand between my legs!'

As if her words were a cue for an actor, Michel glanced down to the thick patch of dark-brown curls brushing over his chest.

'But . . .' he murmured, he was hardly able to speak for the odd sensation of her curly patch against his skin, pressing down on him. Those protruding hairy lips were warm and a little moist. He had no recollection of putting his hand between her legs in the night. Perhaps she only dreamed it. If it was true, he had done it unconsciously.

'Don't deny it,' she said, 'you were fast asleep and stiff as a broom handle from having your hand on me.'

She was rubbing herself against his chest in a gentle rhythm. Michel gripped her thighs and attempted to escape from her, but she had the upper hand and he couldn't tip her off. She mistook his effort to free himself for the squirming of desire.

'You really do want me,' she said. 'You're determined to have my . . .' and at this point she used the short brutal word which he found so offensive for what was to be seen between her legs, and which was sliding warmly over his skin.

'I lay thinking about you, Michel, with your hand between my legs feeling me in your sleep!' she went on.

Her fleshy petals had opened, exposing her bud to the gentle rub against his chest. She was starting to tremble and breathe unevenly as she spoke.

'I thought to myself – if he wants it so badly that he even interferes with me while he's asleep, he must have it! So from now on I'm yours, Michel, all day and all night –

anytime you want me. Touch me, *chéri*.'

Michel desired no more of this, he wanted this atrocious girl to go away and leave him alone with his thoughts – yet he could feel his hard male part straining upward behind her back, avid for action. He could feel throbs of sensation through Solange's body, he knew she had excited herself very nearly to the moment of crisis.

And after that, he thought grimly, when she has satisfied her urgent desire and is limp and trembling, it will be absolutely necessary to roll her on her back and push her legs apart. She will be hot and wet and welcoming . . .

Michel knew he was going to lie on her belly and satisfy his own despairing passion. And not just once . . . seeing her sitting on his chest with her legs apart to show her dark-haired secret had put him in the mood to ride her to exhaustion. He meant to keep her in bed all day long and dissipate his thwarted passion on her body – at least until hunger for food drove them out.

Forgive me, Suzette, forgive me, he said in his mind, *none of this has any significance. It's you I adore, only you, not this girl with the hairy . . .*

He was so unsettled by what was going on that he *thought* that word, the word he disliked so, even while he rolled the ball of his thumb over its slippery wet bud.

ANTOINE
ASSERTS HIMSELF

Suzette's record was played on the radio so many times everyone she knew heard it. They telephoned their felicitations or they sent little notes and flowers. It was no great surprise to hear from Antoine Ducasse. He invited her to lunch with him. Suzette was trying to avoid lunches for a while, anxious to shed a kilo she had put on during her acquaintance with Julien, now happily in the United States.

'Come round about two, if you like,' she said, 'or at one if you have no objection to eating a small salad with me.'

'Marvellous thought! I'll be there at one,' he said down the telephone, sounding ridiculously enthusiastic about the sparse meal she was offering.

Naturally, being an actor, his sincere congratulations covered his true motive for coming to see her. But first he praised the record extravagantly while they ate together – hard-boiled egg chopped with chicory and a lettuce leaf or two, a tiny slice of hard cheese, a single glass of dry white wine.

And because he was an actor he understood perfectly Suzette's need to remain shapely and beautiful – he worried about his own figure in precisely the same manner. Every morning, soon after getting out of bed, he stood naked before the big mirror on the wall of his bedroom and studied his body, anxiously deciding if his waistline was a centimetre more than the day before, if his bottom was sagging ever so slightly . . .

The real reason for his visit, which came out eventually, was his lack of progress with a film-acting career. Things had gone well for him after the premiere Emile sent him to with Suzette, a screen-test had been arranged and one or two important people in the movie industry told him he had interesting potential. Even the great Julien Brocq appeared to be impressed and had gone so far as to say there might be a part for him in a film now under discussion.

After that, nothing. Perhaps Suzette could tell him if he was really being considered? He had heard she was a good friend of Brocq. It was only gossip, of course, now she had made a record and was well on the way to stardom. And at this point Antoine stared meaningfully at the diamond bracelet Suzette wore on her wrist. She laughed and twisted her arm about, so as to make the diamonds glitter in the light.

'But I don't want to be a film star,' she said. 'I'm a singer and I mean to be the most famous singer in France.'

'He offered you a film part, they say,' Antoine persisted.

'And I thanked him and refused.'

'But he gave you that bracelet – are they real diamonds?'

'Yes, they are,' said Suzette, smiling at the thought.

She spoke with confidence because she had taken the bracelet for valuation to a jeweller the day after Julien gave it to her – men are by nature deceivers and it is necessary to be careful in these matters.

'Julien is in Hollywood,' she told Antoine, 'didn't they tell you at his office? He will be away for another month or so.'

'No one mentioned that,' Antoine said, disappointment showing on his face, 'then there is nothing for me but to wait until he comes back. Unless Emile can arrange something elsewhere I must accept a part they've offered me at the Comédie Française. It's Moliere's *L'Avare* – I've done it before and I was hoping to avoid it this time round. I suppose Brocq hasn't said anything to you about me?'

He seemed very downcast at the prospect, Suzette took this to mean he was bored with classical theatre. He said nothing about the influence of Madame Laplace on his stage career or his life outside the theatre. The corners of his mouth were drawn down and his expression became even glummer when Suzette said truthfully that Julien had never mentioned him to her.

To cheer him up a little she reached out under the table and stroked his thigh.

'Ah, you did that to me once before, in the cinema,' he said, though sadly, his expressive eyes staring at her face.

'And your reaction then was the same as now,' she told him, 'you shivered and went hard in your trousers.'

Her fingers played over the instant bulge she had provoked in so tantalising a manner. The moroseness left Antoine's handsome face and a boyish grin appeared. He dropped a hand into his lap to undo his trousers and Suzette's hand crept inside. She stroked his up-risen part while she suggested they went into the bedroom.

In truth, she had another reason besides dispelling the gloom that seemed to have engulfed him. She remembered with amusement the only time they made love and the extraordinary effect that his own reflection in the gilt-framed mirror had on him. Being of an inquisitive turn of mind, as women are, she had a strong urge to discover if Antoine was entertaining without a mirror available to stimulate his narcissism.

They went hand-in-hand to her bedroom, she disengaged herself from his clasp and took her pretty frock off quickly. She meant to give him no opportunity to display indifference or coolness, she was going to put him in a situation where he was compelled to play the masculine role. He stood watching her undress, tiny lines creasing his perfect brow – but whether they were caused by anxiety or bewilderment or panic, there was no way to tell.

Suzette lay on the bed on her back, totally naked, except for the glittering diamond bracelet on her wrist. All her beautiful body was on offer to Antoine, still standing fully dressed and uncertain at the end of the bed., This was not how the scene was played when Leonie Laplace was his partner and he was like an actor on stage who had forgotten his next line and was waiting for the prompter to tell him.

At least he was still aroused, Suzette reassured herself, for the long bulge still showed in his fawn-coloured trousers. Finally a conclusion was reached in his mind – he took his clothes off. But he remained standing, hands on hips, his stiffness sticking out boldly at her, a curious look on his face.

'I've never seen anyone more beautiful than you, Suzette,' he said. 'Your face and body are superb, magnificent, perfection! Have you ever been photographed nude?'

But he was not looking at the beautiful body he was praising. His eyes were downcast and Suzette realised he was admiring his own nakedness. *You pretty little narcissist,* she said to herself in amusement. *The one*

*secret no man can ever keep is his opinion of himself. It
arouses you more to admire yourself than to look at my
body – no woman finds that flattering!*

Yet she was able to understand and even, to some
extent, share Antoine's erotic feelings about himself
precisely because of her appreciation of her own
sumptuous body. And most especially the delicious secret
part of it . . .

'Is that what you want to do, Antoine, take my
photograph?'

To keep her *orchid* smoothly beautiful she gave it
regular attention with a small razor. Afterwards she would
sit on the edge of her bed, knees apart, an ivory-backed
looking-glass in her hand to examine how well she had
eliminated all trace of curls. Then she took a jar of most
expensive face cream and spread a little over those pretty
pink lips. She smoothed it in with fingertips as delicate as
butterfly wings, head bent to observe herself at her ardent
devotions. Her longest finger would slip between satin-
smooth petals and touch her bud, feeling her excitement
swell quickly . . .

'If I had the ability, I would photograph you nude,'
Antoine answered, still regarding his stiffly jerking flesh,
'and paint you as well!'

'No photographs,' she said. 'They would appear all
over Paris as naughty postcards to sell to foreign
tourists.'

'Never,' he said quickly, shaking his head. 'Beauty
cannot be used in that debased way – a man's soul becomes
inspired by it. They choose plain women for the postcards
with drooping breasts and fat bottoms, then nothing
distracts the attention away from the acts they perform for
the camera.'

'Evidently you are an expert on postcards,' said Suzette, her knees moving further apart to present an unimpeded view to him.

'No, no!' he said hastily. 'I have been shown a few by a man I know, only that.'

'And your opinion is that my beauty turns your thoughts away from making love toward a contemplation of the higher spiritual things – is that so?'

'No!' he exclaimed, seeing the trap he had set for himself.

To avoid any further inconvenient questions and answers about matters of aesthetic philosophy, he abandoned his contemplation of himself and sank to his knees at the foot of the bed – moving as gracefully as a trained actor knew how. He put his head between Suzette's open thighs to kiss the bare lips there.

'That's better,' she said softly. 'I was beginning to think you didn't want me, Antoine.'

She was teasing him, but he didn't know it, and making him suffer a little for his narcissism. If there had been a mirror on the wall for him to see his own naked body that would arouse him – he would be lying on her belly. Without it, he remained passive and let Suzette make the running.

But not this time, my poor Antoine, she said to herself with a suppressed smile. *I insist that you are the man here, chéri, not me – at least you have the necessary stiff part. I require that you make love to me, not kiss me and wait like a young girl for me to do things to you. Amaze me, Antoine, make me scream with pleasure.*

She watched him while the same thought dawned in his mind. He closed his eyes and kissed slowly all the way up her body, his lips trailing over her smooth belly and up to her breasts. What was happening in his mind while he did this, who can say? Only Antoine himself knew what images he summoned up to embolden him for what he meant to do to Suzette.

His face was down between her legs again, kissing her with a passion that felt reasonably convincing. His mouth was warm on her tender flesh, his wet tongue protruding to press inside. It was delicious, what he was doing, Suzette told herself, whether his heart was in agreement with his tongue or not. But this was not what she had in mind for her little narcissist.

She sat up on the bed, pulling her knees up, and pressed him away from her. He sank back on his haunches, waiting to be told what she expected. She slid her legs over the side of the bed, spread her thighs and Antoine edged forward on his knees. At last the idea had formed itself in his mind – he understood now what she intended.

His hard-swollen flesh was in his hand. He brought his belly close to hers and guided himself into her. A strong push of his loins slid him in deep. Suzette sighed open-mouthed and put her hands on his shoulders. He was staring down, his hands gripping her smooth thighs to steady himself. This was far superior to a mirror on the wall – kneeling between her thighs he could watch himself making love to her, his stiffness sliding in and out to the swing of his hips.

The sight of his shining-wet flesh thrusting between her bare and clinging lips affected him strongly. He slid in to the very limit of his capability, then out again – again and again until he knew he was very near the end of his course. In a moment the climax would seize him . . .

'*Je t'adore, Suzette,*' he murmured, surprising himself by his declaration. And it was true, true – she was the first woman to understand how to arouse him to a divine madness.

'Oh, Antoine . . .' she gasped, feeling her orgasm overtake her, '*oh chéri!*'

He stared down at his stiff flesh thrusting strongly into her beautiful body – those spasms of ecstasy that shook her, *he* had caused this, *he*, Antoine Ducasse! The scale of his achievement aroused him so intensely he immediately spurted his hot passion into her throbbing belly.

Later that same day while he was with Leonie, the thought came to him that Suzette treated him as a man, not a lap-dog. He had been out to dinner with Leonie, who had told him at length how fortunate he was to have the offer to appear in the Moliere play. When they returned to her apartment, Leonie took his hand as if he were a child needing to be shown what to do.

'Come along,' she said and led him straight into her bedroom and closed the door. It was quiet in there, as still as a great cathedral before the service began. Subtle traces of perfume lingered everywhere; Leonie favoured Piguet's 'Visa' and splashed it about in generous quantities.

There stood her huge four-poster bed with the canopy and the swags of pale gold silk and the golden cords with big tassels – the altar on which her lovers were required to offer homage and reverential adoration to Leonie. Antoine had been engulfed body and soul in that bed many nights – and afternoons! Engulfed by the bed, vast enough for an ordinary mortal man to lose himself in. And also engulfed body and soul by Leonie herself.

Antoine stared at the bed, his face flushed, his thoughts in a turmoil from some words of Suzette's that afternoon. When he asked what he should do, she had said: *Be yourself, Antoine.*

But who was this Antoine? How could *Antoine* be defined? Was he a great actor? Was he a person of value and worth? Or was he only Leonie Laplace's boyfriend – a good face, a well-tended body, a stiff male part?

He had never asked this question of himself before because it had never occurred to him there was such a question to ask.

If Leonie noticed his slight air of abstraction, she ignored it. Her mood today was not for the all-encompassing delights of her magnificent bed – she steered Antoine across the bedroom to a low armchair and made him sit down.

The curtains were drawn across the windows. They were made of an expensive ivory gauzy material and did not darken the room – they protected its secrets from eyes in other windows opposite. While Antoine watched, though with a certain lack of interest it must be admitted, Leonie stripped off her frock and then her white silk underwear.

She was naked except for her transparent silk stockings, a flimsy suspender belt and a very long necklace of blue stones that dangled right down between her small pear-shaped breasts. She smiled solemnly at Antoine and performed a series of poses for him, less for his amusement perhaps than to demonstrate her unfailing power of attraction. Her intention was to madden him with the sight of her body until he threw himself at her feet.

She turned to right and to left, she twisted her body to show off her agility and to push out her elegant little breasts. She raised her arms like a ballet dancer. She thrust out a hip, clasped her hands behind her head and leaned over backwards to force her lean belly forward. She stood with legs apart and her arms akimbo. She sank gracefully to the floor and stretched out like the Egyptian Sphinx, so showing off the lean cheeks of her bottom, superbly taut for a woman of her years.

Antoine looked with no great ardour at her pear-shaped little breasts and at her pale flat belly. He looked at the rich tuft of chestnut curls between her slender thighs – and sadly he was not inspired to cast himself full-length before her and implore her permission to kiss her feet. Or any other part of her body.

Alas, alas, for the fleeting loves of unreliable men! Though Antoine had conveniently forgotten it, the truth was that when he first visited Leonie's apartment, ten years before, he was so overwrought by sitting with her on a yellow striped sofa in her drawing-room that he spurted in her hand the moment she touched him – without ever laying a hand on her! And when for the very first time he had seen her chestnut tuft, he came close enough to spurting again for Leonie to jump on him quickly and get his throbbing part into her before the inevitable happened.

And now? She posed naked – he remained limp in his trousers. True enough, he had made love to Suzette twice that afternoon, but several hours had passed since then. He was perfectly able to respond satisfactorily by now. If it had been Suzette's body stripped for him he would fling himself on his knees and shower hot kisses on the bare lips between her thighs. But it was not Suzette standing here bare-bellied, it was Leonie.

And Leonie had posed quite enough, in her opinion, it was now time for Antoine to pleasure her. She slithered naked along the carpet to where he sat on the low armchair, hissing as she came toward him, like the Serpent of Old Nile. She reared up before him, swaying sinuously, a dangerous cobra about to strike! She wrenched open his well-fitting trousers – her hand darted in to take hold of him.

She found limp softness where she expected strong hard flesh. Her face darkened, she glared up into Antoine's face.

'What is this?' she exclaimed furiously. 'You dare to insult me? I reveal the treasures of my body – and you are as unmoved as a block of wood!'

Before Antoine could think of any sort of answer, not that he or any other man in this dangerous situation could say anything to mollify the scorned woman, before he could stammer words of any sort, the obvious reason struck Leonie like a bullet from a high-powered rifle. He had been with another woman!

She glared at him. Her expression said clearly she wished him dead on the spot. But she said nothing, she clenched her teeth, she bit back the words of hatred that burnt in her throat. What would be the use? To confront him with the truth would simply elicit lies. He would protest his innocence.

Yet Leonie *knew*! In these matters women cannot be deceived – they know for sure when their lover has been with another. The instant they lay eyes, or a hand, on his male part, all becomes clear to them – they know he has been unfaithful!

Perhaps a type of electricity exists, as yet undiscovered by medical science, that clings to this part of a man's body after it has been used to pleasure a woman. It is known to all that an amber rod rubbed with silk acquires a tiny charge of static electricity – something perhaps of this nature also occurs when the act of love is performed?

It is this residual electric charge, if such a thing exists, that causes a shock to a man's girlfriend or mistress or wife, when he comes to her after being with another. No deception is possible – she knows what he has been doing.

The great Leonie Laplace was none of these things to Antoine, of course, neither mistress nor girlfriend. And very surely not his wife. She had made a highly public declaration that never, never again, would she marry – not after the catastrophe of her third husband, not even if the kindest, sweetest, sexiest young man in the world crawled to her feet with ten million francs in his hand as a wedding present for her.

Perhaps Leonie could be said to *own* Antoine, that was more or less her understanding of the position. An unknown minor actor, she had taken him under her protection and created a career for him. And if his understanding of the position was different, it was of no consequence.

Her present rage sprang from the feeling she had been cheated out of something rightfully hers. It was much as if a thief had broken into her apartment and taken an object of value. Not her jewels, Antoine did not rate that high in her scheme of things, nor a valuable painting. Perhaps a porcelain Limoges figurine – something of that sort.

Naturally, this dishonest little Antoine was not going to get away with it! He had to be shown where his duty lay, he needed a lesson in meeting his obligations!

Leonie's sharp fingernails scored along his limp part, making him flinch and groan in anguish. She pulled his shirt right out of his trousers, up to his throat, and scratched his flesh from nipples to groins. And all this time she swayed and hissed like a poisonous snake, spitting out her rage and contempt. Her long blue necklace swung to her movements, sliding over her breasts.

She spoke only once, a few bitter words, commanding him to go hard instantly!

Antoine was not the most intelligent of men, actors rarely do excel in intellectual matters. But even he could not be unaware of Leonie's contemptuous attitude. He felt humiliated by it.

'You cannot treat me like this!' he protested.

Leonie did not deign to reply. She wound the dangling loop of her lapis lazuli necklace tightly round his shameful softness as if tethering a recalcitrant dog. If there had been a leather leash to hand, she would have fastened it in a noose about poor Antoine's neck as a means of control!

She wedged her hips between his knees to keep them apart and her hand was thrust above the wrist into his open trousers between his parted legs. She groped underneath his pompoms – frightening him with thoughts of how she might damage them – but her hand slid deeper yet, till she could force the cheeks of his bottom apart. He groaned as her fingernails clawed in between.

'Leonie – stop this!' he gasped. He was trying hard to sound authoritative. She gave him a scornful look that told him where he stood in her esteem. Far from sounding commanding, his voice was feeble and without determination. He winced and groaned to her cruel assault on his tender areas, his offending male part was being jerked to and fro by the necklace.

In spite of his dismay at this treatment, in spite of all his hatred for her selfishness, Antoine's body began to respond to her vile stimulation. The unwelcome development dismayed him even further, it increased his loathing and it brought gasps of detestation to his lips.

He had no intention of gratifying Leonie, he was no gigolo to be used for her pleasure whenever she decided. He despised her for her insolent possessiveness and her maddening superiority – above all, for her tantrums!

Nevertheless, ripples of pleasure were making themselves felt below his waist.

'I will not be abused like this!' he said – as forcefully as he could. Even to his own ear it sounded more a whimper than a bold statement.

Of course, he was not at that moment in any state of mind to understand the farcical nature of his situation. Nor was Leonie – not that she ever accepted *farcical* as a possible description of anything she did or had done. Her actions, her life, all she was and would be – *dramatic*, yes, *tragic* at times, *sublime* very often. *Farce* – never!

Her fury had achieved what she wanted all along – Antoine was stiff! And when she saw this, she showed her small white teeth in a snarl so furious that he was terrified she would lunge and bite his upright part off altogether! He tried to cover it and protect it with his hands, but she struck them away.

'Leonie . . . please . . .' he pleaded for mercy.

She raised her hands behind her neck, undid her blue necklace and took it off. She wound it round his stiffness and under his pompoms, then pulled on the ends to draw it tight. The polished blue stones pressed into his flesh so very cruelly he expected the string would break under the strain! He prayed it would – and free him from this agony by scattering the stones about the chair and floor.

But it did not break, it held fast. Leonie dragged him to his feet by this leash, making him shriek in anguish. He attempted to seize her wrist, to break her control of him by so sensitive a part of his body but she laughed in his face. She hauled him across the room and he stumbled on unsteady feet, babbling at her, *Please stop!*

His undone trousers slid down his legs after a few steps. He was hobbled at the ankles, he tripped and fell to his knees on the bedside rug. Even then the necklace-string did not give way under the sudden tug. *It must be nylon* was the idiotic thought that flashed into his mind.

Leonie twisted her free hand in his hair and pulled him up on his feet again, to drag him the last metre to the magnificence of her bed. She kept firm hold of the lapis lazuli necklace as she threw herself on her back on the bed and parted her legs.

'No, no, no!' Antoine tried to say, while he stared down as if fascinated at the smooth pale skin of her long slender body and her elegant pear-shaped breasts! How many nights and days had he clasped them in his hands? How many millions of times he had kissed their pink buds!

'No I will not!' he was trying to say but the words stuck in his throat.

Her narrow suspender belt circled her waist, attached to her silk stockings. Antoine's hand reached out to touch her thighs above the stockings. His hand was trembling and responding by itself, not by his conscious will. He realised in the nick of time what he was about to do and dropped his hand to his side, away from the temptation.

But he could not turn his eyes away from Leonie's naked body. He stared, his refusals and denials mumbling in his mouth, meaningless and unheard. Between the slim thighs that were open for him stood Leonie's tuft of chestnut curls, so rich in tint, adorning the long fleshy lips waiting to swallow his hardness.

She has been used by hundreds of men – hundreds! he insisted to himself in a brave effort to prevent himself succumbing yet again to her. Those lips presented for my pleasure, he said to himself, they have been worn thin by the rubbing of a multitude of theatricals and dramatists, intellectuals and critics! And heaven knows who else!

One would truly expect her to be worn to a thread by constant use between the thighs, but there is no trace of her excesses – no indication of the troops of men who have lain on that narrow belly and forced their hard flesh up into her. She is as tender and inviting as a young girl . . . and so warm and soft inside, so very accommodating, so intimately exciting . . .

No, no, no, Antoine rebuked himself sternly, though silently, *I refuse to obey her, I too am a person in my own right, I have a will of my own, I am not her gigolo* . . .

'You are keeping me waiting. Antoine,' Leonie said, her eyes piercing through him like gimlets to skewer his thoughts. 'Take your trousers off and come here.'

She let go of the blue-stone necklace and with a long sigh of relief he unwound it from his tormented parts. His trousers and underwear lay about his ankles. He stepped forward to drop the necklace into her outstretched hand – and by doing so liberated himself from the encumbering garments.

She looped the necklace round his neck in a quick throw while he was leaning over. She pulled hard and dragged his head down until his face touched hers and she could kiss him. It was not a kiss of love. Her mouth pressed furiously against his in a wordless command. He clenched his teeth and squeezed his lips together to prevent her tongue gaining entrance into his mouth.

Never, he was saying in his mind, *you shall not do that to me against my will.* But she brought him under her control with the necklace, she jerked him downward until he lost his balance and fell across her. He was still mumbling unintelligible refusals while he lay upon her cool belly. She could feel his resistance and she pressed her mouth over his harder, till her kiss was so antagonistic it

164

was like a punch in the face.

He had no intention of doing what she wanted. Not ever again. He would not pleasure her, not if she went down on her knees to implore him to take pity on her. It was finished, all that!

But without any guidance from either of them, she dominating, he unwilling, Antoine's jerking stiffness found its own way up between her legs. He was so preoccupied refusing her kiss that he was oblivious of what was happening lower down – until the moment he felt her warmth, her moistness, her readiness.

And at that moment he was lost – he took one long shuddering breath and slid deep into her.

Even now, farce prevailed. He meant to show her that he could not be used like a paid man, she was going to find out that her wishes were not always granted. There had been a time, it could not be denied, when to slide into her like this was so exciting that only a few thrusts were sufficient to bring on his crisis. But not now – not while this dark hatred smouldered deep in his heart!

Let Leonie beware! She had clawed him with her fingernails – clawed him agonisingly, leaving angry red marks down his chest and his belly. Heaven knew what damage she had inflicted on the tenderness between the cheeks of his bottom with her claws – it burned hotly! She had strangulated his proudest part almost to insanity with a stupid necklace! So be it, now it was her turn to suffer!

With all the venom of one whose manhood has been scorned and derided, Antoine rammed into her slippery warmth, furiously and fast, panting and gasping with strenuous effort.

He was not making love to her, he was not pleasuring her, he was ravaging her, violating her, raping her as ruthlessly as he could. He slammed his belly down on hers at breakneck speed. He lunged ferociously into her. He was blind and deaf to all the world except this urgent need to destroy her.

And Leonie? Lying under him, bearing the heavy brunt of his maniac assault, what of her feelings? At first she experienced a shock of disbelief. But then this unexpected vigour of one so unassertive that she normally rode him herself threw her into a mood of delight. She raised her knees and opened her legs wide, her body bouncing on the bed with the savagery of his thrusting.

She writhed beneath him, she released the necklace, she broke off the vicious kiss at last – but only so she could shriek and claw and bite. She bit his shoulders, her hands were inside his shirt to claw down his spine, she shredded the shirt, tore it into strips down to his taut cheeks and sank her talons into them.

Naturally, Antoine's massive assault very soon brought on her climax. She screamed loudly, her belly bumped up at him, spasms of ecstasy shook her. Antoine's reason was swamped by a burning dream of revenge for past slights and in this mood her reaction seemed a clear indication he was succeeding – he was destroying her.

And he was still strong and hard! Every other time with her, when she had used him as her gigolo, his passion had spurted in a very short time and so brought him to a temporary standstill. But not this time. He meant to hold back until he had totally annihilated her, body and spirit, and she begged for mercy. And then he would spit in her face and walk away.

Leonie's ecstasy was over at last. She lay limp under Antoine and endured his relentless ramming. Her eyes stared up blankly at the canopy over her imperial bed, her legs flopped down and lay loosely. Her fingers uncurled, her hands slipped away from Antoine's clawed bottom. She was astounded by his performance. He felt like an iron bar inside her, his energy was phenomenal and undiminished!

She lay still while he ravaged her body and his belly smacked on hers to the rapid rhythm of his attack. She reached up to take his face between her palms and stare closely into his eyes. She could distinguish no expression in them, none at all! Antoine had retreated into his head, into his inner world of vengeance and power. And he was almost at his critical moment, she could hear it in his laboured breathing.

'Ah yes,' she said, 'yes Antoine – I am ready!'

She bent her legs and pulled them high, until her knees were almost up in his armpits, and she opened herself impossibly wide to his frantic slamming. Whether he knew she was urging him on to even greater efforts, who can say? It would surely have sapped his will to know that she *wanted* him to destroy her. His burst of strength and determination sprang from hatred, not desire.

It was a comical moment perhaps – Antoine doing what she wanted while believing he was spiting her. Comic but not unusual. In effect comedy is the natural condition of the dealings between lovers, although very few of them realise it.

Antoine cried out loudly as he reached the peak of sensation. He squirted his hatred into Leonie with furious stabs, she gave a shriek and arched her back off the bed, heels drumming, hands thrashing at him, swept away by a huge wave of sensual delight.

After so enormous a triumph, some little time elapsed before Antoine regained the power of rational thought. He was still on Leonie's belly, his male part shrinking inside her, his face in her hands and her eyes fixed on his in a curious stare.

When he was able to formulate in words what was in his mind, he informed her he had taken a final decision to become a film star – whether she approved or not!

'Whatever you say, *chéri*,' she answered.

Antoine's victory was complete, he had shown her once and for all who was master. She dare not oppose him ever again. And now that was clear between them, it would be a pity to leave her. A consideration of some importance was that she could be useful to him even in the world of cinema. She enjoyed a certain status, she had influential contacts. No doubt of it, her close friendship could be very convenient to him.

Leonie was so deeply and shamelessly gratified by what he had done to her that she saw no point in opposing his silly little notion. For a few marvellous minutes it had been very like when her ex-husband Matthieu made love to her, so excitingly brutal it had ravished her soul! Matthieu had turned out to be a thug to be got rid of, alas, but the memory lingered. Who would have thought, after their years together, that little Antoine would turn into a tiger, capable of the most astonishing endeavours?

He had been with another woman, ungrateful little wretch, no doubt of that, and he had discovered an unexpected violence in himself, that was Leonie's summing up of the situation. His new virtues opened up fascinating possibilities.

It would be important to restrain him at some point before he developed into another Matthieu, the brute who threw her down, day and night, to ravage her body for his own pleasure. But she was certain she understood Antoine's narcissistic nature well enough to control him. His newfound delicious brutality was to be used for her pleasure, not his.

As for the rest, this ridiculous notion of being a film star, well, he would soon find out that without her to help him along in the film business as she had on the stage, his insignificant talent was not going to take him far.

And if he imagined his good looks were enough, how shocked he would be when he saw how many handsome young men were hammering on film directors' doors, begging for an opportunity. Not even the casting couch could help them, there were too many of them.

Ah, my poor Antoine, she thought. *You are mine, you always will be – until I tire of you, chéri.*

Even Leonie's affection had a tinge of malice. She kissed him and rolled him off her belly, his shredded shirt flapping round his waist. She was going to soothe him while he recovered his strength ready to do it again. She stroked his chest where she had scratched him. And between his thighs.

GABY IS
AUDITIONED

After Gaby Demaine came back to Paris from her provincial tour she did not hurry to find another job. It was not that she was disillusioned with show business nor bored with dancing in skimpy costumes for faceless audiences . . . not precisely. But it was true that thanks to the many weeks of travelling between cities and the uncertainty of local audiences and the varying adequacy of cheap hotels . . . well, she felt she deserved a rest.

The curious little pervert Tristan Villette whom she'd met in Lyon was now permanently back in Paris because of her. He lived with his parents and quarrelled with them continuously over his bachelor way of life. He spent as little time as possible with them, he took Gaby to lunch and dinner often. And to chic clubs for dancing.

And shopping – to buy her expensive cosmetics and pretty clothes. That took care of most things, the only large expense left was her half-share of the rent of the apartment she shared with Suzette.

After a time the curiosities of Tristan's love-making ceased to amuse much, as they had once. He was a nice person and she liked him a lot but sometimes it became less than interesting, this obsession of his with the risk of being discovered. It was true up to a point that always having her clothes on when they made love brought a certain feeling of urgency, which added to the excitement. With Tristan there was no time for preliminaries. A hand up her skirt when no one was about, a quick caress, instant penetration – an explosive climax.

Necessarily, the impossibility of the places Tristan selected meant at times that his love-making was over too soon for Gaby. She was left panting and unsatisfied when he slipped out of her and then it was a matter of pleasuring her to fulfilment with his fingers. She found this less than perfect, she preferred the feel of stiff flesh inside her.

There was also a marked lack of comfort in these arrangements of Tristan's. Afternoons in darkened cinemas were all very well – usually it was better than watching the movie – but the seats were cramped and hard, without the least possibility to stretch out and really let oneself go!

Cinema usherettes were not fools, they knew what couples got up to in the dark. Tristan had slipped cash into the hands of a great many of them, to avoid a scene, when a torch had suddenly shone on him *in flagrante*. The strangest thing about him, Gaby confided to Suzette, was that being discovered like that didn't put him off at all. On the contrary, it seemed to excite him so much he wanted to do it again straight afterwards.

'The man's a pervert,' said Suzette, 'and quite insane.'

Eventually Gaby decided she'd been on holiday long enough. An opportunity presented itself by chance. She was with Suzette at the Café Flore about five o'clock one afternoon, on the terrace under the awning, when Angelique Brabant appeared, luscious and ridiculously desirable in an ivory-coloured silk frock clinging to her curves. Her latest boyfriend trailed along behind her, a man with a fixed smile on an otherwise blank face.

Suzette and Angelique kissed each other's cheek as warmly as if they were life-long friends. The newcomers were introduced and invited to sit down and the waiter bustled up to the table.

Gaby learned that Angelique and Suzette had become acquainted at the Folies Bergère. Angelique was a show-girl, posing naked in ostrich plumes, just as Suzette had. And she was still doing it, her major asset being her beautiful body. But she also had a certain talent in bed, as was proved by the presence of Jean-Jacques Chelle and several packages he carried, on which could be seen prominently the names of famous and expensive shops.

Jean-Jacques took little part in the conversation, seeming to be content to look admiringly at Angelique. She explained with pride that he was a property owner, a *rentier* of importance. He owned several blocks of apartments round Paris, mostly in areas where poor people lived. But not all, he was extending his property holdings into the better parts – in fact, Angelique was living with him at present in one of his best apartments, a handsome modern building on the Boulevard Raspail.

'Would you believe it,' she said, rolling her dark eyes upward, 'it's got a sunken bath – in pink marble!'

Suzette and Gaby looked at Jean-Jacques with new interest. He seemed to be a quiet and unassuming person. He was about forty, give or take a year or two, not ugly but not handsome either, a face seen in a crowd and instantly forgotten. He wore a suit of darkish grey, not at all distinguished. To be truthful he could be mistaken for a senior clerk in some dreary office or other.

His role in life was to pay the bills when Angelique went out to eat or shop, that was the impression he gave. And in return he was permitted to fondle her beautiful body, feel her breasts – almost as superb as Suzette's – kiss her belly, throw his leg over her and spurt his desire into her. A nonentity with a full wallet, it might be said – except Jean-Jacques was a man with a sunken pink marble bath!

That was an indication of verve and imagination much superior to what might be anticipated from his very ordinary appearance. In his most secret thoughts he was perhaps a Nero or a Caligula – Haroun al-Raschid or the Emperor Yang – a voluptuary, a sexual despot for whom young women stripped themselves naked and threw themselves into the warm-scented water of his sunken pool to be ridden and ravaged!

Gaby and Suzette stared briefly at Jean-Jacques' lap and then at each other in surmise. He was sitting too close to the table to show much of his legs and his darkish trousers looked loose about his thighs. Whatever was in there was doubtless fairly ordinary, no monstrous part lurking between his legs to rear up when aroused and demand exhausting and unendurable gratification. But it was impossible to know the truth about any man without going to bed with him. He must have secret talents, this property owner – or otherwise Angelique would become bored with him, sunken bath or no. Shopping expeditions were not enough.

But whatever the truth of Angelique's treatment at the hands of her *rentier*, one useful item of information emerged from all her backstage gossip of what went on at the Folies Bergère. One of the dancers had left the cast recently and another was about to go. One short in a chorus line of twenty was hardly to be noticed – but two missing, that was more serious.

Why had Marie left? Who could say? Rumour had it she was on a yacht in Monaco with a bicycle manufacturer –

a small bald man who used to send her flowers regularly. And Chloe, the next one to go, claimed she was off to marry a rich winegrower from Bordeaux, but it was thought she had got herself pregnant by mistake. And by a curly-haired barman with a wife and three children.

Nevertheless, an opportunity was there and Gaby took it. She presented herself backstage next day and talked her way into an audition as a dancer. She was superbly good at it and naturally she was taken on. Strange, she and Suzette said to each other, that she was following Suzette on stage there.

'With your *nichons* on show,' said Suzette with a grin.

Gaby shrugged and returned the grin. At the Café-Mouchard and on tour the dancers had not appeared bare-breasted, though they had worn very little. The usual view in the theatre was dancers might be lean and muscular below the waist but less so above – it could be comical to have unsupported breasts flopping about in the more energetic routines.

The best-known music hall in the entire civilised world had a different view, it selected dancers with small tight breasts so they could show them uncovered.

'The man I danced for said the Folies Bergère had the honour to present the first fully naked woman on stage back before the First World War,' said Gaby. 'Imagine it – all those years ago! I bet that made our grandpapas stiff in their trousers!'

'It was at the Folies Bergère that nudity was elevated to an art form,' Suzette pointed out. Gaby giggled and stared at her friend's sumptuous breasts, an art form in themselves under the thin white pullover she was wearing.

In reality, it was hardly strange at all that the two of them should appear at the Folies – there were not so many places of entertainment in Paris where their talents could be deployed to full advantage. There was the Moulin Rouge, of course, and the Casino and the Lido on the Champs-Elysées. If Suzette had remained a show-girl it was almost certain she and Gaby would have found themselves working together eventually.

Soon after she had learned the dance routines and appeared on stage nightly, Gaby met Remy Courtauld. One of the cast gave a party in her apartment to celebrate her engagement. Though Gaby was a newcomer she was invited and there Remy was, talking and drinking, though mostly he was talking. And Gaby liked the look of him.

If Suzette were asked for her true and candid opinion of her dearest friend, she might admit Gaby was scatterbrained. And, in the matter of boyfriends, she did not always have good luck. If the truth were told completely, some of Gaby's friends had been very unsuitable, regrettably so – and that necessarily included her present friend, Tristan Villette, the man who made love in the streets! Before him there were some equally strange types, Gaby was adventurous in love.

But even Suzette could not complain about Remy Courtauld. He was tall and goodlooking, in his late thirties. He had a broad brow, made more impressive by the way his smooth dark hair receded at his temples. He had a neatly clipped moustache and well-tended, expressive hands. Evidently he was a successful man for he wore an expensive blue-grey suit with a waistcoat.

He seemed to know most of the women at Simone's party though he was attached to none. Gaby decided to make herself pleasant to him – a thrilling experience for any man, to be flirted with by this tall and long-legged charmer, with the supple body of a dancer and silvery blonde hair down to her shoulders. Gaby was beautiful and she knew it, she made sure other people knew it – especially men and most especially attractive men. Like Remy.

Naturally, he took her home with him after the party. She had intended that to happen from the moment they were introduced to each other – but it was necessary to let Remy think it was his own idea to invite her back to his apartment. Because men were so absurd it was necessary to let them believe the initiative lay in their hands. Otherwise they became fretful.

As befitted a successful man, Remy lived in the Parc Monceau district. More exactly, he had a large apartment in a handsome building in the rue de Courcelles, almost next to the building where France's greatest novelist, Marcel Proust, lived while he formulated the plan for *A la Recherche du Temps Perdu*.

Naturally, no one reads it now, except perhaps a professor or two. And it may be no one read it when it was published between the two World Wars. So many volumes, so many words! Yet no one would deny Proust's literary achievement. Those who have heard of him, that is. To beautiful blonde Gaby his name was unknown, his pages unturned. And Remy, with the advantage of a superior education, knew the name and respected it, but that was all. He had never ventured into that prose epic of Parisian snobbery.

And why should it be otherwise? Gaby's mode of life brought her into intimate contact with characters stranger than were to be found in any novel. Literature was too pallid and bloodless an entertainment to interest a woman of her experience. And Remy was a doctor, he had learned more about humanity than any novelist knew, even one who once lived on the same street.

Gaby was intrigued to learn her new friend was a doctor – and a gynaecologist! In the past her acquaintance with these useful people had been formal and businesslike, if lying on her back with her knees up for a middle-aged man in a white coat to push a finger into her private entrance could be described as formal or businesslike. How can any formality be maintained after a woman removes her knickers, even if for an unemotional medical purpose?

Remy's sitting-room was furnished in a pleasingly masculine style – dark green leather armchairs, a plain carpet, hunting prints on the walls, brass handles on the doors. He loaded the autochanger on his radiogram with appropriate records for this late hour alone with a woman. He turned off the main light, made the room pleasantly dim by means of a tall floor-lamp and he poured drinks.

One of the records was Suzette singing *Rue de la Paix*, though Gaby did not mention her close friendship with the singer. That would lead to conversation about her friend – and however proud was she of Suzette's achievement, she had not come to Remy's apartment for conversation.

Not that they stayed for long in the sitting-room. Remy was so delighted she'd accepted his invitation that he wanted her in the bedroom as soon as possible. Gaby lingered on the green leather sofa for only the length of time she thought correct to establish the proprieties, then let Remy understand she was in the mood to view the other amenities of his apartment.

Not to disguise the truth, Gaby adored those charming moments in bedrooms when a good-looking boyfriend worshipped her naked body, kissed her breasts and put his hand between her legs. All the talk in the world, however witty, clever or amusing, was as nothing in comparison with an hour of delicious sensations with a lover who played with her expertly, gave her wild thrills of ecstasy, breath-taking climaxes, back-arching orgasms! And Remy looked as if he was adept in the arts of love-making.

The bedroom was less masculine than the sitting-room. The bed was low and wide and looked comfortably soft. The bedcover was primrose with a pattern of rose-sprigs. This was to the good in Gaby's eyes, it suggested Remy well understood how to make his girlfriends feel at ease and relaxed when he brought them here.

He made a very promising start – he stripped Gaby's beautiful body naked with careful and yet masterful hands. He slipped her short dark-red evening frock over her head without ruffling her silver-blonde hair-do, he peeled her brassiere off to bare her perfectly shaped breasts. He bowed his head to kiss them before he smiled at her and kissed her mouth, almost as an afterthought.

Gaby sighed and half-closed her eyes to feel his elegant hand roaming delicately over her breasts, she gasped at the touch of his wet tongue on their rose-pink buds. All was going extremely well, she could foresee a night of insanely marvellous passion.

Remy sat her on the side of the bed, removed his jacket and eased her over on her back. He took hold of her silk-stockinged ankles and raised her legs until they were upright, then moved closer, so her calves rested against his chest. He took off her shiny red shoes with the high heels and dropped them on the floor.

'So beautiful,' he said softly, 'so very beautiful – dancer's legs, firm lean thighs, well-shaped calves, slender ankles. It was the perfection of your legs that first attracted me to you when I saw you at Simone's party. All the women there are from the Folies Bergère and therefore beautiful,

that's understood, but you stood out from all the others –
I couldn't take my eyes off you.'

Absurd creature, Gaby thought fondly, he really has
convinced himself he picked me up with his masculine
charm!

'You looked at my legs,' she said, 'that was the only
part of me you looked at, naturally. Or did you permit
yourself to look a little higher?'

'Your long lovely legs first,' he agreed, 'and then the
rest of you. Especially your long blonde hair. And your
figure – you are obviously in excellent physical condition.
Every man you've ever met has told you how beautiful you
are, I suppose. What can I say to convey the tremendous
effect you have on me?'

Excellent condition? thought Gaby. *What an unlikely
thing to say! It must be because he's a doctor.*

She was in an exceptionally bizarre position, on her
back on the bed, wearing only knickers and stockings, her
legs upright and clasped in Remy's hands, he standing
there towering above her. Her situation became even
more ludicrous when he slid his hands up her legs to her
ankles and moved her legs apart – like scissor-blades! He
stared down fixedly between her parted thighs, where her
flimsy little black knickers modestly covered her pretty
chatte.

'You ask what can you say to me?' she said with a smile.

She was wondering if Remy's love-making was derived
from some curious book such as the Hindu *Kama Sutra* –
with illustrations, of course, as sold to foreign tourists at
shady shops round the Place Blanche. Was he about to
seduce her into these impossibly named activities of the
Hindus? What an exciting thought! Perhaps the *twining
position* or the *half-yawning position* – or even more

athletic contortions – whatever their ridiculous names may be?

'You can say all the usual things,' she told him. 'Women like to be assured they are adorable, no matter how many times they may have heard it before.'

'You are adorable, Gaby,' he said at once, smiling at her. 'I will say it as often as you like.'

She knew he meant it, she could see the bulge in the front of his trousers. It was throbbing visibly under the wool material.

'And now . . .' he murmured, 'the moment has come . . .'

He lowered her legs, pressed them together, then slipped her little black knickers down her legs to uncover her last secret. As he slipped them over her feet, Gaby bent her knees and moved them apart. This had a devastating effect, as she well knew. It was to fire both barrels at a partridge on the ground one metre away – a guaranteed fatal hit! Remy gasped and stood shaking, her knickers dangling in his fingers.

Like Suzette, Gaby wore the scantiest of theatrical costumes for her work. She too removed her little fur-coat with a razor, but not completely, as Suzette did. Gaby left a charming little tuft on her smooth belly above her *joujou* – and took great care to bleach these remaining curls to the same pale blonde as her hair. The effect was enchanting.

'I never thought I could be so aroused at the sight of a . . .' Remy began, and fell silent, knowing that the anatomical terms he normally made use of were completely out of place here.

'You've seen a lot of them,' Gaby suggested with a smile that made light of his superior knowledge of this part of the female body. After all, he could never know the most important thing – what it felt like to have a man slide his useful stiffness into that tender pink pocket.

'Thousands,' he murmured, 'six days a week women show me this part of themselves.'

'I wonder you're not bored to distraction by them,' Gaby said with a giggle, 'but perhaps you are. Cream gateau with kirsh is very nice – but who would want it ten times a day?'

'Every one I see is different,' Remy said softly, 'blonde or brown or black or ginger, plump or flat, matronly or virginal. I adore them, every single one. I can never, never be bored by the sight of a woman with her legs apart for my inspection – it is impossible.'

'An enthusiast!' said Gaby. 'A man who loves his work!'

'Oh yes, yes,' he breathed softly, missing the gentle mockery in her voice. As well he might, he had other things on his mind at that moment – as evidenced by the throbbing in his trousers becoming stronger.

He stared and stared down between Gaby's open thighs – until she began to be bored with this strange adoration. But eventually he arranged her legs in the way he wanted them, with her knees bent up, her feet well apart and tucked back till her heels touched her bottom. This remarkable posture he chose had the effect of presenting Gaby's *belle-chose* for his attentions over the side of the bed.

Yes, she thought, *it's one of those curious Hindu positions, the congress of the mango fruit or some such impossible way of doing it – and why not if he does it really well? He must know everything about anatomy, being a doctor – perhaps the pressure on nerves and sinews in this position makes the sensations more intense . . .*

His fingers were sensitive, they played over the smooth flesh between her splayed thighs, palpating the soft lips with gentle care, feeling them between his fingertips as if to estimate the thickness and length. In the usual way of things Gaby's lovers were so impressed by the beauty of her *joujou* they went down on their knees to kiss it amorously.

Remy had not done so. That could be taken as an affront. But he was doing such clever things with his fingers that he could be forgiven – his fingers were kissing it, one might say.

It was so strange, yet marvellously exciting, the way he felt her. He parted her lips with a most delicate touch and slid his middle finger a mere centimetre inside.

'Ah, what a very pretty colour!' he murmured, sounding more thoughtful than impassioned. 'This rose-pink seen against the silver-blonde little curls. Perfect. And to make it even more so you have added Art to Nature. The warmth of your skin exhales the heady perfume of Dior or Chanel you dabbed in your groins when you dressed this evening.'

His fingertip touched her secret little bud with delicacy, it sent shivers of pleasure through her body. His finger entered a little further, slowly, almost imperceptibly, as if feeling its way. And then a little further still. When it reached perhaps five centimetres inside her, Gaby arched her back and sighed to feel the delicious touch. Her dark blue eyes were closed – her body told her Remy was using both hands.

A long middle finger had advanced deep into her belly, while a fingertip was stroking her bud. The combined sensations were so delightful she sighed continuously, her legs shaking.

'Excellent reactions,' Remy murmured, 'first-rate.'

He was speaking to himself, he was in a world of his own – he was making judgments! At this moment the thought struck Gaby – almost as if he'd slapped her bare belly with his palm – he was not making love to her at all, he was *examining* her! He seemed to have confused 'girlfriend' with 'patient' in his thinking!

And the thought forced itself into her awareness that Remy's excitement wasn't the usual preparation to sliding into her and bringing them both to a shattering crisis of pleasure – not at all! He was deriving a perverse pleasure of his own by staring between her legs and fingering her. This was atrocious!

'Make love to me or leave me alone!' she gasped. He had made her so aroused she wanted to scream but she restrained herself for a little longer, glaring up at him.

The dreamy expression left his face, he appeared startled for a moment, then grinned wryly. He stepped closer, knelt up on the bed between her knees and took his stiff flesh in his hand. She held out her arms toward him in welcome, to embrace him and pull him down on her body. But it was not to be so. He crouched over her like a predator and slid his hands under her bottom to lift her until he could manoeuvre into her wet and open lips.

Gaby groaned in pleasure as he slid all the way up inside her hot belly. She wanted to clutch at him and hold him, but he was outside her reach. Because of the way he was holding her up her loins were higher than her head – he seemed to have no use for any part of her except the slippery pink split he had forced to open wide between her legs!

Yet, why not? All Gaby's delight was concentrated on the same part of her body at that moment – and Remy's strong thrusting into it gave her such thrills of pleasure it no longer mattered whether he kissed or hugged her . . . Nothing mattered so long as he kept on stabbing his hard flesh into her.

He said not a word, labouring above her in his waistcoat and tie, his hair falling forward over his brow. His face became a bright scarlet and his eyes glared insanely. Gaby felt her lean belly begin to clench in the first pang of ecstasy. She adored what he was doing to her and gasped out *More, more!* Perhaps he heard her, he went faster yet, then she saw his eyes roll up in his head and his body jerk sharply to the sudden spurt of his passion.

'Yes, *chéri*!' she shrieked in orgasmic delight.

Afterwards he seemed fatigued to the point of exhaustion and Gaby thought this was probably more an emotional reaction than a purely physical one. It seemed to her that love-making was not the simple pleasure for Remy it was for other men. There were obsessions in his mind.

She herself was very contented – although matters had started oddly and continued even more so, the eventual climax he had given her was marvellous. She stretched out on the bed to ease the tightness out of her leg muscles which had been so forcefully bent and cramped by Remy's posture. He lay quietly beside her, wearing two-thirds of his expensive suit, his shoes and socks!

Gaby turned on her side towards him. His eyes were closed and he was breathing deeply as he recovered from his furious exertions. She unbuttoned his waistcoat with gentle fingers, unknotted his silk tie and pulled it off. Remy didn't move, he lay with his eyes shut and let her make him comfortable. As she sat up to untie his shoelaces and slip his shoes off her perfect round breasts swayed above him but, if he knew it, there was no response from him. His arms stayed at his sides, it was as if he were asleep.

His trousers were undone all the way down but his male part was not displayed – he had tucked it back inside after slipping out of Gaby.

'So that's how you treat your friends,' said Gaby. 'At least it's original. I thought when you started you were a *Kama Sutra* devotee and would make me stand on my head with my bottom up in the air while you had me from behind – or some laughable Oriental love-position. But nothing so fascinatingly bizarre – the truth is that you are a gynaecologist for twenty-four hours a day! Let me see what you've got.'

She slipped her hand into his open trousers and held his limp and sticky part in her hand. It seemed to her to be of a decent length and thickness, but it did not respond in any way to her touch, not even a flicker. Remy was similarly unresponsive. He lay with his eyes closed, a faint look of satisfaction upon his face, but he said nothing.

Gaby stroked him for some time without any evidence that his interest in her was returning. An idea came into her head – if Remy was as entirely devoted to his profession as he seemed to be, she knew how to arouse him. In an instant she was on her knees over his head, her pretty *joujou* poised no more than five or six centimetres from his face.

'Open your eyes, Monsieur le Docteur,' she said, 'I need your expert opinion.'

Remy's eyes opened slowly at first, then they stared hard at the smooth bare lips and pale blonde tuft between Gaby's legs.

'Oh!' he said softly. 'Oh!'

Then he was unable to say more because she sank down a little and pressed the smooth bare lips on his mouth.

'What do you think, doctor?' she asked.

Remy made a noise like *mmm*, his hands sliding behind her to grasp the taut cheeks of her bottom and lift her up enough for him to recover the priceless faculty of speech. Her bottom was of no interest to him. Perfect though it was, he did not deign to squeeze it or stroke it. As soon as she was off his face his fingers went straight to the fleshy petals between her legs and caressed them delicately.

'I must make a complete examination before giving an opinion, mademoiselle,' he said gravely, 'but first appearances suggest you have made love very recently.'

'Anyone could say that to me, any day of the week,' said Gaby with a little shrug, 'and it would be true. You are the expert, what are your reasons for saying it?'

He was well into his obsession, holding her open while he did delicious things to her with expert fingertips.

'The moistness of sexual arousal is very marked,' he said in a professionally calm voice, 'there is a pinkness that suggests recent friction. And there are other unmistakable indications of a male organ penetrating here within the last twenty minutes or so. In short, mademoiselle, there can be no question of it – you have engaged in sexual intercourse.'

Remy's voice was the only part of him that remained calm. A glance over her shoulder showed Gaby his fleshy stiffness stood out of his open trousers and pointed boldly upwards.

'What you say is true,' she agreed, 'but it has not calmed me at all. Quite the reverse. Can you treat my agitation?'

'A simple matter,' he pronounced, and before she could begin to ask how he intended to relieve her tension, his busy fingers had completed the treatment and made her cry out shrilly as the sexual crisis swept through her body.

She was still shaking and gasping as he pushed her away from his face and arranged her in his favourite position, two large square pillows under her bottom to raise it. He bent her knees and placed them apart. Gaby found herself staring up the length of her own beautiful body at Remy on his knees, still wearing his shirt and trousers, presenting the purple head of his stiff flesh to the wet bare lips between her parted thighs. His face was crimson with emotion and he was panting slightly.

'*Bon Dieu!*' Suzette exclaimed when Gaby told her of this new friend and his curious ways in the bedroom, 'another one who is demented! Where do you find them, *chérie*? Outside a madhouse? You take impossible risks with a man who only makes love in the hope of being arrested for public indecency – and when you tire of him you find a gynaecologist with an insane power-drive! It is too much!'

'Yes, that's it, now I understand!' Gaby said with a giggle. 'Remy demands power over women's bodies – or at least over one part of them. For the rest, he has only a passing interest but that one part fascinates him – he is compelled to dominate it.'

'A gynaecologist who needs a psychiatrist. Get rid of him, if you want my advice,' said Suzette, pursing her sensuously shaped lips in disapproval.

For as long as Suzette had known her, Gaby insisted she loved being dominated by a man. And she believed it herself, although Suzette didn't. She preferred to think Gaby amused herself with a harmless delusion.

'Get rid of him? Are you mad?' said Gaby. 'It was the most exciting experience I've had for ages, being gripped so tight I could hardly breathe while Remy controlled my body and used me for his demented fantasy. I adored it! I could hardly wait for him to recover and do it to me again!'

Suzette shrugged, she knew her friend too well to

imagine she could change her adventurous ways with men.

'There is a certain bizarre interest in this situation, for a time anyway, I can see that,' she said. 'It must be intriguing in a strange sort of way to know your looks are not important. There is no need for make-up or hours at the hairdresser and no need for pretty clothes or sexy knickers – nothing matters to him except this perverted desire to dominate and control the few centimetres between your legs!'

'Perverted? What nonsense!' said Gaby. 'That's what all men want to do – get you to open your legs for them to dominate the bit between. With Remy there is no pretence or deception – he grabs you and holds you helpless while he does exactly what he wants to do. And it's marvellous!'

'Evidently his profession has unhinged the man's brain,' said Suzette. 'Too many women have taken their knickers down to show themselves to him – he has lost touch with reality and believes he is a Casanova instead of a doctor.'

Gaby shrugged and said it was her impression matters were the other way round.

'I asked him,' she said, 'and he told me he'd been fascinated by that part of the female body since he was thirteen. He spent years training to be a doctor and then a gynaecologist, just to make sure he'd have plenty of opportunities every day to observe the subject of his mad devotion.'

'He told you that?'

'He makes no secret of it. When he has a day off he finds it difficult to survive without going into a frenzy of frustration at not being able to touch his favourite thing.'

Suzette laughed and asked how frequently the Doctor required his intellectual gratification. She was sure his desire was of the mind, not a physical need.

'You know how men exaggerate these things,' said Gaby with a grin, 'how can one ever be sure what to believe? According to him, on average he sees ten patients a day. What can be said for certain is he makes a tremendous amount of money from them. And, after he decided he could trust me, he explained how he arranges to make love to two a day on his examination table.'

'Two women a day? Every day? *Oh la la!* But surely there is a nurse present at these examinations?'

Gaby shrugged again.

'Yes, but his nurse adores him, he says, and has no objection to his methods. She slips out for ten minutes when he gives her the nod, leaving him alone with whoever's on the table with her knees up.'

'They never complain, these patients, when something thicker and longer than the doctor's finger is pushed into them?'

'Not as far as I know. I think he must choose his women with care. I imagine he probably picks married women who are feeling neglected and can't find a suitable lover. Some of them pretend not to know what he is doing to them, or so he claims, although they keep coming back for regular appointments.'

'This nurse of his, evidently he pays her extremely well for her silence. If she ever lost her loyalty, she is wonderfully well placed to blackmail him for everything he owns.'

'As I understand it,' said Gaby with a grin, 'he ensures she never stops adoring him by having her climb up on his table for regular examination. Every single day, after the last patient's gone, he says, but he might be boasting.'

'All that and a salary too? She must think herself lucky.'

'From a gynaecological point of view,' Gaby said with

a broad grin, 'she is expertly and thoroughly attended to.'

'And so will you be, if you see him again. Do you mean to?'

'I most certainly do. You haven't heard the half of it yet!'

Nor had Gaby, of course. There were many unusual things about Dr Remy Courtauld – of which she had as yet no suspicion – but which she learned as their friendship developed further. One that he revealed after only a week or two made her smile – he owned the largest collection of photographs in France, perhaps in Europe, of that part of the female body which fascinated him. In close-up and life-size, nothing less could satisfy him, in leather-bound albums, one to each page.

Underneath each photo he had written a first name and a date. He flicked through the pages of an album to demonstrate to Gaby the extensiveness of his professional researches. It amused her to see the seemingly endless variations possible on a natural theme as portrayed in these pages. There in living detail were recorded the physical secrets of Madeleine, Zita, Marie-Lise, Renee, Martine, Denise . . . and so on, and so on.

It occurred to Gaby that in some mysterious way Remy judged the character of these women from the part that intrigued him so entirely. But what could anyone make of these pictures, even he – these plump, flat, protruding, thin-lipped, tight, gaping, recessive, bushy-haired, wispy variations?

Did Remy correlate tight lips with an ungenerous spirit? Or protruding inner lips with eagerness? Excessive hairiness with fertility? Ginger curls with fast climax? But experience must have taught him by now that women were complex creatures. They were not to be categorised by simple physical traits. The idiot of a man who did that would encounter great surprises and some unnerving shocks. And Gaby laughed at the thought.

Naturally, Remy was very keen to add Gaby to his collection – she had the prettiest he'd ever seen, he said, blonde and pink.

MADAME CHAMPLAIN
MAKES AMENDS

Tristan Villette was desolated when he came to understand Gaby no longer wished to play his dangerous games. She was very fond of him, she explained, but these public performances . . . no, all things considered, she could not continue any longer. There had already been two disastrous incidents – in an alley at the back of a shop and under a tree in the Luxembourg Gardens.

For him it was amusing, she knew that, but for her it was too embarrassing to be caught with her knickers down in public. And if it had been a policeman who saw them, what then? *Bon Dieu* – for a woman to acquire a police record was a catastrophe! From now on she must decline to see him, it was regrettable, but she had no choice in the matter.

Naturally, she did not upset Tristan by mentioning she had a new friend, a handsome beast of a gynaecologist who held her in a grip of steel while he did marvellous things to her that sent her into shrieking orgasms. After all, it would have been most unkind to distress Tristan unnecessarily – he was sufficiently heartbroken already by learning his friendship with Gaby was to be discontinued.

And having said what was necessary, but no more, Gaby put the telephone down and did not answer when Tristan rang back in two seconds. However frequently he rang for the next three days, he was not able to speak to her. Mostly no one answered, but once or twice he found himself persuading Suzette to intervene for him – to beg Gaby to think again about her decision. His heart was broken, his life was in ruins, he was unable to eat, sleep or think. And so on, in the normal way of men whose girlfriends have left them.

Suzette refused politely to become involved. When he said he loved Gaby to desperation and he was sure in his heart that she still loved him – and similar idiotic statements men produce in these circumstances – Suzette informed him of a simple truth he appeared not to know.

'Love lasts while it lasts,' she said and even Tristan could hear the shrug in her voice.

She didn't tell him so, but she was pleased Gaby had resolved to get rid of him. He was not entirely sane, that was certain. Who on earth needed a boyfriend devoted to outdoor activities? Generous he might be, amusing and pleasant – all that and much more perhaps – but in Suzette's opinion Gaby was well rid of him. Let him go back to his door-mat of a fiancée, the girl with the domineering mother, that was more his style!

Alas, poor Tristan, the truth was he had no fiancée to go back to any more. Some weeks had passed since he had seen Lucile, the day after they were at the races at Longchamp and she disappeared. She had refused outright to give any account of herself, why she left, where she went. But she made it clear, painfully clear, that their engagement to be married was at an end.

First Lucile, now Gaby – it was too much! Tristan loved them both, he was absolutely certain of that. Loved them both at the same time and now, wretched fate, his heart was twice broken! Had he expected too much of life, he asked himself, was Nemesis making him pay for the mad pride of wanting *two* beautiful women to love him? He gave the question anxious thought and decided to throw himself on dear Lucile's mercy, pour out his heart and convince her of his undying love. And beg her to marry him.

On the way to the Champlain apartment he thought of the last time he had made love to Lucile, before the dreadful day at the races when he had lost his girl – and a thick wad of francs he bet on a sure winner that ran fifth.

That last day of their happiness together they took a picnic basket to Versailles. It was an early-summer weekday with not many visitors there that afternoon, which pleased Tristan of course. He and Lucile wandered through King Louis' imposing palace, by the Parterre with the fountains and through the gardens, on past the Petit Trianon – till eventually they found a secluded grassy spot to enjoy their picnic and open the wine.

Suitably refreshed, Tristan was ready to proceed to the real purpose of the outing. He drew Lucile into his arms, they were lying on dry warm grass with trees around them, to kiss her and stroke her breasts through her thin blouse. Lucile was in high spirits, he recalled, she had giggled and slipped her hand down the front of his trousers. Ah, the memory of that delicious giggle, how it pained him now to think of past happiness with her!

'You are impossible,' she murmured, letting him put his hand up her skirt to caress her. A red-hot flush of passion made him catch his breath when his exploring hand touched her bare flesh – she had come on the picnic with no knickers! How he adored her, darling Lucile, she seemed always to guess what would most delight him!

He caressed her until she sighed and trembled at the

approach of ecstasy – but before he could roll her on her back and slide on top, she rose to her knees and turned to present her back to him. Tristan's bone-hard length stuck out of his open trousers where she had opened them wide. He watched in shaking delight while Lucile pulled her skirt up round her waist and arranged herself on hands and knees.

She turned her head to smile at him over her shoulder, a grin rather than a smile, an impudent and suggestive grin – inviting him to feel the neat round cheeks of her bare bottom. What more could a man ask? A pretty girl, a sunny day, a secluded spot and the prospect of immediate joy! His stiff flesh jerked as he rose to his knees behind her and put his hands on her bottom to stroke it. And between her thighs there was just a glimpse of brown curls and pouting lips.

He gripped her hips while he jerked forward and slid straight into her wet warmth. The smooth clasp excited him intensely and he went about his pleasure with vigorous enthusiasm. Lucile braced herself on straight arms to stand the onslaught, she pushed her bottom at him to receive his thrusts.

A day to remember! Yet how miserable was his plight now, without darling Lucile! She had changed overnight, one day she did all she could to please him, the next day she didn't want him ever again. It was too confusing! And it must stop, he insisted she must return to him now. He would refuse to accept a denial.

One of the most obvious of truths is that things rarely work out as they should, yet life continues. Tristan arrived at the Champlain apartment with a bouquet of yellow roses in one hand, a large bottle of excellent champagne in the other, prepared to woo Lucile back into his arms and celebrate the reconciliation. But Lucile was not at home and her mother frowned when she saw the former fiancé at her door.

It is hardly necessary to say that Tristan had never found Madame Champlain a sympathetic person. In the days when he was engaged to be married to Lucile he had speculated more than once, with an element of fascinated dread, on the inconveniences of having Madame Champlain as a mother-in-law. She was a large, heavy-built woman in her early forties, with short fair hair, a determined jaw and the type of domineering approach such women often have.

When she was angry, as now, she was formidable. Anyone not so determined as Tristan might well have muttered an apology and run away. But not him, he was intent on regaining Lucile's love and affection, he stood his ground while Madame glowered at him – her arms folded, face flushed, her heavy bosom swelling under her grey-striped frock.

She declared she did not know where Lucile was nor when she would be back.

But evidently she knew who Lucile was with and that made her angry. She didn't *ask* Tristan to come in and sit down, she *told* him to. In the drawing-room he perched nervously on the edge of a chair and tried to meet her glare without flinching. She sat exactly opposite him, staring balefully at the bouquet and the bottle he had put on the floor beside him. There appeared to be contempt in her stare – as if these little tokens of love were to be scorned and condemned.

As if that were not bad enough, she took a malicious pleasure in conveying what she knew of Lucile's present companion. Judge of Tristan's utter astonishment when

Madame Champlain informed him Lucile had fallen in love with another woman!

'What are you saying!' he exclaimed, red-faced and outraged. 'It's impossible! I do not believe you!'

'Whether you believe me or not, it is true,' Madame Champlain said with cold fury. 'My daughter is besotted by a woman named Gruchy – Nicole Gruchy, ten years older than herself. This harpy is rich, she lives in the Avenue Victor-Hugo and I think she is married. The position is dreadful beyond words.'

It was impossible to doubt the sincerity of Blanche Champlain in this extraordinary matter. Tristan stared with bulging eyes, his mind in a most fearful commotion. He tried to picture dear Lucile being kissed passionately by another woman – but no, it was out of the question! He thought of a woman's fingers, with rings and polished nails, undoing Lucile's brassiere to stroke her pretty breasts. It was unimaginable!

He imagined this perverse woman's hand up Lucile's skirt and in her knickers, playing between her thighs. Lucile arching her back, as she did in her moment of supreme ecstasy, surrendering herself to a woman. *Ah, non, non, non, quelle horreur!* he said to himself in a rage of shocked disbelief.

'I hold *you* entirely responsible,' said Madame Champlain. 'If you were more of a man, this would never have happened.'

The barbarous injustice of her accusation dumbfounded Tristan for some moments. *If he had been a man indeed!* And whose fault was it that certain problems had developed in love-making? The unreasonableness of her words threw him into a blind rage. With a shaking hand he reached down and wrenched his trousers open!

His purpose was to make Madame Champlain understand the extent of the desperate injury she had inflicted on him the day she burst in while he was making love to Lucile. This unnecessary and ill-considered interference had caused a trauma in his mind that inhibited his natural ability to become hard at the right moment with a woman unless the circumstances were repeated – which is to say, when the risk of being caught at it was ridiculously high!

For this reason he was compelled to make love to Lucile – and to Gaby – in public places. In the Bois, in the cinema, on the Metro, under the Seine bridges . . . and now neither of them would go with him. Lucile had met someone to adore her in more usual settings, it seemed. And Gaby too, had tired of *alfresco* love.

In effect, he thought furiously, Madame Champlain might just as well have taken a knife that day and cut off his pompoms, as wound him psychologically! Very well, she was going to be told what she had done and made to accept responsibility herself for the train of events that brought Lucile into a woman's bed. And here was the proof – here in front of her eyes!

But with amazement Tristan saw the evidence was otherwise. On the instant he opened his trousers, out sprang his male pride – long, hard, throbbing!

'But, but, but . . .' he stammered, unable to comprehend the new development in his sorry tale of love thwarted.

'Uh, uh, uh . . .' Madame Champlain stammered like an echo – she was as amazed as he at the sight of his uprearing part but for very different reasons. A deeper tinge of crimson touched her cheek, her eyes goggled and she stared at Tristan's revelation.

How long had passed since she last saw this interesting

part of a man's body, who could say? She had been twelve years a widow, grieving no doubt for the late Monsieur Champlain. But whether a regard for the proprieties and the injunctions of religion caused her to deny the promptings of human nature for so long . . . that was a secret she shared with no one.

'The fact is . . .' Tristan began, but he was no long sure what the fact was.

'What fact?' she asked faintly. 'Why are you doing this?'

'You robbed me of the power to make love normally to Lucile,' said he. 'You are entirely to blame for what has happened. You have destroyed my life and you have destroyed Lucile's life.'

The astounding truth was, Tristan at this moment realised, he was wildly excited. In his turbulent mind was the memory of how Madame Champlain had burst into Lucile's room to find him lying on her daughter's belly, her clothes up round her waist, at the very instant she writhed in orgasm.

She had stared in outrage and revulsion at the scene, at her dear daughter underneath a man, and Tristan's eyes had met her horrified eyes at the very instant he had given a huge gasp of dismay and spurted his throbbing passion into Lucile.

The scene was still so extraordinarily vivid in his memory it overrode the paralysis of will that had afterwards descended on him. His excitement took him past the bounds of reason. Before he knew himself what he intended to do, he slid forward from his chair and was on his knees at Madame Champlain's feet.

His hands were on her knees, decently covered by the skirt of her grey-striped summer frock. At his touch her face was bright red – she stared wildly at him as if he were a criminal of the worst type, destined for the guillotine before he was forty! He slipped his hands under her frock, up her thighs and found the soft bare flesh between stockings and underwear. Her legs remained firmly together, she meant to protect her virtue until the very end.

Tristan did not try to separate them – natural cunning alone told him a wrestling match was ridiculous, when a little gentle persuasion could achieve the same result. He reached higher yet under her frock, his hands feverishly stroking her meaty thighs, until his fingers touched the edge of her knickers. There was an irrational smile on his flushed face.

Perhaps it was the smile that galvanised Madame Champlain to retaliatory action, mirth of any type was so out of place at a moment like this! She swung her arm and hit him. It was not a slap on the cheek of the sort women rebuke male impoliteness with – for a pinch of the bottom, perhaps. This was a hard blow to the side of the head with her palm and it made his head ring like a bell. She was, after all, a solidly built woman, who weighed in at a good many kilos more than he did.

'Ah!' he groaned. '*Ah mon Dieu!*'

His head still rang with the shock when she swung her other arm and landed an equally heavy blow on the other side of his head. He groaned again, he was dizzy and his vision had become blurred. Nevertheless, she had not dislodged him. Far from it, he had managed to get a hand over the top of her knickers and his hot palm lay on her fat bare belly.

Madame Champlain had lost the power of speech, it seemed. The violation of her honour was having the most devastating effect, reducing her to gasping incoherence. It would have been simple to hit him again, right and left to his head, left and right, a fusillade of blows that would eventually render him unconscious on the floor at her feet. But she had shot her bolt, she could do no more. In fairness to her, never in all her life had a man conducted himself towards her in so relentless a manner. It had disoriented her.

Tristan's hand was down inside her knickers, he could touch a broad expanse of thick hair! And then he pushed lower still, forcing his whole hand and wrist down between her plump belly and the material of her underwear, until his fingers found her long fleshy lips. Madame Champlain's body jerked violently when he touched there and her eyes rolled upward in her dark-red face, as if she were at the point of apoplexy.

Whether she opened her legs or kept them together made little difference now – Tristan had penetrated her secret against her will and he was feeling it with a look of surprise on his face. He subjected his speechless victim to a determined stroking and in a minute or two she began to utter cavernous sighs.

But sighs of what? The question not easy to answer. Sighs of chagrin? Of horror? Of resignation to her cruel Fate? Sighs of detestation of Tristan and what he was doing? Doubtless she knew what her sighs indicated but there seemed no obvious way for him to understand what they meant, the long heartfelt sighs of this ridiculous woman – this monstrous prude who had ruined his ability to make love normally to Lucile, this tyrant mother who had destroyed his serious love-affair with her daughter!

Crimson of complexion, with her breath rasping in her throat, Madame Champlain succeeded at last in speaking a few words. She called Tristan unpleasant names, of which *voluptuary* and *pervert* were the least offensive.

His furious emotion grew stronger at this unwarranted attack.

'I am what you have made me,' he retorted. 'I was happy once, I was in love with Lucile and she with me. But you had to spoil it with your stupid morals and restrictions and your notions of what must be refused before marriage!'

His strength surged through him, with one hand he forced open her legs and rose on his knees to display to her startled eyes the hard and throbbing part sticking out of his trousers.

'Take a good look!' he said ferociously. 'You destroyed that wonderful ability. For years I have been compelled to make love furtively in parks and back streets, half-hoping to be found at it. That was the ultimate excitement, to be in fear of the shame and embarrassment that would follow.'

Whether Madame Champlain understood what he was talking about may be doubted. She stared with bulging eyes at his stiff flesh as if petrified. And he meanwhile ripped open the buttons down the front of her thin grey-striped frock, from the little white collar to the black patent-leather belt round her bulky waist. He thrust his hands behind her back to unhook her brassiere – a very capacious garment, the largest size available!

Her immense breasts spilled out into his hands, pale-skinned, soft-fleshed and drooping under their own weight. Tristan with one long sigh reached out for them, he wanted to roll their bounty in his hands, he wanted to nibble the faintly blue-veined flesh and to lick the dark pink buds . . .

Madame Champlain was of a different mind, she was

prudish in respect of her oversized breasts and she tried to cover them with her hands. It was a hopeless cause, they were too large for any mortal hands to protect. And when Tristan persisted she stood up quickly to avoid his attentions, taking her remarkable bosom out of his reach – but in so doing she put her belly and thighs on a level with his face.

Naturally, he seized this golden opportunity at once. He put both hands up her frock and had her pink silk knickers down her legs before she knew what he was doing. His head was under her frock, he was kissing her bare thighs, his finger pressed into her warm cleft. She made a gurgling sound in her throat, it was impossible to guess what she wanted to say, even if Tristan was listening. Perhaps it was *please*, and perhaps not.

He butted his shoulder against her and pushed her off balance against the chair so that she collapsed heavily into it with a gasp of outrushing breath. With confident hands he forced her thighs open and he moved in to pierce her. There was never a shadow of doubt in his mind – she had deserved this! She had ruined his love affair with Lucile, ruined it beyond repair and now he would have something from her by way of compensation – though the use of her middle-aged body was grossly inadequate as a substitute for darling Lucile . . .

Her hands were in her lap, trying to stop him, but he was so aroused he was unstoppable. He brushed her hands away, he came nearer still, he thrust his jerking hardness at the broad patch of hair between her massive thighs. She stared horrified into his face so near to hers, her mouth opening and closing without a sensible word escaping.

He was inside her, pushing forward hard. Her hands were again lying on her drooping breasts to safeguard them from his touch. As he sank into her soft warmth he stared into her eyes, only a few centimetres from his own. He saw her eyes were soft and brown, glistening with what? Rage, perhaps? Unshed tears? Some more complicated emotion? But there was an expression in those eyes Tristan could not misunderstand, it sent him into a sexual frenzy.

It was just like the day she had caught him in Lucile's room, lying between Lucile's legs. He had glanced up when the door opened and his eyes had met Madame Champlain's glare across the bedroom. A look of indignation met his gaze, of revulsion, of resentment, of that same expression which was there in her eyes now. It made him feel guilty, it racked him with feelings of shame and turpitude – these emotions were so delicious he moaned loudly and spurted his hot humiliation into Madame Champlain.

And she – when she felt his frantic release inside her body – she gasped and shuddered in deep embarrassment. She felt an emotion so complicated she could not have understood it if she could ever have brought herself to think about it calmly. For Blanche, it was impossible to contemplate these indecent matters. But it was undeniable they had certain bodily consequences.

And so it was then – even in the midst of his ecstatic throes Tristan felt a tide of orgasm sweep from Blanche's shuddering loins up to her heaving breasts, then back again to her loins! Her back arched as she pushed her big round belly at him hard and she bit her lips to stop herself shrieking in her climax.

Tristan knew he had turned the tables completely. By seeing her at this intimate moment he felt he had caught her out, just as she caught him out with Lucile at the instant Lucile wailed out her climactic sensations. Now he had exposed Blanche's own innermost emotions, he had destroyed her malign power, he would never fear her again.

When her crisis was over at last she slumped in the armchair, breathing unsteadily, her eyes turned away from his face. She was unable to meet his eyes now. She knew Tristan had the upper hand.

He intended to take full advantage of the position. He was of the opinion Madame Champlain had done him great harm and he had every right to take his revenge. He slid out of her wetness and got to his feet. He took hold of her hanging breasts, a handful of soft flesh clutched in each hand, pulling at them to get her up out of the chair. Armchairs and sitting-rooms were all very well, they had their useful purposes for passing liaisons, but a woman was finally conquered in her own bedroom, on her back.

He took her into her bedroom and made her strip naked and lie on the bed. He looked at her as if she were an exhibit in an art gallery – a nude by Gustave Courbet, perhaps, or a sketch by Jean Dubuffet. Ah, the sheer lubricity of those vast shapeless breasts, the biggest he'd ever seen. The lasciviousness of that impossibly wide and fat belly, of her immensely plump thighs!

He told her to open those fleshy legs. He wanted to look at her patch of dark-brown hair, curls so thick he could draw his fingers through them . . . and those long lips that seemed to pout in invitation . . . *Ah mon Dieu, there is so much of her,* he said to himself, his male part stiff again and bounding impatiently. *So much flesh . . . so much woman!*

It goes without saying she had found her tongue again by now, no woman is ever silent for long, it runs entirely contrary to their nature. She used her restored power of speech to condemn Tristan, what else?

'What you have done to me is utterly despicable,' she

said in a most aggrieved tone. 'You have embarrassed me so much I shall never be able to look a man in the face again. I give thanks to the good God you never married my poor Lucile. You are a brute and a degenerate – you have the instincts of the gutter.'

There was a good deal more in this vein and Tristan paid little attention to it, he was too preoccupied rolling her monsters of breasts in his hands. Although he had made her strip herself naked, he was still fully dressed except for his jacket. He even wore his striped bow-tie and his shiny two-tone brown shoes. She no longer attempted to shield her breasts or hide them from him – perhaps she thought there was no point in objecting to a little handling, now the worst had happened.

Her face was flushed pink, her breathing was still unsteady – the rise and fall of her chest made her breasts wobble in a highly diverting way. Tristan slipped a hand between her fat thighs and the look in her eyes brought a twisted grin to his face.

'Blanche,' he said, addressing her boldly by her name for the very first time, 'because of your stupidity I was driven out of the comfort of bedrooms into the furtiveness of snatched loving in alleys and cinemas and on staircases. Now I have broken your spell, you owe me more than you can ever repay. You may regard the last half-hour and the next two hours as a down payment.'

'This is atrocious,' she said, 'I owe you nothing, you are a depraved beast.'

In her mind at that moment – apart from the indecency of what was being done to her – was perhaps nothing much. But Tristan's words had stirred in his own mind thoughts of Lucile. Once she had been his to embrace and kiss and love, now she had turned to someone else – and not another man! How was it when her new friend, this Gruchy woman, made love to Lucile? Tristan wondered. Did Lucile stretch out on her back with her legs wide open, as her mother was doing now? And did Lucile give herself without shame? Did La Gruchy kiss her between the thighs – kiss her little bud until she shrieked with delight?

Between Blanche's thick thighs the plump lips were slippery warm and half open to Tristan's fingers. He, of course, in the foolishness of male pride, had the mistaken idea he had made a total conquest. The truth was more complex, naturally, because it involved the deep secret emotions of a woman. And women are not such simple creatures as men.

Blanche had grown up in a more restrictive time, one less inclined to accord much freedom of action or decision to women. To make matters worse, her parents were over-religious and too obsessed with morals and similar social myths. She had been imbued with the need to seek male approval and, though she was now over forty years old, attitudes instilled in youth are not easily changed.

Tristan had gone far beyond giving approval to her orgasm, he had forced it on her brutally. The responsibility for anything that happened to her was entirely his – he had *made* her do it! She found the thought intensely arousing. When she was sitting in the armchair he had only just got inside her before her climax overwhelmed her! She had never known it to be so fast before – it was all his fault, she was powerless – thus she comforted her awkward conscience.

Naturally, she didn't want to lie here stark naked for him to stare at. It was highly embarrassing, exposing her body in this manner! No decent woman ever let herself be seen in this state – not even by her husband! To reveal everything like this – it was dreadfully immoral. But she had no choice, Tristan *made* her do it. And he was forcing her to become excited all over again with his touching and stroking . . .

The reason Tristan kept his clothes on was to demonstrate his dominance over Blanche. She was his to do with as he pleased, he was the master here. She was naked to prove her submission. All of her body was exposed to him, to touch or pinch or stroke or smack – drooping breasts, fat belly, massive thighs – his to use in any way he wanted. If he wanted to stand up on the bed and plant a nattily shod foot on her belly to prove her complete subjugation to him, he could!

And would! But later, not right now – what he was doing was too pleasant to stop. He was holding the lips of her prominent and hairy mound open with two fingers and the thumb of one hand and dabbling inside with two joined fingers of the other, making it wetter and wetter. Blanche was rolling her bulk from side to side on the bed, her eyes closed and her strong legs trembling.

She had surrendered herself to him – her will, her body, her conscience. The shameful sensations that held her in their grip were not of her choosing. Some thought them pleasant, but she knew it was disgraceful to give in to them. Because they led to that unbelievably embarrassing moment when all control was lost and a sexual climax resulted . . .

It had taken her by surprise when it happened to her in the chair. Tristan had pushed his hand down her knickers and touched her *there* and she'd thought she'd die of shame when she'd felt the instant surge of desire in her belly and realised what was happening to her body! Mercifully he didn't seem to notice her jerking, he was too wrapped up in his own despicable emotions.

But he certainly had noticed what happened to her the second time, when he was inside her – he was staring into her face at the very instant the orgasm took her! To be observed at such a moment was too shameful for words! She was mortified more than ever before in her life! And even that wasn't enough for him. She was being shamed again now, he was touching her – oh how he was touching her! It felt as if he was turning her inside out, it was impossible to be opened like this, impossible!

'Look at me!' Tristan said sharply. 'Open your eyes!'

Triumph could never be sweeter than this. He was getting his own back, he was annihilating her pride and self-esteem just as she had ruined his. She obeyed him and he could see the expression in her eyes, the dread and the embarrassment – and also the desire as his fingers rubbed her to shuddering orgasm. Her chubby legs kicked and thrashed at the bed, she was moaning words without meaning.

She was not in the least beautiful, of course, this oversized middle-aged woman with the great flabby breasts and wide paunch of a belly. Her face was too broad and her jaw too squarely set and determined. There were tiny beads of perspiration trickling down her chest between her breasts and on her belly, where the excess flesh made deep folds. She was pink all over, baby pink, a smooth overfed pink, only her red buds and the dark hair down between her thighs were different.

Yet, beautiful or not, she was enormously arousing to look at on her back, chubby thighs apart, swamped by orgasmic sensation and oblivious to the entire world. Tristan stared open-mouthed at what he had achieved, his stiffness throbbing and ready for immediate action.

Before her belly had subsided he was on her, bow-tie in position, trousers decently in place, only the front open wide to allow his stiffness free play. She was so wet and open he was in her with an easy push, cushioned on her broad fat belly as if on a feather mattress. She was sighing and panting, wriggling under him as he took a massive soft breast in either hand.

'Blanche, Blanche, you are my toy,' he gloated over her. 'You are a slave, a mattress, a doll, a *thing* to be used!'

To prove his point he stabbed brutally hard and fast into her yielding flesh.

She heard his words and guilt showed in her eyes, guilt and a keen lust. The consciousness of lust made her feel more guilty.

'I *hate* you,' she gasped while her orgasmic throes shook her as if she were truly a doll to be played with.

Whether Tristan heard her words or not, who can say? But the look in her eyes, the delicious mingling of lust and guilt, was enough to sweep him from his vaunted superiority and pitch him into ravening sensation. His body convulsed so strongly he was afraid his back was broken. His loins thrust frenziedly without any co-operation from him – he felt himself spurt in Blanche's capacious belly as if he would never stop.

And while he was savouring the shame and mortification in her eyes, she was peering closely into his, observing his emotions at that critical moment. She saw his feelings and his thoughts, his urges and desires, his precarious self-esteem, his pride in being a man. In those climactic seconds she learned more about Tristan than in all the time he had been her daughter's fiancé – and when she knew all she needed to know, she closed her eyes tightly, and let herself be carried away by the surging tide of passion.

It goes without saying that Lucile, the starting-point of the confrontation between Tristan and Blanche, was wholly forgotten by now. Earlier on there had been some vague idea in Tristan's mind, when Blanch had told him about Madame Gruchy, that he would storm into this dreadful woman's apartment and rescue Lucile by main force. An equally vague thought had occurred to Blanche – perhaps Tristan could be spurred into going to the woman's home to save Lucile from whatever unnatural acts were committed upon her young body.

But all of that was forgotten. Lucile could carry on with her new-found friend as long as she liked, Blanche and Tristan were too engrossed in the strange events between them to care about Lucile's moral welfare.

In effect, Blanche had reached a satisfactory decision. She had endured the worst Tristan could inflict upon her, this fool of a man who had stolen her daughter's innocence, this son-in-law who never was! First he had defiled Lucile's body – and now he had defiled Blanche's own body. To be sure, this business with bodies was contemptible, a mere rubbing of skin on skin, a game for the degenerate – but it was also very pleasant.

Much more pleasing in fact than Blanche could recall from the days of her husband's attentions to her in bed, when twice a week he raised her nightgown to feel her breasts. Tristan had aroused passions she had never experienced before. And since what was done could never be undone, she might as well continue and ascertain just *how* pleasant this despicable indulgence could be.

Tristan was a strong young man, well-fed and in good physical condition, to judge by his looks. It would be possible to tell more when his clothes were off. Blanche meant to encourage him in his pursuit of revenge on her naked body. After all, perhaps there was some little truth in his claim she had done him harm. If she was in his debt morally, as he seemed to think, then she must repay, it was her plain duty. And this way of repayment he had chosen was, she had to admit, exquisite, if indecent.

'The wine you brought with you,' she said, 'bring it here and we will drink it together.'

Tristan rolled off her body and sat up, very surprised.

'What?' he said.

'And two glasses.'

'But it will be warm,' he said, uncertain how to interpret an invitation to drink champagne with her when she ought by rights to detest him. Her broad face was without expression, there was no clue there to her mood. In some manner he did not understand this neutral state of hers was spoiling his act of revenge. He wanted her to rage at him.

After a pause for confused thought, which achieved nothing at all, Tristan slid off the bed and went to the sitting-room. He returned with the bottle of champagne intended to celebrate his reconciliation with Lucile. He had no glasses with him, but he brought the bouquet of yellow roses.

He advanced to the bedside, bottle in one hand and flowers in the other, to glare down on Blanche. She lay passive, her great naked body fully exposed, her eyes meeting his.

'I hate you,' said Tristan. He had worked himself into a rage during his brief walk back to the bedroom. 'I was in love with Lucile and you made sure it came to nothing. I see it all now – you never meant me to have her! You wanted me yourself! Well, as you've already had what was hers by right, you might as well have these flowers I brought for her!'

So saying, he pushed the bouquet of roses between her massive thighs. Most fortunately the florist had wrapped the stems with several layers of green paper, to protect the buyer's hand from thorns, or the skin of Blanche's baby-pink thighs would surely have shown long scratches and droplets of scarlet blood. But as it was, only a single sharp thorn on a stem pierced the paper – its fierce point scraping across the fat lips between her parted legs. She gave a shrill cry of anguish and her loins bucked upward in sudden spasm.

Tristan paid no heed, he was engrossed in getting the wire off the champagne cork – and shaking the bottle vigorously to raise the pressure! The cork flew out with a loud pop and struck the bedroom ceiling, Tristan laughed furiously and sprayed foaming champagne over Blanche's naked body – over floppy breasts, big round belly, down round the bouquet of yellow roses!

As the frothing wine cascaded over her, Blanche screamed, and her heavy body arched up off the bed in shaking orgasm. No one had ever stirred her imagination or raised her dormant passions so bizarrely. Tristan's brutal triumph turned into blazing desire as he saw her body writhing in ecstasy. He let the bottle drop from his hand and flung himself on her throbbing belly.

SUZETTE MEETS
A SONG ARRANGER

What amazed Suzette was the headlong speed at which her career advanced when her record of *Place Vendôme* was released. It was played on the radio every day and in the shops it was selling like hot croissants for breakfast. She was asked to sing live on the radio and Emile negotiated the fee. Polydor offered a contract for another record and an option on a third – and all this in a few weeks!

The money was starting to pour in. And if her luck held there was much, much more to come. This inspired mixed emotions – the simple pleasure of realising her ambition to be a big-name star might well be fulfilled but she had curious thoughts about the money. As a child growing up in Belleville – not so long ago, she was still only twenty-three – her family were destitute. Suzette knew all about the miseries of poverty.

At fifteen she had a job in a small drapery shop, only a street or two from where she was born. The proprietor was Monsieur Meran, a middle-aged man with a drooping moustache, and he took every opportunity to feel her bottom through her clothes. No doubt he would have stroked other parts of her if events had been favourable. When nobody else was in the shop he would open cardboard boxes to finger the unstylish knickers he stocked, while he made remarks that were suggestive.

Without doubt he wanted to get his hand up Suzette's clothes, this pot-bellied draper, for a feel of her young charms. Perhaps he thought an offer of free underwear would be enough to secure her willingness. But young as she was, she had already received offers from much better-looking men than Monsieur Meran. Offers which had convinced her she owned something of immense interest to men of all ages.

And because life was a hard struggle in the back streets, she did not propose to squander this priceless asset on mean-minded shopkeepers with dreary moustaches, not when it was all she had to improve her social position.

Meran was a timid man and his wife was well acquainted with his proclivities. They lived above the shop and she was able to keep a sharp eye on him. For this Suzette was grateful, she did not wish to lose her job by annoying her unattractive employer. Yet all the same, this lack of interest in him did not prevent Madame Meran deciding that the shop assistant was too pretty by far and getting rid of her.

It put a useful idea into Suzette's head, being told she was too pretty. Everyone knew about artists needing models ready to pose naked for them and it was to be presumed they would prefer to paint pretty girls rather than plain ones. And for a model who had been sacked for being *too* pretty, they ought to pay well.

Naturally, artists did not have their studios in Belleville. They were to be found in Montmartre and Montparnasse, which was all to the good as Suzette was anxious to leave the neighbourhood as soon as possible. She made enquiries, she even earned a few francs from a painter named Boguette for standing about naked in his draughty attic hour after hour while he daubed away. Now she knew she was very pretty, she had no shame about taking her clothes off.

What she learned from talking in the local cafés to other models was that these so-called artists never had any money and never paid more than a pittance. And to crown insult with outrage, after a long session, when a poor girl's muscles ached from head to toe from remaining absolutely still, the self-styled artist usually expected his model to lie down and open her legs for him!

That did not suit Suzette at all, she saw no career prospects in lying down for garlic-smelling artists in miserable studios. If she wanted to be a whore, the easiest thing was to remain in the rue de Belleville. There was a continuous demand for fresh young bodies. Nearly half the girls she was at school with had taken up this means of earning a living.

The other half were either married to unemployed young drunks who beat them senseless, or were living without the approval of the Church with men who did precisely the same. Needless to say they were all pregnant at sixteen, some for the second time, married or otherwise.

By asking around, by perseverance, by refusing to be put off, Suzette found employment at the Ecole des Beaux-Arts. She sat or stood or knelt or whatever the professor decided, while the students sat round her in a circle and drew her. She was naked, it goes without saying – what student-artist wastes his time in drawing women wearing cheap clothes? The advantages to Suzette of this employment were evident: there was a proper rate of pay, there was never an argument about getting her money and no one expected her to lie on her back afterwards.

The life classes were very popular with the students.

Most of the time they were required to sit in the big domed gallery and sketch the classical statues standing around – gods and heroes of antiquity, in Greek drapery or Roman armour. It was somewhat more interesting for them when the subject was a nude Venus or Apollo in a helmet and nothing else, though still a statue.

Naturally the life classes had a live subject, more often a woman than a man for the professor enjoyed an ordinary Frenchman's enthusiasm for the naked female body. In Suzette's observation the models were pleasant-looking women, mostly in their thirties, a little plump of belly and behind, not over-endowed with bosom.

Nevertheless, the students flocked to the life classes. Being penniless, their experience of naked women was restricted to the occasional tart picked up in Latin Quarter alleys. And that was necessarily brief for the tarts wanted to be back on the street as soon as possible. They were hard-working and had no time to sit around chatting after the client had had his money's-worth.

To be able to stare openly at a naked woman for a couple of hours and sketch her, that was a pleasure for the students. The classes were well attended, even for the plainest of models.

Needless to say, Suzette was a sensation. The first time she mounted the rostrum and slipped off her newly bought dressing-gown to show herself naked, there was a collective sigh of admiration. At least a quarter of an hour went by before a pencil touched paper, the students were totally occupied with staring at her beautiful face and body.

Even the women students stared at her in grudging admiration. They probably intended to become architects or designers, these young women, rather than artists as such. But they liked to go to the life class almost as much as the men. The men, it hardly needs to be said, were as stiff as if a second pencil had been pushed down their trousers.

The professor was beginning to think he had made a mistake in accepting Mademoiselle Bernard as a model. She insisted she was eighteen, though he guessed she was younger than that. But *mon Dieu* – that body, those breasts, those thighs! If the professor were younger, he would have offered to set her up in an apartment of her own in return for calling on her two or three times a week – and not to paint her portrait, that was sure!

While he was trying to summon up the necessary resolve to get rid of her from his life classes, the perplexed professor came under her enchantment, much as his students had. He ignored his objection to her – that to look at her was so arousing that the students very nearly forgot they were there to draw her, not to indulge themselves in erotic fantasies about her.

He let her stay on for he too enjoyed the sight of her. He was a man, after all, though over fifty and a professor of Fine Art. He sketched her himself when he thought no one was watching him.

At nineteen Suzette was taken on at the Folies Bergère, her beauty and her self-assurance when naked were her talents. Show-girls are never paid a fortune, it must be said, but it gave her true independence. She teamed up with Gaby and between them they could afford the rent of a proper apartment with a bathroom. But for such necessities as silk underwear, chic clothes, jewellery and expensive perfumes – and the many other luxuries essential to beautiful women – they were still dependent on finding well-to-do boyfriends.

But not any more, it seemed, not for Suzette, not now she was well on the way to becoming a singing star. Money was piling up at a rate she thought incredible. On the other hand, various commitments she'd never even dreamed about were also piling up. For example, she received scores and scores of letters from fans and unknown admirers, well-wishers, religious fanatics warning her against pride and sinfulness, beggars with heart-wringing tales, cranks wanting subscriptions to charitable causes they had invented – and demented men explaining in detail what they wanted to do to her after they'd ripped her clothes off.

Emile advised her to get a secretary to read all this rubbish and deal with it. This seemed strange to Suzette and she asked Gaby for her opinion. Gaby was in favour of anything that would shift the mountains of unopened letters stacked on the sitting-room floor. But to pay someone out of her own pocket – just for reading letters from strangers – Suzette had great difficulties in accepting that. In the end she found a compromise, she asked plump Arlette in the apartment upstairs to take on the work for so much an hour.

Blonde-dyed Madame Saumur agreed willingly. She was always in need of more money than her circle of regular men-friends could provide. And she had the time for it. All her friends had jobs, none ever called to see her in the mornings. For the most part they visited after five in the afternoon to indulge their pleasure with her. Except the one who liked to drop in during his lunch-break from the Ministry of Public Works and one who visited on Sundays only, telling his wife he went to a football match.

'He's a strange one,' Arlette confided about her friend from the Public Works. 'He likes to tie me up in pink ribbon, metres and metres of it. This makes him aroused very quickly. Ah well, it takes all sorts, as they say. He's easily the politest man I've ever met.'

So it was agreed. The reproachful backlog of yearning letters was moved upstairs into Arlette's apartment to be read and some to be answered. And once a day she came down to collect further deliveries.

'We all know men are crazy,' she said one day, reporting her progress, 'but I'm amazed at the number who've only heard your records, who've never seen you, who write proposals of marriage to you. They include complete details of their jobs and family. Take your pick – this week you can have a cinema projectionist, a butcher with a shop in Clichy, a bank clerk from Nancy who is divorced, a bookseller who says he has a secret method for ensuring total satisfaction ten times a day without fail . . .'

'Enough!' said Suzette, laughing at the list. 'They must be insane, all of them.'

'Those are just the nice ones,' Arlette said, 'I write them a little note to thank them and say you don't want to be married. It's the others who are truly insane. They want to perform some of the most bizarre things I've ever heard – to demonstrate how they adore you! They make my poor Daniel, tying his pink ribbon round my bosoms, sound totally saintly!'

Suzette had to laugh again and this time Gaby laughed with her – not at the ridiculous antics of men in general but at the picture Arlette had conjured up for them. Arlette's *nichons* were as big as melons, they rolled about under her clothes when she moved. The mere thought of these monsters bared and trussed up in pink ribbon by her civil servant was comic beyond words! They would look like two fat geese plucked and ready for the oven!

What did he do next, this Daniel? Suzette asked herself. She caught Gaby's eye as they laughed and she knew her dear friend was pondering the same question. Did he want to truss her plump belly and her bountiful bottom with his pink ribbon? Did poor Arlette have to be bound and helpless before he rolled her over on her back and penetrated her?

'I hope you don't answer the crazies, Arlette.'

'No dear, they never put their address on their letter. Well, one did, he said he'd buy you a diamond bracelet, as in the song, on condition you went with him for a week to a nudist resort on the coast somewhere, not far from Biarritz, I think. He said he's been going there for years and enclosed a snap of himself in the altogether. There's not a lot to be proud of, if you ask me, but he seems pleased.'

'Thank Heaven they don't know my address!' said Suzette. 'Or there'd be a queue of men right up the staircase wanting to get married and madmen wanting to act out their fantasies!'

Her fans were not only in Paris, of course, they lived in all parts of France. And in Belgium and even some in Holland. They sent their effusions to her care of the record company or of the radio station, where the usual arrangements existed to pass on to her this daily tide of trash.

But it was not impossible to find her address, if anyone was determined enough. One morning she had a phone call from a man who introduced himself as Raoul de Montmilieux-Pontillard. The name was as counterfeit as a nine-franc note, but Suzette knew who he was. In fact, she had met him, though from his manner on the phone it was evident he had no recollection of that.

He called himself a song-arranger, this Raoul de Whatever. He had for years played a large and important part in the success of Armand Regence, France's best-known export to the world. At one time Regence was the civilised world's leading heart-throb, the charmer for whom girls ran away from home and married women abandoned husband and children!

Alas, nowadays he was a little too old for that. Twenty years too old, if the precise truth needs to be stated. But he was still an international star, he was still paid phenomenal fees to appear on stage. His song-and-dance act had become more of a song-and-shuffle act but his charm was as sugar-sweet as ever and his knowing wink could still make female hearts go pit-a-pat.

Raoul de Quelquechose was the man behind the scenes who took indifferent words and tunes and developed them into songs which the cracked voice of Armand Regence could record as top-selling hit records! And he wanted to come and talk to Suzette.

She had met Regence once and he was charming, as always. She had met the improbably named de Montmilieux-Pontillard at the same time and he was rude and overbearing. She guessed that was his usual manner to people he considered his inferior, especially women.

On the telephone he was reasonably polite, though he found it impossible to conceal his favourable view of himself. He wished to discuss an important matter with her, he stated, it would be to her benefit. Suzette guessed he was promoting a new song and wanted to persuade her to sing it.

She said she would expect him at 2.30 that afternoon. He came half an hour late, without even one word of apology, evidently straight from a restaurant where he had enjoyed the cuisine and the wine in handsome measure. Especially the wine.

He looked exactly as Suzette recalled him, a big round-faced fat man with dark hair slicked straight back with brilliantine. He wore heavy horn-rimmed glasses and had small ears. His suit was of a beautiful pearl-grey, with a blue shirt and a bow-tie.

Not only was there no apology for his lateness, he behaved in an unpleasantly superior manner, starting by demanding a glass of cognac. He glanced round the sitting-room with a curled lip. Evidently nothing he saw pleased him, not even Suzette herself.

He downed half the cognac, shrugged and admitted grudgingly that for a complete beginner she hadn't made too much of a mess of things. Suzette began to seethe at this unwarranted rudeness – who the hell did this fat fraud think he was, coming here to insult her? But she contained her anger for a while, she still wanted to know why he was here. Show-business riffraff like him didn't make social calls, there was always some sort of scheme going on in their minds.

'Your voice isn't much,' he told her with a sneer, 'you won't ever sing like Piaf. As for your songs, perhaps it is possible to do something with them, but it will take a lot of work. What ham-handed idiot composes the tunes for them – the chief of the fire brigade brass band?'

'How kind of you to call round to offer your felicitations,' Suzette said in a tone so ice-cold it should have shrivelled up Raoul de Wherever's pompoms. 'Goodbye now, don't bother to send flowers when my next record comes out.'

Raoul was too well-protected by his lunch-time wine to notice her sarcasm. Or perhaps he was born with an exceptionally thick skin. A hippopotamus in spectacles!

'I've seen plenty like you in my time,' he said with a sneer, 'here today and gone tomorrow. Those little songs of yours will dry up. Whoever writes the words has no talent, anyone can tell that. Who is he?'

'A friend,' said Suzette, outraged to hear Michel's abilities as a poet slighted by this fat and overdressed drunk.

'Dump him,' said Raoul, 'he's a liability to you.'

'Get out of my apartment!' Suzette said, loudly and clearly, getting to her feet to urge him on his way. 'You are a slug and a dirty pig and I want you out!'

Naturally, her early background had provided her with a range of more devastating invective than that, but she was determined to remain calm and moderately polite.

Raoul stayed where he was, sitting plumb in the middle of her sofa, his fat thighs spread, an empty glass in his hand, a look of indifference on his round moon face. He explained how lucky Suzette was to have the benefit of his advice. In the ordinary way of things, aspiring singers, song-writers and other would-be stars had to wait six months to get a few minutes of his time. If he agreed to see them at all. Usually his secretary threw their letters straight into the waste-bin.

'Perhaps I'm sentimental,' he said, not very convincingly, 'I may perhaps be a complete idiot, but I thought I saw a spark of potential in you. It won't be easy by any means but I think I can make something of you.'

'If you don't go, I'll make something of *you*,' Suzette warned him, 'and it will be squashed toad.'

'Don't take that tone with me!' he retorted. 'I know who you are, I've checked up on you. You used to be a show-girl flashing your *nichons* at the Folies Bergère. When you crash as a singer, what will you do then? Go back to that, if they'll have you? A few years and even that will be finished. By the time you're thirty your arse will be sagging

225

and the *nichons* dangling down to your belly button. I've seen it all before.'

'You should know,' Suzette retorted in her most cutting tone. 'Anyone can see it's happened to you already.'

'I've got talent and brains and contacts and a track record,' he bragged. 'My looks don't matter. What have you got, girlie? A pretty face and a nice pair of *nichons*, that's all.'

While Suzette stood speechless at his insufferable arrogance, he made the offer which was his reason for wanting to see her.

'We'll sign a contract,' he said. 'I'll manage your career. I find the song-writers, I decide what you sing, I look after the bookings, I choose what you wear. You decide nothing, you do as I tell you, understand? In two years I'll make you a star. All I want is fifty percent of everything you earn. Agreed?'

Suzette's anger had turned into contempt. She told Raoul what he could do. She told him in the unambiguous terms of her early years in the back streets, that he could kiss her behind. Though it wasn't as polite as that, the way she put it to him.

A person as important as Raoul believed himself to be was not accustomed to brusque suggestions of that kind, most especially from nobody singers! The shock of the words penetrated the slightly drunken haze that shielded him from reality, they rang in his mind with fearful directness. He stared at Suzette with round eyes, his mouth opening and closing like an ornamental carp in a pond, but nothing came out, not even a bubble.

'What?' he gasped at last. 'What was that?'

Suzette repeated her suggestion, making it sound insulting to an unbelievable degree.

To her amazement his muddy eyes rolled up in his head and he gasped *Yes!* In another instant he slid from the sofa on to his knees and clasped his arms round her thighs.

'Get off, *crapaud*!' she said in haughty disdain. She was not in the least afraid he would rape her, anyone as overfed and so obviously out of condition as Raoul de Pigsty could be felled instantly by a well-aimed blow between the legs.

He had positioned himself ideally for that, down on his knees and close to her. She had only to swing her leg and deliver a crushing kick to his vital parts. What a pity she was wearing flat-heeled sling-backs and not pointed-toe shoes! He was sure to have folds of fat protecting his necessities – but a really determined kick might incapacitate him permanently.

The thought was a very pleasing one. Consequently she made no particular effort to shake him off, she let him cling round her legs in the hope he would give her an excuse to neuter him with a well-directed foot. And then, she told herself, when this fat pig lay squealing and writhing, she would drive him across the floor on his hands and knees and out of the apartment, by hard kicks to his backside.

And then all the way down the stairs, kick after kick, brutal revenge for the dreadful things he had said to her. Out of the street door – if she was still feeling malicious at that point – and out on to the pavement!

But that wasn't what Raoul wanted at all, to get her down and rape her. Her contemptuous words had seized his fuddled mind to the point of obsession. His facade of conceit had crumbled and the natural servility of his personality revealed itself. His only desire was to do what she had said!

The words were spoken in contempt on her side, of

course, but to Raoul they did not seem a dismissive expression, a mild form of swearing at him. Not at all! His mind was addled – a common condition for so strange a person – her derisive words had the force of a law, an unavoidable injunction.

Suzette had no inkling of how strange a man he was, this song arranger named Lasse who had baptised himself *de Montmilieux-Pontillard*. Nor of how disorganised his imagination had become. It was impossible to know that her words were taken by Raoul to signify that he owed her a sort of perverted homage.

She was dressed very simply for the meeting with him – in a silk blouse in palest pink with a frilled front and a pleated dark-grey skirt. While his arms held her legs she considered all the agonies she would inflict on him the instant he revealed an intention to violate her.

But he was shuffling round behind her on his pudgy knees and, instead of putting his hand up between her thighs, he lifted her skirt at the back. He uttered shrill sounds like a piglet while he pawed at the silk-covered cheeks of her bottom.

'Ah, would you!' she cried. 'Take that!'

She found that swinging the leg backward to connect with the heel was a far less satisfactory manner of assault than kicking forward. And in sling-backs! Her heel connected with something flabby, but Raoul clung to her, his determination undiminished. Perhaps it was only his thigh where her blow landed.

True, he gave a long sigh, but it was not the sound of agony, far from it. Suzette was craning her neck to see down over her shoulder in order to aim her backward kicks better, but she was unable to see his face. Otherwise she would have seen his look of bemused delight – caused by his close-up observation of the manner in which the thin silk of her knickers was caught in the cleft between the cheeks of her bottom.

Suzette kicked again, this time he grunted, she was getting a little closer to the target, perhaps. But that did not stop him pulling her knickers down below the rounded cheeks. In one more moment his lips touched the smooth flesh he had uncovered – and Raoul de Montmilieux-Pontillard was kissing her behind!

'What do you think you're doing!' Suzette exclaimed, she was beginning to understand that the song-arranger was not exactly normal. She ceased to try to cripple him with kicks for now.

'I didn't mean you to take me at my word!' she said and she had to grin at the ridiculous situation. 'Get up, you fool!'

Raoul said nothing to that, down upon his knees in his act of homage, his mind whirling as he kissed Suzette's perfect rump. Everyone privileged to see it when she used to appear naked at the Folies Bergère was an eyewitness to its natural beauty.

'Get up,' she said again. She was struggling not to laugh at the fervour of his repeated kisses on her bare bottom.

'You are cold and cruel,' Raoul babbled, 'you hate me!'

He was filled with a perverse enjoyment, his legs had turned weak and he knew if he tried to stand on them he would collapse on the carpet. He felt he was on the verge of fainting because his blood had withdrawn from his brain. He was sure his wildly beating heart was pumping the blood into his swollen male part to make it grow bigger – and to make it pulsate in pleasurable desire that was also half-torment.

Suzette's voice reached him through his sensual confusion.

'I despise you rather than hate you. But if you continue what you're doing, I'm sure I can manage hatred as well.'

Out of her sight, he was unzipping his trousers with one hand – the other holding her pleated skirt up to her waist, his lips pressed to her bare skin in a heart-felt salute. But he did not extract his stiffness, he kept it hidden and clasped it tightly in his hand.

The distressing truth was that in this respect Raoul had been treated niggardly by cruel Destiny. Not to conceal the facts, he lacked the usual fifteen centimetres. His sexual endowment was no longer or thicker than his own little finger! By nature he was sensual. Through his profession he had easy access to hundreds of pretty young women trying to make a career in show business. Most of them would give themselves to him for his assistance. Many came to his office wearing no brassiere and dressed thinly enough for their dark buds to be visible. Some arrived wearing no knickers. But alas, Raoul had little to offer them.

Over the years his character had become warped – how could it be otherwise? Like Tantalus in the old Greek myth, he had been consigned to a special Hades of his own in which exceptionally delicious pleasures were offered to him continuously – but even at the moment he grasped for them, these delights receded from him. He knew to his bitter chagrin the look of astonishment on a girl's face when she felt nothing inside her, even with Raoul lying heavily on her belly and reaching his critical moment.

He rained kisses on Suzette's bare bottom, hot ardent kisses, tremors shaking his plump body as his hand moved briskly on his stiff little part. It would be soon, soon, he told himself in a silent cry of pleasure inside his head, his hand moving faster on his taut flesh, the pace increasing with the beating of his heart, the tension in his body and soul stretching tighter.

'Get off me!' Suzette said loudly.

The joke had worn thin in her view, she did not know that for Raoul it had become immensely serious, this furtive affair of a snatched pleasure.

'I hate you!' she said sharply. 'You are a mean contemptible pig without manners or sense!'

She kicked backwards with her heel again and this time, by chance, she connected with her intended target. Raoul squealed – not in anguish but in sudden ecstasy – the open contempt in Suzette's words and the kick had carried him over the edge. He collapsed in a gasping heap, backward at first, until his thick thighs and his fat rump stopped him from going any further. He swayed gurgling for some moments, then toppled over sideways.

Suzette turned to glare down at him, her leg drawn back for a second disabling kick. But what she saw halted her foot in mid-swing. Raoul was rolling on the sitting-room carpet in a tight ball, knees drawn up to his fat belly, his eyes staring blindly behind the heavy spectacles. One hand was thrust deep into his undone trousers and from the spasms shaking his body it was easy to guess he was spurting a perverse passion into his underwear.

'Pah!' Suzette exclaimed. She was affronted by this fat slug of a song-arranger and his miserable little pleasure in kissing her bottom. She kicked as hard as she could at the bulge under his trousers. Her sling-back flew off and skimmed right across the sitting-room and her silk-stockinged toes struck with a thump. The back of Raoul's busy hand absorbed much of the blow but it was not wholly

231

wasted – the sudden impact jarred through to his pompoms.

He squealed again, his eyes rolling up behind the horn-rimmed glasses till only the whites showed. Stronger spasms shook him, faster writhings and he rolled over face down, his entire body heaving like a beached whale. *Merde!* said Suzette, for she saw she had merely intensified his climactic thrills.

She turned on her heel and went to the kitchen, smoothing her skirt down at the back where Raoul raised it, looking to see if it had wrinkled. She was furious with him for using her for his bizarre notions – and she was angry with herself for permitting him to get close to her without guessing what his motive was.

Her hand trembled with fury while she poured a small glass of cognac. She sat at the kitchen table while she drank it slowly, waiting for Raoul de Quelquepart to get up off the floor and go away. A quarter of an hour passed and all was silent, he must surely have departed in shame and ignominy. Or had he? She had not heard any sound of footsteps or the apartment door closing.

Was it possible her final kick had paralysed him? Could the repulsive toad still be lying on the floor? What if it became necessary to send for an ambulance to move his wretched carcase out of the apartment? Or the police, or the fire brigade – or whichever officials dealt with these incidents!

She went to look. He was still there, but not on the carpet. He had recovered sufficiently to crawl to an armchair and there he sprawled, a foolish smile on his moon face, his glasses halfway down his nose. His trousers were done up, at least.

When Suzette saw she had not crippled him, she was determined to chase him out of the apartment – with words if possible and with kicks and punches if need be. But he took her by surprise. He beamed at her as if they were the very best of friends.

'You are the most adorable woman I know,' he said, 'you must let me represent you. I'll make you a bigger star than Regence ever was and bigger than Mistinguett in her best days.'

'You?' Suzette said, astonished by his blind arrogance. 'You represent *me*? I wouldn't let you kiss my . . .' she broke off her outburst at this point. After all, he'd already done that.

'Forget what I said about fifty percent,' said he sweetly, as if unaware she was about to explode. 'That was only a joke. Not to be taken seriously, I assure you. Because I believe with all my heart you are destined to become an international star, because I see in you great talent not yet properly developed, because I am fascinated by your potential – for all these reasons I offer to represent you and I make no stipulations. I ask for nothing, only ten percent to cover my expenses.'

'What am I to do with this buffoon?' Suzette exclaimed, her shoulders rising in a shrug of despair. 'He is insufferable!'

'That may be,' Raoul agreed. 'I am also indispensable, if you truly wish to reach the top.'

'You were drunk when we met before,' she said, 'I suppose you are drunk now.'

'Have we met before? When was that? I don't remember it.'

'The last time Armand Regence came to Paris. He did six weeks at the Folies Bergère to prove that everyone adores him still – and to promote the sales of his record. He gave a party for the cast before he went back to

America. You were there – it was in the big apartment he rented in the Boulevard Lannes.'

'So many people,' said Raoul, 'but how could I miss *you*, even in a crowd? I must have seen you on stage hundreds of times. I don't know why I didn't recognise you with clothes on. You *were* dressed, I suppose?'

'You recognised me. You called me Suzy and told me I'd a nice pair of *nichons*! You wanted to feel them.'

Raoul pushed his glasses up the bridge of his nose with one pudgy finger and assumed a tragic expression.

'I can't remember any of it,' he said. 'Imagine – feel a pair like yours and not remember it afterwards!'

'But you didn't, I can assure you,' Suzette said at once, she didn't want the idiot to get ideas like that. 'You were on the bed in Regence's own bedroom, with two girls. They had stripped down to their knickers, both of them, but you were dressed. And very drunk!'

'I hope I had a feel of the girls,' he said with a grin, 'not that I can remember a thing about that party. Except there was a row afterwards with Regence, I'm not sure what it was about.'

'Probably about making a mess of his bed. One of the girls was pouring champagne down your throat and the other one had opened your trousers and was pouring champagne in from another bottle. Most of it was going on the bed, I imagine it was soaked before your games came to an end.'

'Now that does bring back a memory!' he exclaimed. 'A bottle of champagne in my trousers – I woke up wet through and thought I'd had a little accident.'

A cloud passed over his round face as the implication of what Suzette had said occurred to him. His trousers were open – she must surely have seen! Was that why she despised him? She had told him very forcefully she despised him and hated him! That was what aroused him – that and kissing her bare bottom.

'Did you stay and join the fun?' he asked cautiously. 'No, I suppose not, once you'd seen what was on offer. The other girls didn't seem to mind so much – I mean, it's all a bit blurred in my mind but I'm pretty sure I had both of them.'

Suzette didn't believe that for a moment. He'd been too drunk to go stiff – what she'd glimpsed was as soft as boiled spaghetti. The girls were in much the same condition, giggling like idiots while they poured champagne into him. He might have wanted to, perhaps even thought he had, but he was incapable.

As for what was on offer, as the shamefaced owner put it, she remembered clearly that his white shirt had been pulled up over his fat belly and the champagne was cascading on to dark curls plastered flat to his pale skin. And there lay a small and limp item. At the time she hadn't given it a thought, in retrospect she concluded that poor Raoul was undersized and ashamed of it.

The problem was his, not hers. Long or short, thick or thin, she had not the slightest interest. She wanted him to leave. He was a pig, an arrogant repulsive pig, she had no time for men like him. As for this business of wanting to represent her, it was a stupid lie to get her knickers down. He'd demonstrated in the most obvious way what he was after. He wasn't going to get it.

'Out!' she said, seizing his left earlobe between finger and thumb. '*Fiche-moi le camp!*'

She dragged him from the armchair by his ear. He squealed and grabbed her wrist but was unable to break her grip. She led him across the room, got the apartment door open and manoeuvred him round to push him out on to the landing.

'But my offer!' he said shrilly. 'Let's talk about it – I'm very sincere about representing you. Please listen to me!'

'Pigs are usually led by a ring through the snout!' Suzette informed him. 'As you've forgotten to have one inserted, an ear will have to do. Out!'

He was fumbling in an inside pocket, he pulled out a handful of business cards and thrust them at her.

'Phone me when you've thought it over,' he begged, he sounded very anxious. 'Here's my number and office address. I'll expect to hear from you. You're going to be a big star, I promise!'

With one hand she held his ear to control him, the other hand was on his chest to push him backwards through the door. Seeing she was not going to accept any of his business cards, Raoul in despair tried to tuck them down the front of her pink blouse.

Naturally, she thought he was groping her breasts. It was too much! First he molested her bottom with his nasty kissing, now he was attempting to feel her breasts – God alone knew what he would do next!

'*Sale cochon!*' she spat. 'Get away from me!' and she jabbed upward with her knee between his legs.

This time there was no protecting hand over his necessities. The pleated skirt hampered Suzette's movement a little, but she felt her silk-clad knee thud into his pompoms. He gave voice to a long shrill squeal and staggered backwards, helped on his way by a vigorous push of her hand under his double chin.

His back was to the wall, he was groggy and swaying. One step to his right would tumble him head-over-heels down the stairs. He was holding himself tenderly between the legs with both his hands, his eyes blank behind his heavy spectacles.

'Suzette!' he gasped. '*Je t'aime, je t'aime!*'

It was incredible, he was unzipping his pearl-grey trousers! His hand slid inside, an expression of cherubic pleasure slowly crept over his round face. The thump seemed to have stirred his emotions again – he was giving every sign of wanting to repeat his perversities! Standing out there on the landing!

Suzette closed the apartment door quickly, then bolted it top and bottom. He was a degenerate, this Raoul, she told herself, he confused pleasure and pain, he blustered and bullied, but *au fond* what he really desired was to abase himself.

At least he hadn't bitten her bottom when he had her knickers down to kiss it! That was something to be thankful for.

JULIEN
RETURNS

When Julien Brocq got back to Paris he sent Suzette an enormous flower arrangement in a tall-handled basket and with it a note congratulating her warmly on her success. Evidently he had kept up to date with events during his absence. He did not suggest a meeting and that pleased her. She preferred him to be a friend and not a lover. But there was a scribbled postscript that said: *If ever you change your mind about being a film star, call me.*

Julien, it went without saying, did what she predicted on the evening they went to the Folies Bergère and afterwards to a bar to meet some of her friends. He went to the bar again after the show one evening to look for Jasmin Bonaventure. She was very beautiful, after all, or she would never have been a show-girl.

He had no way of knowing it, but his approach was well timed. Jasmin had become disenchanted with the acrobatic juggler from Gaboon who was in the show with her. The promise of his bulging white suede *cache-sexe* was more inspiring than its performance. And in her view he was mean with money – he said he had to send most of his earnings back to his village in Africa. His father and his mother, his six brothers and eight sisters depended on him, he said, they were poor people. But when she'd come to

239

know him better, Jasmin thought it more likely he had a wife or two back home and a brood of chocolate-skinned babies.

She welcomed the overture from Julien Brocq when he turned up in the bar looking for her. An approach from almost any wealthy man would have pleased her just then, but most especially these signs of deep interest in her by a man who was important in the film business. Who could say where that might lead to?

In fact, hand on her heart, Jasmin could imagine no reason at all why she shouldn't be a film star. Or as it was not Jasmin's heart on which her career was based, then with her hand on her *bijou* she could think of no reason why she shouldn't be a film star. She had the looks for it, no doubt of it, the pretty face and the beautiful body that made men drool.

She moved with elegance, she was sexy, she knew how to please men – there was no great trick in that, she thought with a grin of faint contempt. The only reason she wasn't a film star was the lack of the right opportunity. Standing about in ostrich plumes and sequins every evening while the men in the audience played with themselves through their trousers – it paid the rent but it was not a longterm career.

But here was Monsieur Opportunity in person, Julien Brocq the movie mogul! He wanted to take her to a late dinner after the show, he said, meaning he wanted her to lie on her back for him. *Him and half the men in Paris!* Jasmin said to herself with a grin and a shrug. Naturally she accepted the invitation.

They had a delicious supper in an expensive little restaurant near the Opera. They ate nothing heavy, in view of proposed later events – just a few escargots and a lobster shared between the two of them and a bottle of chilled and sparkling white wine. That was enough, except for a morsel of Brie and a glass of Armagnac.

He took her to his suite in the Ritz, where else? And Jasmin glanced round the bedroom and nodded in silent approval. It was precisely the right setting for her, she decided, the luxurious surroundings she needed and not a tiny two-room apartment in a very inferior district. She wanted servants to wait on her, to appear when she rang for them and bring bottles of champagne on ice, maids to tidy up, make the bed, take care of her clothes – all the boring domestic chores she hated.

Dear Julien could make all that happen for her – if he wanted to. He could get her into movies, where she'd very soon become a star with a mansion on the Avenue Foch, a long white car and a chauffeur in uniform, a sable fur coat, all new clothes twice a year from Dior and Chanel, stacks and stacks of jewels . . .

She looked at Julien with an interest as consuming as that of a boxer weighing up an opponent before the bell rings to begin the contest. How to get past his guard, to weaken him, to bring him under control? She knew where he was vulnerable – the area between his thighs, that was her natural target. Get through to that and he'd be down for the count, twitching and gasping.

Meanwhile he'd be trying to finish her off – and he looked as if he knew plenty about women and how to put them down on their backs. Jasmin understood she was only the latest girlfriend to be brought here to this bedroom by him. Who could say how many had preceded her? Julien evidently had an eye for beautiful women.

Suzette had been here before her, to spread her legs on that elegant bed of patterned and polished wood. And he'd given her a diamond bracelet she never took off, Jasmin reminded herself. There were good prizes to be won, even if the competition for Julien's devotion was ferocious. He'd known too many beautiful women to let himself be seriously enchanted.

But Jasmin intended to show him what he had been missing. She stared at him thoughtfully, taking his measure. He was a heavy-set man, solid of shoulder and hip – about fifty years old in her estimation. An age at which the fires of youth were less fierce and an age at which he would be grateful to the woman who could stimulate him to greater endeavour and wilder gratification.

He took off his jacket and his foulard silk tie. Jasmin stood by the bed while he kissed her and undressed her completely. He slipped her stylish little black frock over her head, hardly glancing at the butterfly brooch on the shoulder. It was crystal and not diamonds, alas, but that might change, she considered.

When she was naked he gripped her waist between his hands and took in the beauty of her body with shining brown eyes. She was the taller, but no more than a centimetre or two. Her reddish-brown hair came loose while he was undressing her and fell to her shoulders. He kissed her breasts avidly, delighted by the curious dark-red of their buds. After the performance she wiped off the cosmetic she used to tone them down for the stage. She was proud of their real hue and expected lovers to admire it.

She lay down on the bed, on the pale blue satin bedspread, and Julien stood looking at her in admiration for some moments. And most particularly at the red-gold curly-haired delight between her long thighs. Like all the show-girls at the Folies Bergère she kept her natural little fur-coat trimmed small, so not even the narrowest sequin-spangled *cache-sexe* let the customers see more than they had paid to see.

Julien feasted his eyes on her charms until it was impossible to contain his emotions any longer. He lay beside her to stroke her thighs and feel between them. She was ready for him – a man had only to look at Jasmin to make her become moist between the legs. The right sort of man, that is, not just anybody. Men who could treat her well and take her to interesting places and buy things for her – when that type stared at her, her knees shook.

In another moment Julien was going to slide over her and drag his trousers open. *Too ordinary*, she thought, even as prelude to a night of extended pleasure. It was like letting the opponent wind you with a punch to your midriff, it was points scored for him, it gave him confidence he was going to win. But he wasn't going to master her. Jasmin was determined he was going to give in and beg her to accept everything he could offer – jewels and an apartment and clothes and a leading role in his next movie.

'Take your clothes off,' she said in a slinky temptress tone, 'I want to feel you naked against me.'

He was off the bed at once, shedding shirt and trousers. When he was naked Jasmin stared in surprise at his hairiness of body – the thick pelt of brown curls covering him from his thighs up to his shoulders. Men with hair-matted chests Jasmin had seen before but never anything to match this! Down where his legs met, his male part stood up stiffly out of an imposing bush.

'*Formidable!*' she said breathlessly.

Before he could lie down beside her on the bed and resume his *ordinary* lovemaking, she threw her marvellous legs up over his shoulders. Julien wasn't going to call the tune, not if she had anything to say about it. She wanted him to become used to the idea of following her lead.

'Oh yes!' he murmured, his hands gliding over her belly and under her to squeeze her bottom – which was lifted well up from the bed by her position. Then his thumbs were in her, deftly opening her down by the red-gold tuft. He was parting her fleshy petals to plunge into her and see himself doing it.

In another moment he had done it – he had penetrated her, his hard-swollen part was in her. Jasmin sighed to see how he made his stiff flesh slide into her. She felt his rigid length push deep and open her belly. She watched it sliding in and out. She saw the wet sheen on the pale skin, the way it seemed to throb, the little blue veins on the sides, she saw how it grew harder still and thicker as the moment approached.

And, truth to tell, although Jasmin observed all this she was not detached – she was immensely aroused by the sight of Julien bending over her, his hairy torso swinging in a strong rhythm to thrust in and out of her beautiful naked body. With her legs on his shoulders and his hands grasping her thighs, she was at his mercy, helpless . . . It was just like children's storybooks, she was being savaged by a wolf in the forest and he was devouring her ferociously, ravishing her flesh from her bones – and she loved every moment of it!

She was ready for the supreme moment, she wanted to feel him spurt inside her and release her from the fierce sensations he was provoking. *Yes*, she moaned, *do it, chéri, do it now!*

Julien gasped and began to thrust harder, his eyes bulging as he watched the fast movement of his swollen part stabbing into soft wet flesh. He raised his eyes for a moment and saw how her superb breasts bounced to each stab, and on her face he saw the look of naked desire.

'Yes!' he answered hoarsely. 'Oh yes, Jasmin, now!'

She was driven to the ultimate peak, wailing as her orgasm took her – and at that very instant Julien spurted his ravening desire into her quaking belly in six fast gushes then collapsed on her. They panted and gasped, both their bodies were slippery with sweat and they were lost in sexual satisfaction. Yet they were unable to let the pleasure go. They clung together avidly, Julien's belly gliding on her belly, her breasts sliding under his hairy chest. It was if they were making love a second time.

Needless to say, Julien was delighted with his new girlfriend and she with him. He took her to dinner twice a week, he took her dancing at exclusive nights clubs, he took her shopping and bought her pretty underwear. He gave her presents, but nothing as impressive as Suzette's diamond bracelet. He took her to his suite in the Hotel Ritz and made love to her. But there was not a word about making her a film star.

When she raised the question herself, tactfully of course, a casual enquiry whether he considered she had talent enough for a career in movies, Julien smiled a charming smile and shrugged his shoulders and turned it aside with a vague *we shall see*.

Jasmin tried everything she could think of, every little game in a bedroom she knew or had ever heard of. She was determined to capture Julien's heart as a necessary step to being the star in his future films. He adored everything she suggested, he was an eager participant in her little games.

He was enchanted when she smeared sweet Belgian chocolate on the curiously dark buds of her breasts and had him lick it off. Naturally, she enjoyed this enormously. Julien took it further, he smeared chocolate between her thighs and licked it off – she lay on her back, legs apart, the chocolate beginning to melt in the warmth of her body even as he put his tongue to it.

Before he had licked her clean she cried out in orgasm twice and she trembled as he slid his hairy belly on to hers.

Yet, however delighted he was with her, the question of films never arose. Jasmin consulted her friend Angelique, who had won the heart of the *rentier* with the sunken marble bath and lived with him in luxury on the Boulevard Raspail.

'He's done it all before,' said Angelique with a shrug. 'He's had more women than you and I have had dinners. Nothing much is going to impress him, not unless you can think of something you can't buy a postcard of in the Place Pigalle.'

They discussed the problem for some time, they compared their past experiences of doing it *this way* and *that way* and what the effect was on the partner at the time. Eventually Angelique had a notion that sounded interesting – suppose it was arranged for Julien to have them both together? Two beautiful women naked, at the same time, that ought to stir him!

'Why not?' said Jasmin, shrugging prettily. 'Stranger things have happened in the Hotel Ritz, I'm sure.'

'Perhaps he'll offer both of us parts in his next film,' said Angelique dreamily, 'important parts, I mean, not just as walk-on extras, that's no good to us.'

'But what about all this?' Jasmin asked in surprise, waving a slender hand to indicate the flashy grandeur of the apartment Angelique was sharing with her property-owning boyfriend. 'Have you got bored with Jean-Jacques already?'

'In a word,' said Angelique, pouting her perfect lips

into a sign of discontent, 'yes. He's too tied up in his business – he never has time for me, except when he wants to climb on top. So I'm looking round for someone else. Your Julien could be useful to both of us.'

'That's all very well . . .' Jasmin said doubtfully, 'but what a fool I'd look if I agreed to let you get in bed with us and he preferred you to me afterwards.'

'No chance of that,' Angelique reassured her. 'After he's had two of us at the same time, he'll never be content with one on her own again. Trust me, I know – I've done this before.'

'With who?'

'Someone you don't know, Nadine Leclos. We worked together in a strip-bar in Pigalle for a while. She had a boyfriend who was threatening to leave her and go back to his wife and she was so desperate about losing this idiot that she begged me to join in a threesome, to show him what he was missing if he dumped her.'

'Did it work?'

'Like a charm. We got his clothes off and rolled all over him till he went red in the face and shot it over my *nichons*. Then we started on him all over again . . . what can I tell you? After an afternoon of being raped by the two of us he'd do absolutely anything Nadine said, just to hang on to her and me. She'd got him right where she wanted him.'

'But what happened when you moved on, Angelique?'

'Nadine had to find a replacement. By then her precious idiot of a boyfriend – Bertrand, his name was – found it so boring to make love to only one woman that he couldn't do it! Only with two together. What a comedy!'

'It's worth a try,' said Jasmin. 'I'll suggest it to Julien – and if he agrees, it's a night at the Ritz for you.'

'Why not here?' Angelique asked.

'Here in Jean-Jacques' apartment? But why? It's madly risky and there's no point. Julien would never agree to that.'

'For the pleasure of having the two of us at the same time he will fall over himself to agree, I promise you. Men are capable of anything when you-know-what is standing up hard. You know it as well as I do.'

'So what's the point – if there is one?'

'Just to enjoy a little gloat, nothing more. If Jean-Jacques can't find time to roll me around the bed, I'll find someone to do it for him. He'll be away on Thursday and Friday, he's going to view some property on the coast. It's a run-down hotel, he's got the idea that summer holidays in France for foreigners will be big business in a year or two.'

So it was arranged. Julien was astounded at first when Jasmin suggested including a friend of hers in their pleasures. But he quickly became fascinated by the idea, as any man would. On the occasion of meeting Angelique, he insisted on taking Jasmin and her to supper at Maxims! He said the idea of two women in bed with him was so divinely *fin-de-siècle* decadent that Maxims was the only truly appropriate setting for such an adventure – with bottles and bottles of their best vintage champagne!

He believed his two stunning show-girls would accompany him to the Hotel Ritz afterward, and they didn't tell him of their own plan until the bill was brought and signed. For a moment Julien hesitated but, as Angelique predicted, he smiled and agreed the three of them would take a taxi to *her* apartment. Naturally she told him the apartment was hers, she could see no necessity to mention the absent Jean-Jacques.

With these two beauties at his table, one to his left and

one to his right, it was impossible for Julien do anything else but agree. Jasmin was stately and slender in an off-the-shoulder frock he had bought her, her wealth of reddish-brown hair swept up on top of her head. She wasn't slender where it mattered most, of course – her breasts under the thin satin frock were sumptuous.

And her friend, Angelique, a dark-haired charmer with a beauty spot near one corner of her mouth, huge luminous dark eyes, her hips subtly rounded under her clinging black chiffon creation – and such breasts! For the privilege of kissing them bare a man would break the most heart-felt vow he had ever made. Or so Julien thought, afloat in a euphoric haze of champagne and desire.

They understood just how to arouse a man, these two Folies Bergère lovelies, he thought. They knew what clothes to wear, they knew how shiny black satin suggested the erotic quality of a wet and naked body. They appreciated how well soft chiffon clung to the body to outline the breasts . . . they understood the mysteries of lace and silk underwear against smooth-fleshed thighs . . .

In the taxi he sat with an arm around the waist of each, head turning from side to side to kiss them in turn, passion surging through him from a hand on each of his thighs, stroking him. He paid no attention to his surroundings when they arrived at the building, or even to the apartment itself. Angelique had removed all the obvious signs of the real owner, everything was hidden in one of the wardrobes with Jean-Jacques' clothes – and the wardrobe was locked.

With Jasmin on Julien's right and Angelique on his left, they settled themselves very comfortably amidst ten or twelve circular down-stuffed cushions on an enormous half-round hideous pink velvet sofa in the sitting-room.

There was soft music on the radio and the wall-bracket lights were dimmed.

It seemed only right and proper that Jasmin should start the proceedings. Her hand on Julien's thigh caressed up towards the long swelling in his trousers. Angelique watched with a grin on her pretty face, awaiting her cue, while Jasmin unzipped Julien and brought out his hard-standing part.

Never a passive man, he responded by sliding his hand up Jasmin's frock, up the silk stocking to the bare thigh above – then he gasped in surprise. Where he expected to touch silky underwear, his fingers found warm flesh. He explored gently until he knew she was wearing a tiny silk triangular *cache-sexe* instead of knickers. His fingers crept under it to feel her and he lay back on the cushions, his face toward Angelique to bring her into the love-making.

Angelique laughed and slid down on the pink sofa till she was almost lying on her back, her long legs spread as wide apart as her frock permitted. Julien stared in delight and slid his hand down the top of her black chiffon to caress her superb breasts, the equal of Jasmin's, he thought in delight. He caressed them with his free hand, the one not engaged with Jasmin!

He put his hand under Angelique's skirt and stroked her warm belly. He slipped it down her knickers to feel her *jouet*. It was delicious in its plump fleshiness, it was so *accessible*. It was in his mind Angelique's was one of the most lascivious he'd ever felt – a conclusion causing his stiff part to leap in Jasmin's wet mouth – she having twisted herself about to bring her face close to his thick-haired belly.

Angelique's charm was fully available to his touch by

the way she held her legs apart. Julien stroked the fleshy lips pouting boldly forward, as if about to kiss any male part that was near enough. His fingers caressed up and down, then slid inside, to find her slippery secret bud.

'Ah, you like the feel of me,' Angelique said with a chuckle. 'He's playing with me, Jasmin – he's put two fingers inside me, he's going to make me feel very happy in a minute!'

'Good, I'll help him,' said Jasmin.

She released her hold on Julien and slid to her knees between Angelique's feet. She pushed up the black chiffon frock as high as Angelique's lap and assisted Julien to draw her frilly silk knickers down her legs and off. Julien was enchanted by the neatly trimmed little tuft of dark curls above the smooth lips between her legs – he sighed in pleasure to see how Jasmin's long-fingered hands stroked her friend's thighs above the tops of her stockings. He touched the pouting lips gently, hoping to see them open of their own accord.

Angelique's eyes were closed to experience fully the movement of two pairs of hands on her voluptuous body. Whose were whose, who could tell? There were fingers in her soft groins, fingers on her belly, fingers parting her fleshy petals .. it was sheer delight, moments of pulsating happiness . . .

Julien and Jasmin looked into each other's eyes and kissed in ardent passion as they caressed Angelique, their hands touching as they went about their intimate work. Fingertips met for just a moment, a palm slid over the back of a hand, a thumb entwined itself around a thumb and glided away again.

Julien's trousers were gaping wide. Angelique opened her eyes as she felt herself near climax, she glanced at his up-rearing part and slid her legs even further apart. Without hesitation, Julien stood up and loomed above her as she sprawled on the pink sofa, poised to plunge into her.

'Yes!' Jasmin exclaimed, her fingers pulling Angelique open for him.

'Yes!' Angelique exclaimed, her half-covered belly writhing.

But it was too late, they had aroused her too intensely – she moaned and twitched in orgasm even before Julien could push the purple-swollen head of his male part into her. She moaned again in delight and it was all over before he had probed her depths. She lay squirming and sighing while he butted against her belly until his frenetic desire spurted into her.

While they were recovering, Jasmin stood up to undress. She took off her sheath of a frock and the rest of her clothes. Though that is not to say much, for this *rest* amounted only to a flimsy lace brassiere that did nothing to conceal her luscious breasts, the tiny triangle of black silk that only just covered her darling *chatte*, her garter-belt and her silk stockings.

Julien lay half-bemused by delight and anticipation upon the sofa, his arms about Angelique. He watched Jasmin's undressing and sighed in admiration at her beautiful thighs, so perfectly shaped, the satin-smooth flesh gleaming in the subdued light.

She turned her back while she leaned forward to take off her stockings, so displaying the round fullness of her bottom and the shadowed dimples he longed to explore with the wet tip of his tongue.

He too stood up to undress and took Angelique by her slender wrists to pull her to her feet. Soon all three were naked. They lay entwined on the velvet sofa, moving slowly against each other, enjoying the feel of skin on skin, belly on belly, hand on breasts, thigh against thigh. There were only three of them yet it seemed as if a dozen mouths were kissing and fifty fingers were playing over hot flesh, that there were a score of tender openings to explore, to stroke, to kiss . . .

At first, when Jasmin had proposed Angelique as a partner in the revels, Julien had wondered if she might become jealous to actually see him with another woman, even her friend. But when it came to the moment, she urged him on with kisses and little caresses. And now he must pay her in pleasure for what she had done for him.

The threesome on the sofa, their limbs entangled, their minds dizzy with sexual delight, were not far away from a moment of delicious crisis. Julien felt himself ready to spurt all his desire into the hot mouth that enclosed his leaping part. Both the women were so hot and wet he knew they were close to orgasm – it was time to reward Jasmin.

He clasped her body between his hands and turned her face-to-face with him. She knew what he meant to do. She sighed, put her mouth to his and slipped her hand down her belly to prise herself open for him. He hooked an arm under her leg and raised it high to let his stiff flesh slide up into her wetness.

'Julien, yes, yes, yes,' she murmured into his open mouth.

Angelique was not to be left out. She was behind Julien, her breasts pressed against his hairy back. She pushed at him hard when he was embedded in Jasmin, forcing him to roll over on top of her. Then she was on his back, her weight pressing him down on Jasmin's belly, ramming her loins against his bottom to push him deeper into her friend.

'I've got you both now!' she gasped out, and her breath

was hot against Julien's ear.

She bounced up and down on him fast, forcing him and Jasmin beneath him to the very brink of orgasm. And the rub of his hairy back on her breasts and belly, the roughness of it between her widespread thighs, the feel of it against the bare lips – this was rushing Angelique herself to the same brink.

When she was only two heartbeats from her climax she stopped bouncing abruptly and let herself lie heavily on Julien's back, panting and perspiring. Jasmin shrieked loudly in protest – she was left halfway into the sensations of orgasm, frantic for the *coup-de-grâce*. She was uncontrollable, she thumped her belly up against Julien, continuing the rhythm faster and stronger.

Julien, too, was in the frenzy before the critical moment. While Jasmin bucked below him, he felt Angelique's hands slide under his belly, feeling for the point where his stiff male flesh slid in and out of Jasmin. She wanted her fingers to touch the hardness and the stiffness, the wet slipperiness, to feel the in and out, to share in the giving and receiving.

Jasmin cried out shrilly as the spasms of her climax wrenched her belly and arched her back. Julien gasped loudly to feel his own moment arrive. At Angelique's fingertips his thrusting part leaped and jabbed as she moaned and smacked her belly up and down on his bottom.

Some time passed before any of the three was capable again of rational thought. Angelique slid sideways off Julien's back and lay beside him and Jasmin, one arm round his neck and the other under Jasmin's. When Julien's male part had shrunk small and limp, he rolled off Jasmin to lie facing her, a hand on her breasts. And when they were eventually ready to move, it was Angelique's suggestion they went to the bedroom. It was more comfortable in bed, she informed them.

Jasmin knew why the suggestion was made – Angelique wanted to have another man in her absent *rentier* friend's bed. She wished to spite him in her thoughts, to give herself a memory to gloat over the next time he deserted her for his business. Julien did not know any of this, of course, but he was no fool. Angelique had said this was her apartment, but he could guess at the rent and he knew a show-girl from the Folies Bergère couldn't pay it from her salary.

A man was involved. She was being kept by someone, he had no doubt of it. The thought did nothing to stop his enjoyment of the delights she offered. If the pink sofa and bed were another man's, so much the worse for him!

The three lovers made their way into the bedroom, arms around each other's waists, Julien in the middle, a thick-bodied hairy man between two sleek naked beauties, dark-haired Angelique and reddish-brown-haired Jasmin. They left their clothes where they lay scattered on the floor – frocks, neck-tie, frilly knickers, trousers – all tangled together.

The bedroom was spacious, furnished with the same indifference to good taste as the sitting-room. On the floor were two large white polar-bear skins complete with heads, jaws open to show yellow fangs. The bed between the flattened bears was the equal of the pink velvet sofa in misdirected imagination – it was low and perfectly circular with black satin sheets!

Julien stared at it in silent surmise – what sort of man had bought this, he asked himself? Then with a grin he slid across the smooth satin when Angelique turned back the cover. It felt cool and slippery and he knew the answer to his own question. The man who paid for this had a Pasha-complex, his desire was for a harem of naked slave-girls. Angelique was his harem of one and she was busily betraying her missing Pasha. Julien grinned, the situation was deliciously comic.

The women knelt on either side of him, stroking his thighs. They examined his limp part, small, soft and innocent – they stared at each other with their eyebrows raised. So far he had made love to each of them and he was a man of fifty. Could he do more?

Jasmin nodded to Angelique over his body and winked briefly. It was why they were here, after all, to entice him beyond the furthest point he had attained before and to overwhelm him with pleasure – and addict him to having two women in bed.

Julien was on his back on the black satin. Jasmin stretched a slim arm over him and put her hand between Angelique's thighs.

'Look at this pretty little bush, Julien,' she said, a smile on her face. 'She clips it with nail scissors to keep it short, you'd like to do that for her, I'm sure. As for your big thick bush, if we trimmed that there'd be enough to stuff a cushion.'

She was running her hand over Angelique's thighs, then up to her belly button. Julien watched in fascination. He sighed when Jasmin's fingers caressed the dark little tuft of curls and the pink bare lips below. Her middle finger pressed slowly between them and sank into Angelique. Julien sighed again when the long forefinger joined the probing one – and Angelique sighed too, to feel Jasmin's fingers teasing her little wet bud. She closed her dark eyes and parted her legs wider.

'Ah, you're going stiff, *chéri*,' Jasmin informed Julien with a chuckle, and her left hand was between his legs to tug at his lengthening part.

'*Je t'adore*, Jasmin,' he murmured.

'A little exhibition, that's what you like,' she said.

She let go of him to have the use of both hands on Angelique. Julien propped himself on an elbow between the women, all the better to observe their pleasure. Angelique's knees were well apart upon the shiny black satin sheet and Jasmin had spread her petals wide to expose the pink flesh of the inside and her firm little bud. She was caressing it with a fingertip and Angelique's breath was coming in short sobs as she became more and more aroused.

'*Ah, mon Dieu* . . .' she was moaning, 'don't stop . . .'

Jasmin's knees were hard up against Julien's hip and she was leaning over him, completely engrossed in what she was doing to Angelique. Because she was bending forward those beautiful breasts of hers swung below her and Julien reached up to fondle them, but without letting his eyes stray away from what was happening to Angelique. Her head was thrown back, her eyes were closed, she was caressing her own breasts, plucking at their firm buds with feverish fingers.

'You're going to do it now, Angelique,' Jasmin breathed, her hands fluttering between her friend's thighs. 'Show Julien how you do it, *chérie!*'

The onset of ecstasy threw Angelique into spasms, her smooth belly heaving, her hands clawing at her breasts. She wailed like an amorous cat on a roof at night, her back arching like a bowstring.

'Good, good, good!' said Jasmin. 'That's it!'

At last Angelique's throes ended. She opened her eyes to look down at Julien with a knowing grin, then let her beautiful body collapse over him. Her hot belly pressed over his now fully stiff part. She rubbed herself against it a little, persuading it to leap against her skin.

'You're ready again,' she said, grinning at the open-mouthed expression on Julien's face. She changed position until she had her breasts over his hardness, she squeezed it between them.

'Ah, you like that!' she exclaimed. She saw the look in his eyes, delicious sensations quivering through him from what she was doing. Julien gasped, certain it would not require much to make him spurt over her breasts.

When Angelique saw she had him furiously aroused, she got off him so Jasmin could take her place. He squirmed and babbled in delight as Jasmin straddled his hips, her petals slippy against his skin.

'Watch this, Julien,' she said.

She drew the engorged head of his hard-standing part between her spread thighs, touching the wet lips he was trying to feel beneath her red-gold tuft. Her hand slid up and down, rubbing the head against her exposed bud.

What she was doing aroused him to a pitch of frenzy — it was impossible for him to remain passive any longer. He reached out to sink his fingers in the flesh of Jasmin's beautiful thighs. He held her fast while he gave a tremendous upward jerk of his loins that drove his stiffness through her clasping fingers and up between those slippery lips she was holding open.

The climax was instant. Jasmin cried out to feel his passion spurting into her. She bumped up and down heavily on him until she had all his fifteen centimetres inside her, jerking to the urgent spurting of his desire. She screamed shrilly and she, too, dissolved in ecstasy while Angelique squeezed her breasts.

Very soon after that Julien slid into contented sleep, a

warm female on either side of him beneath the black satin sheets. He was pleased – and just a little surprised – he had been capable of doing so much. Twenty years ago, ah yes, that was a story of another colour – in those days he was tireless! And fearless! Beautiful film stars, sexy starlets – he made love to them all and flicked his fingers at boyfriends or husbands who imagined they had a prior claim.

They had restored his hot-blooded youth, these two enchanting creatures from the Folies Bergère – a miracle to thank God for. Individually they were so very desirable, he would be fortunate to have either as a girlfriend, Jasmin or Angelique. Together – well, it had to be admitted that the combination was completely devastating! A matched pair, like book ends with him in between – delicious thought!

Delightfully fatigued though he was, when he slept he dreamed of them, so intense was their hold on his imagination. And when he awoke he was alone in the big round bed. Daylight showed at the windows and he heard traffic noises on the boulevard below. He slid out of bed, stretching like a cat pleased with itself and went in search of the women. He thought his clothes were probably still in the sitting-room where he had taken them off. He explored the apartment barefoot and naked.

He heard voices. He opened a door and encountered a sight to gladden the heart of the Caliph of Baghdad. It was a bathroom – but such a bathroom! It was large and completely carpeted with a long-haired white substance that he took to be goat hair. And there in the centre was the bath – circular and of pink marble, sunk into the floor.

Just like a film set, Julien said to himself. He felt at home. In the bath Jasmin and Angelique sat side by side,

259

their bodies gleaming pearl-pink through warm scented water. They had large-sized breakfast cups in their hands and were drinking coffee as they soaked and chatted. Julien sat on the edge of the bath, up to his knees in the water, looking at them in admiration.

'*Bon jour, chéri*,' said Jasmin, smiling over her cup at him.

Julien put his hands to his mouth and blew kisses at both of them. He eased himself into the bath and lay down between them, his arms round two perfect pairs of shoulders. Both women gave him a smacking kiss on the cheek at the same moment. They were like two sleek seals smoothing themselves against him, perfect breasts breaking the rippling surface.

'Not that it matters,' he said, 'but what time is it?'

'Who cares?' said Jasmin. 'About midday, I think.'

'I'll get you some coffee,' Angelique offered and she heaved her long wet pink body out of the bath. She knelt on the side to kiss his forehead, her superb breasts dangling toward him. Julien slipped a hand between her thighs for a moment and she laughed and padded away on scarlet-nailed bare feet.

'What do you think, was my idea to invite Angelique along to join us a good one?' asked Jasmin, her fingers playing lazily with his limp part.

'It was a magnificent idea!' he said. '*Je t'adore*, Jasmin.'

'Do you want her to come with us again, sometime?' she asked very casually.

'But of course, *chérie*! From now on, I want you both together every time.'

Jasmin said that was outrageous. A little frolic one evening with a friend who was on her own with nothing to do, yes. But as a regular arrangement? *Bon Dieu* – nobody had two girlfriends! It was unheard-of! A look of disappointment came over Julien's face and he appeared so very mournful that Jasmin knew she was on the right track.

Even if she herself agreed to this irregular proposition, she told him, Angelique might not be willing to become a member of a threesome as a steady arrangement. And, apart from that, there were other difficulties.

At this moment Angelique returned to the bathroom, bringing a large cup of *café-au-lait*. She left wet footprints on the way out but not coming back, Julien observed, delighted to see how her hips swayed as she walked. She got back into the bath – and while Julien sipped the fragrant coffee, Jasmin explained what she and Julien had been talking about.

'What you want is impossible, Julien,' said Angelique. 'Even if I could be persuaded – and I do not know whether I can be or not – there is a formidable problem. You have seen my apartment for yourself. It is not a miserable little room in a tenement. It belongs to a man who wishes to marry me.'

Jasmin nodded in sympathy, even though she knew the chance of Jean-Jacques Chelle wanting to marry Angelique was zero – or of marrying anyone come to that! She thought it very probable the *rentier* was already married and had a family somewhere out of sight and out of mind.

Julien accepted the story at face value, his mind had become subservient to his desire for the beautiful duo sitting in the bath with him.

'I understand perfectly,' he said, 'that you could not continue to live here. Do you love this man?'

Angelique shrugged her shapely wet shoulders.

261

'I have a certain affection for him,' she said, 'otherwise I would never have agreed to live in an apartment he pays for. As to love, that is something else.'

'You may be assured I would provide an apartment just as good as this one,' said Julien sincerely, 'for you and for Jasmin to share. It would be necessary for the three of us, when we make love together, to have space and comfort and privacy. There is no need to worry about apartments.'

'That's a very generous offer Julien is making,' said Jasmin to her friend, her hand stroking idly under water between his legs. 'You ought to think about it very seriously.'

'That won't stand up again,' Angelique commented, grinning as she nodded in the direction of Julien's submerged belly.

'If that's what you think,' Jasmin retorted, 'you're wrong – I know what he can do. It's starting to go stiff already.'

'Perhaps you can persuade me to become part of this *ménage-à-trois* that you want,' said Angelique, sliding down in the bath until only her head and a rounded hip showed above the scented water. 'I have a very affectionate nature, Jasmin can tell you that – and I like you very much, Julien.'

'Then I shall do everything in my power to persuade you,' he said, 'and Jasmin, whom I adore to distraction, will help me.'

'Of course, *chéri*,' said Jasmin.

Julien's head rested on the marble rim of the bath on a small pink cushion. His eyes were closed, there was a contented look on his face as Jasmin stroked him. She winked at Angelique, to signify events were very much in their favour. Angelique winked back and grinned. This was not the time to talk about becoming film stars, that would come later when Julien had installed the two of them in a nice apartment and was addicted beyond cure to making love in a trio.

'Let me feel what you've got down there, Jasmin,' she said in a sexy voice. 'Is it really stiff again? Oh, Julien, it is!'

MICHEL IS
RECLAIMED

When Solange Barbot moved into Michel's dismal little room with him it was to be just for the night, until she made other arrangements. But sharing his narrow bed changed her views and several hours of making love to her next day changed his. It was not that he discovered an ardent passion for her, in some ways he found her deeply unsympathetic but she was immediately and permanently available.

In contrast, the great and overwhelming love of Michel's life, Suzette Bernard, was not. True, she was happy to see him when he went to her apartment and she let him make love to her and matched his desire with her own. But she didn't return his love – she was fond of him, that's what it amounted to. And to be so deep in love and that love un-requited – ah, what desolation for the sensitive young poet!

Solange didn't love him either, he had no illusion about that, but she was always there, day and night, ready for him to put his hands up her roll-top black pullover and fondle her little breasts. She was a free spirit, Solange, she wore no brassiere to hinder him. And whatever the time of day, she never refused to sit on his knee for him to slip a hand up her skirt and feel her – she had no underwear to get in the way!

If the truth were told, she could afford neither brassiere nor knickers, nor any clothes other than her Existentialist uniform of drab black. She had no employment, no skills and no interest in acquiring either. Her few material needs were solved by moving in with young men who could afford food. And a bottle of cheap wine, of course.

Though she was never a student, Solange at eighteen had learned the central doctrine of Existentialism from students she slept with – existence has no purpose except to do what is pleasing to the individual. This lesson she applied with simple and devastating logic to her own daily life. After her quarrel with the artist-genius, she moved in with Michel Radiguet. He had been brought up in a conventionally religious family and found it impossible to make head or tail of her modern philosophy but that was not important. From her viewpoint Michel was an improvement on the painter, he was better-looking, he was easier-going, kinder and less temperamental.

In the important matter of contenting her in bed, Michel was more diligent than Jules the genius had been. The reason for it was easily seen – the artist-student attended classes from time to time and he also spent hours painting pictures of tremendous significance. Michel had given up all studies, he did nothing, all his energies and imagination went into pleasuring Solange.

As for money, there was nothing to choose between them. Jules and Michel both depended on an allowance from home. It paid the rent and bought simple meals in cheap restaurants. For Solange that was enough, she lived for the moment and never looked beyond. Whether it was enough for Michel, he didn't say. His grief and disappointment over Suzette were his secret, he never mentioned these misfortunes.

But there comes a day in human affairs when an annoyance long ignored insists on forcing itself upon the attention. And this day came for Michel after only a few weeks with Solange. It was in the afternoon on a fine sunny day and the streets of the Latin Quarter thronged with interesting people strolling nowhere.

Though the sun was shining, for Michel and Solange it was not a fine sunny day at all – in fact, a squall was approaching. An unfortunate sequence of events began in bed that morning, when Michel woke to find Solange down beneath the sheet fondling his upstanding part and touching the wet tip of her tongue to it.

The majority of men would be delighted to be woken up by such affectionate attentions – and why not? After all, Solange was eighteen years old, slender of body, enthusiastic for sexual pleasure – and stark naked in bed. Ordinarily, Michel too would be happy to be woken by her in this intimate manner. But alas, the touch of her hand turned his sleeping mind toward Suzette and he dreamed about her.

They were in her bedroom, the shutters and curtains closed to create a secret perfumed world of desire. He was lying on his back on Suzette's bed, she had opened his trousers and was playing with his stiff and throbbing part. She was murmuring that she loved him, she wanted him to be with her forever, she would never let him leave her again. The touch of her hand was sending delicious thrills through him, he felt his male pride growing stronger with each flick of her fingers. Any moment now she would roll over on her back and open her legs to receive him.

Then he woke to find himself in his own hard and narrow bed – the fingers stroking him, the lips kissing him, were Solange's. He stared up bleakly at the cracked ceiling, disappointment in his heart – and a certain vague feeling of dislike for Solange, who had brought on the wonderful dream which she was unable to fulfil. She had cheated him, this Solange, she had aroused his deepest emotions, only to destroy them merely by being who she was when he awoke, instead of the woman he truly loved! It was hateful, hateful of her and he loathed her!

But after all is said, he *was* aroused, and she was in his bed and naked and extremely willing . . . only a fool would refuse the pleasure of her warm young body. He slipped his hands into her armpits, where she was unshaven and natural, he pulled strongly upward to bring her up the bed until he could kiss her. She had not troubled to remove the cosmetics on her face before getting into bed with him the night before. Young as she was, her white face and eyes heavily rimmed with blue-black gave an appearance almost of a clown at the Cirque Medrano!

When Michel got his hand between her thighs, he found she was moist and ready. He guessed she had caressed herself before he woke up – she had woken him with caresses precisely because she had aroused herself and wanted another satisfaction beyond that she could provide herself. Early in their brief friendship he had discovered this was something Solange did without shame, and often.

If they spent an evening in a cellar listening to the singers and drinking cheap wine, and he was a little too tired or just a little too drunk to make love to her before they fell asleep, she turned on her back and put a hand between her spread thighs – and rubbed herself to a gasping climax. Sometimes this roused Michel from his torpor, as no doubt it was intended to, and he rolled on to her bare belly and jabbed into her.

As he did this morning, when he woke in disillusionment

from his dream of Suzette. But his fifteen centimetres of hard flesh were not disillusioned – by no means! That part of him rarely failed to respond when called upon to do its duty, and then only occasionally, late at night after a heavier than usual intake of cheap red.

He lay on her, his cheek against her pale cheek, her slender legs wound tight about his waist, and thumped away gladly until he satisfied them both. All the while he was doing it, his eyes were closed and he thought of Suzette and pretended it was her underneath him. As a result, he was very miserable afterward.

A poor start to the day! And it got worse. They were without money – Michel had spent his month's allowance and had nothing until his father sent the next instalment which was not due for a week. Meanwhile he and Solange had to eat and pay the rent, although that could wait, he thought. He'd sold the shirts Suzette gave him, all except two, to a second-hand clothes dealer. They had gone weeks ago. The only item of any value either he or Solange now owned was the St-Christophe medallion she wore round her neck.

It wasn't worth much, not being gold, only gold-plated and on a long chain of similarly little value. But perhaps it could be pawned for a few francs. Enough to buy a loaf of bread or two, some cheese and a bottle of red – food for a couple of days if they were careful. Except there was a problem – Solange didn't want to part with her St-Christophe.

For a girl who claimed not to believe in anything whatsoever, who said religion was only superstition, she was oddly attached to the memory of the burly saint who carried people on his back across a river somewhere or other. She believed he looked after her, guided her footsteps and saved her from harm. This she had been taught as a child, of course. It would bring dreadful bad luck to pawn St-Christophe, she told Michel.

They wrangled over this for some time, Michel hungry and in a wretched state of mind, Solange ruthless in determination not to forfeit the heavenly protection of the Saint. At last an idea occurred to her – she would ask Aunt Berthe for a loan to tide them over until the mail brought Michel's next money from home. Who was Aunt Berthe? he enquired and learned she was a sort of cousin of Solange's mother. Michel shrugged, what did it matter what sort of relation she was so long as she had cash to lend?

Solange said her aunt lived in the 14th Arondissement. Michel was not a Parisian and had only a hazy idea where that lay. And as they had only ten centimes between them, it was necessary to walk. Without breakfast, not even a cup of coffee, they set out on their journey. First to the Boulevard St-Germain, then along the rue de Rennes, long and straight between fine buildings and shops, heading toward the southern suburbs.

They came to the Montparnasse cemetery and went on past it on the Avenue du Maine. Neither Michel nor Solange knew, nor cared, that many famous Frenchmen were buried here in the Montparnasse cemetery. Guy de Maupassant, who wrote some stories of brothels and expired in his forties of an unfortunate malady acquired in one – and also the celebrated poet Charles Baudelaire, who found a strange beauty in the ugliest of street-women, or so he said in his verses. He, too, came to a sad and early end for the same reason as Monsieur de Maupassant.

But let it not be believed that the Montparnasse cemetery was the last resting place only of men-about-town. The memorials of other famous unfortunates are to be found here, as for instance Colonel Alfred Dreyfus, who either was or was not a traitor to France, but who was most certainly transported to Devils Island after his court-martial. Then he was brought back to be pardoned after the novelist Emile Zola caused a fuss in the newspapers.

Perhaps the most unfortunate of them all is the great explorer Dumont d'Urville, who braved every danger in the early nineteenth century when he voyaged right round the world. He returned triumphant only to perish in a train crash in the suburbs of Paris.

On the Avenue du Maine Solange began to look a little anxious – she thought they should take the next street to their right – or perhaps the one after that. From this hesitation Michel saw she did not often visit her Aunt Berthe. His conclusion being that they were not on such friendly terms that lending and borrowing money was merely a matter of asking. At least she was certain the street they wanted was off to the right.

It was a little street with the promising name of Maison-Dieu and from there they turned into an even narrower street. Michel wrinkled his nose and glanced about warily. The houses were all old and shabby, the pavement was cobbled and broken. In several of the doorways, as Solange led him down the street, he saw women standing together. They were bold-faced women with meaningless smiles in cheap-flowered print frocks, smoking cigarettes and leering at men passing. There was no mystery about their vocation or about what went on in the houses behind them.

In a fit of post-war morality the Government may have passed a law to close the brothels, the celebrated establishments that were part of the heritage of Paris, but no government can stop the commerce between men and women. If any evidence was needed, this little street of dingy houses provided it. It was improbable in the extreme that Baudelaire or de Maupassant ever came looking for diversion in this miserable *quartier*.

Solange shouted *Auntie Berthe*! and waved at someone further along the street.

Aunt Berthe sat on a straight-backed wooden chair, outside a house, on the cobbles. She was about forty, plump, round-faced, with dark coarse hair cut short and frizzed up in front. A string of fake pearls dangled down to an imposing but excessive bosom.

She got to her feet and hugged Solange to her, seized Michel and hugged him too, squeezing him against the cushions of flesh under her thin cotton frock.

They went inside into an ordinary sitting-room, very much to the relief of Michel who didn't know what to expect and feared there might be a double bed for instant use when customers came in. There were chairs and a table, old and shabby, a threadbare sofa and a framed coloured print on the wall of General de Gaulle, evidently cut from a popular magazine some years before.

He was even more relieved to note that Aunt Berthe displayed a certain affection for Solange – it suggested a small loan was not perhaps out of the question. And when Berthe offered coffee he was convinced that they had come to the right place in their dire need even though he was not included in the conversation between Solange and her aunt. Far from it – he found he was the subject of it and they talked as freely about him as if he weren't there at all!

How did he keep Solange if he hadn't got a job? Auntie wanted to know. A student? Had he been kicked out of the University? Where were his family? Was he in trouble with the police? The questions were very direct and the answers unnecessarily frank, in Michel's opinion.

Berthe studied his slim body and sensitive features with some doubt on her face and asked Solange if he was any use in bed.

'He doesn't look up to much,' she said, 'he's got no flesh on his bones.'

Solange laughed and told her Aunt he was a good performer and a very regular one, not a day missed.

'That's good,' Berthe said with an approving nod of her head. 'Make him do it all you want – it's the only thing men are good for. And some of them aren't even good for that.'

Perhaps it was Aunt Berthe's mode of life that gave her this unpleasant view of men, Michel said to himself. He maintained a calm expression and said nothing as Solange grinned and surveyed him in a proprietorial way. Berthe stared with bold eyes at the front of his trousers, evidently estimating his size.

Michel found it impossible to guess what type of men thought Berthe's overblown charms worth paying for. In his imagination he stripped off her floral-pattern frock to see her naked – the round fat belly with deep creases across it, the massive thighs and the coarse doormat between, the ridiculously large breasts flopping down . . . no, no, no! Even if she undressed and offered him a free ride on her tub of a belly, he would not be able to avail himself of the doubtful pleasure! His pride would refuse to oblige, it would remain limp and small when confronted with so huge a challenge.

Eventually, after much personal and exasperating chat between Solange and her auntie, the purpose of the visit was mentioned. A look of horror appeared on Berthe's round face. The notion of lending money, even to a blood relative, upset her. It might be said, though the comparison

273

seemed unlikely, Berthe was feeling all the outraged revulsion of a pious young virgin when a young man for the first time attempts to slip his hand up her skirt!

Solange pleaded, she even offered to leave St-Christophe as a pledge she would return and repay the debt. Michel expected to receive money from home in a week or ten days – the debt would be repaid instantly! And what was a week to auntie? It mean nothing. Surely she did not want the niece who adored her to go hungry?

The look on Auntie's face was still very unpromising. Solange got up and went to kiss her cheek and wheedle. Seeing all this, Michel became more dejected. What the devil was he doing in the house of a . . . of Berthe. Had he sunk so low as to be dependent on the whim of this fearsome woman?

It galled him to know he could ask Suzette for money and she would give it to him without hesitation. She believed he should have a share of what she earned, because he wrote the words for her songs. But in Michel's mind, his poems for her were sacred, there could be no question of accepting a cash reward – it was utterly impossible to defile his passion for her in this way! And to creep back to her, after staying away for weeks – no, he would be too ashamed to look her in the face!

Aunt Berthe proved to be not entirely without heart, although it took her some time to discover it. She patted Solange's face and kissed her and handed over twice what she had asked for. As a loan, it must be understood, and only for ten days. As for the medallion, she wouldn't for a moment consider depriving Solange of St-Christophe's protection. For herself she had always found St-Sulpice to be a sympathetic saint and ready to grant favours when requested.

They parted with hugs and kisses, Michel was clutched to that pneumatic but sagging bosom again. And as they left Berthe even pinched his bottom.

'You make sure you look after my niece right,' she admonished him, 'give her a good seeing-to when you get home.'

It was not necessary to walk all the way back, they travelled by the Metro from opposite the cemetery. And though Solange was delighted by the success of their visit, Michel was in a sombre mood. The Metro carriage was full, they stood near the door and Solange pressed herself against him. Evidently she had taken to heart her auntie's parting instructions to Michel and was eager to be *seen-to*!

No one paid any attention to them, of course. Lovers are part of the urban scenery of Paris, they are unnoticed as they kiss, hold hands on buses, caress each other in the parks – and even when they enjoy a complete stand-up union in an alley. Solange pressed the palm of her hand against Michel's trousers, cupping his male part through the cloth, grinning up in glee while she rubbed him to make him stiff.

It took no great effort to achieve that. She was a young and pretty girl, he was a young and hot-blooded man. Dislike her as he might – and he almost loathed her at that moment – his flesh responded without demur. It stood upright and hard in a moment.

'We won't eat in a restaurant,' she whispered, 'we'll stop in a shop to buy a bottle of wine and bread and cold meat and take it to bed. I'm going to wear you out with love.'

It was Solange who had the cash, naturally, she had put it in a pocket in her black skirt. She would be the one to spend it – Michel would never get his hands on a *sou* of it. Yet he was the one who would repay Auntie when his student money arrived from his father back home in Fecamp. Student! He had given that up because of Suzette, now he had given her up! What would it all lead to, what was his life to become?

These and similarly miserable and self-pitying considerations occupied Michel's mind. He stood on the pavement outside a shop waiting for Solange to buy food and a bottle of wine and there on the opposite pavement, standing on the corner, he saw a band of street singers.

There were three of them, two women and a man who played the music on an old accordion. He had thin wavy hair, this man, and a pencil-line moustache, evidently he saw himself as some type of heart-throb. A cigarette hung from the side of his mouth and he kept his eyes closed while he played. One of the singers was in her forties, a thin-faced, sharp-nosed woman with a bush of dark hair held back with cheap slides. The other was young enough to be the accordionist's girlfriend. She wore a white blouse with red spots and her long hair was tied back with a ribbon to hang in a ponytail.

Their voices were not very good, the accompaniment left a lot to be desired musically, but the song brought tears of chagrin to Michel's eyes. He heard the familiar words of '*Place Vendôme*', Suzette's hit record, based on the poem he wrote for her before he even knew her. And hearing this cracked version by a trio of street musicians, he realised for the first time what a success she had become. She was a star.

And this was the beautiful woman he loved to distraction. He had run away from her with a broken heart after writing '*Rue de la Paix*' for her. That too had become a hit – it was on the radio daily. And he, the poet who made these successes possible, what had he done? Why was he standing outside a little shop while his thin and untalented girlfriend bought cheap food to eat in bed after he made love to her? Without a thought for his own well-being, he had exchanged fascinating and sumptuous Suzette for Solange.

'*Merde!*' he said loudly, angering a man passing by, who took this as some sort of insult directed at himself. He stopped and retaliated in grossly abusive words.

But Michel was gone. He was running along the street, down in the gutter to avoid the slow-moving pedestrians, honked at most furiously by drivers of cars, who considered no one had a right to use the road except themselves. Michel didn't care, he knew where he was going. Nor did he care what Solange would think of him when she came out of the shop with a long loaf under an arm and a bottle of wine in her hand.

He was going to see Suzette, he was going to beg forgiveness for deserting her. He loved her, how could he have been so very insane as to leave her? And though she didn't love him in the same way, she was very affectionate to him, and that would have to be enough. An arrangement could be reached.

Needless to say, this impetuous decision of Michel's to visit Suzette caused certain problems, as unexpected decisions always do. Her apartment on the rue de Rome, by the Gare St-Lazare, from where he was on the Left Bank was just as far as the walk earlier that day to where Auntie Berthe lived. And to walk was the only way he could get to there – Solange had the money they had gone to borrow.

Michel shrugged and said *Merde* again and walked determinedly along the Boulevard St-Germain. His intention was to cross the Seine by the Pont de la Concorde and on past the Tuileries into the rue Royale and keep on going. He was hungry as a wolf, he'd eaten nothing that day. There had been no money to buy even a single bread-roll for breakfast and Solange's auntie had given them *café-au-lait* but no food.

By the time he reached Suzette's apartment and climbed up the staircase and knocked on the door, it was after six o'clock in the evening. He met a response he had not expected after coming so far to see her – no one answered his knock. She was out. And so too was her dear friend Gaby, who at least would have asked him in to sit down and rest his weary legs.

What to do? Return to Solange and his cheap room on the Left Bank? But for what purpose? He had ceased to have any regard at all for Solange. If he ever did go back there, then he would of course sit her on his knee and put his hand up her roll-top pullover to feel her soft little breasts. And up her skirt too – but that would be without any significance, merely a pleasure of the body, much like enjoying a meal in a restaurant.

As for possessions, there were none to go back to collect. He had sold his books long ago, most of the clothes Suzette had bought for him and everything of any saleable value he had brought with him to Paris when he arrived as a student two years ago. All he could leave for Solange was a towel worn very thin by use and a safety razor. She was welcome to both, Suzette would equip him in style.

He sat down on the uncarpeted landing to rest his aching legs and leaned his head against the wall. And promptly fell asleep. It had, after all, been a tiring day. An hour or more passed before a hand shook him by the shoulder and he woke with a start, unsure where he was for a moment.

Then he smiled his charming smile to see it was Suzette standing over him, a tiny frown of surprise on her perfect face. She looked ravishing, her hair shone raven black under a tiny three-cornered hat, her tailored summer suit was of rough peach silk, belted in closely at the waist and smooth over her long thighs. Michel's heart bounded, something stirred in his trousers.

'What are you doing here, Michel?' she asked.

'I walked all the way,' he said, trying to explain to her his feelings. 'I fell asleep waiting for you. I adore you, I cannot live another day without seeing you and telling you I love you. Will you forgive me for running away? I am a complete idiot.'

'Yes,' she said seriously, 'I know that. But leave it for now – come inside. You look thin and hungry.'

The good corduroy jacket she had bought him was sadly in need of cleaning and pressing, so were his grey flannel trousers. He needed the attentions of a good barber and his curly dark hair was too long over his ears and the nape of his neck.

He agreed he was hungry, though without further explanation – he was too shamefaced to provide details, even if she asked. He followed her into the apartment and into the kitchen. He sat at the table while she set a plate for him and a knife – there was crusty bread and Normandy butter and from the refrigerator she brought sliced cooked veal and salami and sausage. She mixed a salad of radish and chives and found Dijon mustard. She poured him a glass of cool white wine and set the bottle on the table.

She left him eating greedily to go and change from her superb Dior suit into something more casual. She returned ten minutes later in a thin white woollen roll-top pullover and a swirling taffeta skirt in pink and grey checks. Michel stared, thinking what a world of difference there was between Suzette in her pullover and Solange in her sombre black version. As to what was under each rolltop – Suzette's clung to her sumptuous breasts in the most provocative manner while poor Solange had little to display.

'Lucky for you that you came to see me today,' said Suzette, she was leaning against the door-post, watching him eat. 'Next week I'll be gone and the apartment will be empty.'

'You are moving to a better apartment,' he said with a little nod. He understood at once she had selected a superior address now she could afford it. 'Where is it?'

'Boulevard Lannes,' she said proudly. 'An apartment that looks out over the Bois de Boulogne.'

Michel was impressed. He didn't know what the rent was for an apartment in so very superior a location, it had to be a barrel of money, he was sure of that.

'Not the Avenue Foch?' he said, grinning at her. One of his poems had that title, it had been made into a song she had sung many, many times. It told of beautiful woman walking her fluffy little white dog on the Avenue, pausing under a tree. Her lover was waiting eagerly for her return. There were no names in the poem, but naturally the woman was Suzette and the lover Michel.

She smiled and said nothing, she wasn't going to tell him she had chosen the Boulevard Lannes because she was once at a party given by Armand Regence in an apartment there and she intended to prove she was as big a star as he was. Or would be one day.

Michel finished eating at last and gazed ardently at Suzette. He wanted many things from her. He wanted forgiveness, love and a place in her life, he wanted money to pay for a hotel room to keep him away from his former girlfriend and he wanted to make love to her. On her bed, on the kitchen table, on the sitting-room floor – no matter where. His desire was more than physical – he felt his soul and body crying out for the sublimely erotic sensations she could give him, he was desperate to be accepted by her.

But things had changed between them. Only a few weeks ago, if she saw that look in his eyes she would have stripped naked for him without a word said. But today she asked if he had brought a poem for her.

'No,' he said, abashed. 'I haven't written anything lately. I haven't been able to.'

'What a pity,' she said sweetly, 'well, now you've had enough to eat, perhaps you should write my new address down before you leave.'

Michel almost burst into tears to be treated so very casually by the woman he adored to distraction. He knew he had deserved it from her, he had behaved badly, he had been a terrible fool. He had hoped for forgiveness but it seemed Suzette was not in a forgiving mood. It was impossible to be sent away like this – he would die of a broken heart before he got to the foot of the stairs, he would be found face down on the pavement outside . . .

'Suzette, *je t'aime*,' he said. 'I cannot be away from you, my life has no meaning apart from you. I fell in love with you the first instant I saw you, the evening I heard you singing in the cellar in Montmartre. I followed you out into the street and my entire life was changed. We stood in a doorway and kissed – you cannot have forgotten those moments!'

'I remember them well,' said Suzette with a faint smile. 'You took my knickers off in the doorway and when we parted you kept them – they were in your pocket. You brought me good luck that night, Michel, I shall always be grateful to you for that.'

Gratitude was not what he wanted, he stared round-eyed at her and tried to control his aching disappointment. This was by no means how he had visualised their reunion during his long walk here from the Left Bank.

'And *you* brought me luck, and happiness,' he said, with a sad little smile. 'Because of you my poems have become hit-songs.'

'Then you must write more,' Suzette said firmly. 'Your talent demands it, your public demands it, I demand it.'

He drew in a long shuddering breath when she stooped to reach under her skirt with both hands. She slipped her knickers down and handed them to him. His hand trembled as he held silk warm from her beautiful body. It was a charming little confection of peach silk and lace, chosen to go with the Dior creation she wore when she returned to the apartment and found him asleep on the landing.

'You must find your luck again, *chéri*,' she said. 'Tuck these in your pocket, like the first time, and who knows? I hope you will be inspired to write poems again.'

Michel kissed the peach silk fervently, wishing with all his heart he was kissing the soft flesh it had covered. Suzette had a cool expression on her face as she stood leaning against the door-post, it was not the look of a woman about to ask him into her bed.

'But I shall die if you send me away like this,' he murmured, 'I only live when I make love to you.'

This ridiculous male sentimentality had no effect on Suzette, since she was sixteen men had been declaring themselves at the point of extinction – unless she saved their lives by letting them do the usual. It was not necessary to take that seriously. But she wanted something from Michel, she wanted him to write verses to be made into songs.

Jacques-Charles could compose the tunes for these words, when he was sober. The idiotic Raoul had a genius for turning simple little tunes and words into instant hits for her. But she knew neither could do anything without words to work on. Michel was important to her.

But not important enough to stroll in and out of her life as the mood took him. Dealing with Raoul she had learned a useful lesson about keeping control of men who could contribute to her greater success. Raoul was a toad, he could only be controlled by blows and contempt. Michel had a sensitive heart, he was all too easily discouraged. It was necessary to guide him into the right direction with a delicate hand.

He was still kissing her knickers reverently. She told him to lie down on the floor. The kitchen was not large, but there was room between the table and the cooker for him to stretch out at full length on the black-and-white squared linoleum. He stared up wide-eyed from this lowly position, hardly able to believe a turn in his fortunes was at hand.

Suzette kicked off her shoes and straddled him, with her feet on either side of his head, her legs apart.

He could see up her skirt, the wide taffeta skirt she had put on, he stared up the smooth columns of her silk-stockinged legs – right up to her superb bare thighs. *Ah*, he breathed, *Ah* ... he began to gasp and babble mindlessly when he saw her naked mound and the smooth-shaven lips where her thighs joined.

'So you only live when you make love to me!' she said with a faintly mocking tone in her voice. 'We shall see, *chéri*.'

She put her hands on her hips and she twisted her body from side to side, as if exercising. Her superb breasts swayed underneath her thin white roll-top pullover and she stared down at them in pride and thought the rhythmic wobble was very arousing. If she had been a dancer like Gaby, she could have stiffened every man in the audience by shaking her *nichons* about!

Michel saw nothing of this heart-stopping hula-hula dance of her breasts. His entire attention was focused up her skirt. He was watching in fascination the movement of her bare thighs. He babbled and panted. Suzette glanced down at him without a pause in her Hawaiian dance and saw the long bulge in his trousers.

She crossed her arms to slide her white pullover up over her breasts, then over her head. She held it at arms' length and let it fall to the floor, she undid her close-fitting brassiere and threw that after the pullover.

She adored her breasts, their firmness and size, the elegant shape, the red-brown buds that stood proud of the pale-skinned flesh. She twisted a little faster, her eyes turned downward to admire how her unsupported charms swayed so magnificently from side to side. Ah, but they were adorable, her two beauties!

She felt Michel's hands on her ankles, gripping her tight as he moaned and stared up her swirling skirt. She looked down and saw his loins thrusting in a steady rhythm. His back was arched off the floor as he balanced on his shoulders and the cheeks of his bottom.

The bulge in his grey flannel trousers seemed impossibly big. Suzette guessed that the regularity of his movement was sliding his furiously hard part against his loose underwear.

'I wonder what you are thinking of, Michel,' she

murmured, to herself, not to him. 'I have a surprise for you, my friend.'

She clasped her breasts and stroked them until the sensations flickering through her body were too adorable to continue. She ceased to gyrate her hips, she hitched her skirt higher and she bent her knees more – and more. She allowed herself to descend slowly toward Michel's face. He shrieked like a girl and raised a trembling hand between her thighs. His tremulous fingers touched the long bare lips.

She had wondered what he was thinking of, though only to mock him a little in her mind. It would not have pleased her to know what images were filling his head. He was recalling how Solange woke him the first time she slept in his bed by sitting on his chest, her knees on his biceps to pin him to the hard mattress. Her thighs were splayed wide to let her thick brown curls touch his bare chest.

It seemed so extraordinary then, the unfamiliar touch of warm and hairy lips rubbing gently against his skin. In fact what he remembered best was a feeling of dislike, almost repulsion. But the sight and the touch aroused him soon enough. And observing Solange's self-induced climax on his chest spurred him to roll her on her back and slide on top.

Here with Suzette he was on familiar territory – no matter he was on his back on the kitchen floor! Above him, moving slowly ever closer, was no patch of curly hair – just smooth skin and the elegant pink *orchid* that was the centre of his universe!

Suzette's knees were bent almost double, she was a centimetre or two above his face. He turned his head to bite at the tender insides of her thighs in a frenzy of desire. She maintained her position, watching the frantic movement of his loins while he tried to pull her down close and kiss her. But she wouldn't let him. She braced her leg muscles and resisted – she tantalised him with the impossible.

She could hear the note of desperation in his babbling as his excitement soared higher. His fingers were probing eagerly into her, front and back together, rubbing and sliding, pulling her open, tugging to bring her down within reach of his mouth. Her climax was two seconds away, the golden sensations were growing irresistibly in her belly. She gritted her teeth and held fast, her face bright pink with effort.

Leave her for another woman, would he? Ah, the wretch! The ingrate! How was it possible to turn away from her perfection of face and body? And to imagine he could come back and plead for forgiveness and his betrayal would be forgotten? Did he think he was in a church, whispering his transgressions to a priest?

Before Michel was admitted back into her favour he had much to learn. The insolence of him – he imagined he'd come back and inside ten minutes have her on her back? It was time he learned he had to keep writing useful poems if he wanted to remain her friend. This little demonstration, raising his desires and only in part satisfying them, ought to teach him the truth!

Michel screamed shrilly and Suzette saw his grey-trousered loins jerk up off the carpet. He was spurting into his underwear, pumping his thwarted desire under his shirt and up over his belly!

'Good!' she gasped. 'Very good!'

She was very close to her orgasmic moments, the tremors were already in her belly – but she did not let herself succumb yet. She waited till Michel's frantic jerking had subsided, till she was sure he was finished and his sticky desire drained away. His hands fell away from between her thighs. His legs were twitching but that was only a reaction of the nerves.

Michel was done for – subdued and put in his place. With that thought in her mind she brought on her own pleasure. Her hands clasped her breasts, fingertips flickering delicately over the buds that stood so proudly. Down between her thighs the orgasm exploded almost at once. She shook and fell forward on Michel's limp body, her face resting on his thigh. Her loins throbbed in the long after-throes of her climax and she was smiling.

SUZETTE
AT HOME

Suzette's new apartment in the Boulevard Lannes, not far from where it met the Avenue Foch at the Porte Dauphine, had ten rooms and three bathrooms. The main rooms commanded a view over the Bois de Boulogne to the lake and beyond – in all, it was an elegant home for a star!

The move was very necessary. Because of her rising success an amazing number of people wanted to talk to her, and it was not only people who wrote songs and music and people with proposals for concerts and public appearances. There were also reporters from the popular press and from the radio, wanting to interview her. The little apartment in the rue de Rome was inadequate for this daily throng of people. And the fan mail was fast becoming too much for Madame Saumur in the apartment upstairs to handle.

Suzette persuaded Gaby to move with her, though not without a certain reluctance on the part of the dancer.

'Impossible, *chérie*!' Gaby said when Suzette first suggested it. 'I can't let you keep me!'

'I'm not suggesting it,' said Suzette. 'I shall expect you to pay rent, that's only fair.'

'But I can't afford half the rent of an apartment like that! You know how much they pay me at the Folies Bergère.'

'It's more than they used to pay me, because you dance

289

and I could only stand about naked to be stared at. But that has nothing to do with it. I only ask for the same as you pay here – half the rent of this little apartment we have shared for so long.'

'That's absurdly generous! I would prefer to live there, of course. Just think of the look on a man's face when he suggests taking me home and asks where I live. Boulevard Lannes, I say – being very casual, of course! He goggles at me, he thinks I'm joking. Or he's misheard. He asks me to repeat it . . .'

The idea amused the two women greatly, they both laughed.

'But I don't think it will work,' said Gaby. 'I know we have been the best of friends for a long time now but you are going to be a big star, rich and important, and I shall always be a dancer in the chorus-line. I do not wish to be a dependant, one of your entourage, a sort of paid companion.'

'Naturally,' Suzette agreed, 'your life is your own. You come and go as you wish, nothing will change. But it is important to me that you are there when I need to talk to you.'

'I know nothing about being a star – I'm only in the chorus! What assistance could I ever give you?'

'You said there will be an entourage around me. Already it is forming. I shall be surrounded. There will be managers, agents, music-directors, song-arrangers, dress-designers, hairdressers, publicists, accountants, magazine writers, photographers – who else, God knows! There will be an army of them, from morning to night. They will all want something from me – and they will all lie to me. I need someone I trust absolutely, someone for whom there is no point in telling me lies. Someone I can talk to and giggle with. Someone I really like. In short, you, Gaby.'

'If you put it like that . . .' said Gaby. So it was agreed
and they embraced and kissed each other on the cheek.
They went out to sit on a café terrace in the sunshine and
sip a glass of *kir* while they discussed domestic
arrangements. Both were in total agreement they never
wanted to do housework again.

Suzette was opposed to having servants live in the
apartment. It was too inconvenient – and how embarrassing
if a maid walked in at a critical moment on a sofa with a
man!

'We'll get a couple of good strong cleaners to come in
every morning,' she said, 'but not too early, we don't want
the noise of vacuum cleaners at nine if we didn't get to bed
till three.'

'One of them could bring fresh rolls in and make the
coffee,' Gaby pointed out.

At the time of the move Gaby was still on good terms
with her gynaecologist friend, Remy Courtauld. When he
saw the apartment for the first time, he was impressed. The
Boulevard Lannes was where he would like to live given
a choice but, alas, it was a little too expensive. He was
unaware Gaby was beginning to tire of him slightly – she
suggested to Suzette that she might find it amusing to try
out his curious style of love-making.

'Hah! The gynaecologist who needs a psychiatrist! You
want me to take him off your hands? You are bored being
dominated, is that it? Overmasterful types are not much to
my taste, you know that.'

'But you like men who play games,' said Gaby with a
knowing smile, 'just as I do. And with Remy it is even more
interesting because he doesn't know he is playing a game.
For him it is all very serious – which makes it comical.'

'All you are telling me is that he is slightly insane,' said Suzette, pouting her beautiful lips.

'Not insane, merely absurd, like all men,' Gaby reassured her with a shrug. 'Try him – his obsession will make you giggle.'

It was easy enough to arrange, of course. Suzette had met him several times already with Gaby. In the ordinary way of things she would have considered him an excellent boyfriend for Gaby – he was good-looking, distinguished in fact, with his smooth dark hair and neatly trimmed moustache. He was making a good living, so it was unlikely he would want to borrow money from Gaby – that fatal failing of so many men in the theatrical world! He was very well-educated and good-mannered, not a man to beat his girlfriends.

But he was also totally obsessed, according to Gaby, never sure whether a woman with her knickers off was a girlfriend or a patient. Well, it would be interesting to experience this obsession of his and discover how far it went. So, when he came to the new apartment, Gaby winked at Suzette and went to her own room for something she had forgotten, she said, giving Suzette the time to mention to Remy that she would be alone the next afternoon after five.

Needless to say, Remy was enormously impressed by Gaby's dear friend, especially now she was halfway to becoming a star – and evidently making formidable amounts of money. To say nothing of the inescapable fact she was stunningly beautiful. And when she murmured that she would be alone next day, not for a moment did he display any vestige of loyalty to Gaby or the least scruple in betraying her. He smiled suavely and bowed.

There he was at the door punctually at five o'clock the

next day, smelling of expensive cologne and wearing a well-cut suit in a shade of tan, a bow-tie of maroon silk and a small yellow flower in his button-hole.

Suzette offered her hand to shake and Remy kissed it. He did so with a wariness that indicated he was a little uncertain. She had said nothing the day before, given no hint of her reasons, only a plain statement she would be alone after five. She smiled to herself to see his hesitation, some men would have embraced her by now. It would be amusing to tease him.

The long and elegant sitting-room was furnished in a style he found a little too . . . well, too contemporary, perhaps, for his own taste. The furniture was upholstered in soft white leather, the floor was of glossy black tiling, with white goat-skin rugs scattered about. Remy's own preference was for the traditional in the decor of his apartment, as in his attitude toward women.

They chatted for a while of nothing very much, Remy listening for some guide to what was expected. And eventually, keeping a straight face, Suzette announced she would prepare herself for examination. Her bedroom was the second on the left – he should come there in five minutes. A look of astonishment passed over his face, this was not what he had expected.

'Examination?' he muttered, eyebrows rising. 'But it was not made clear to me . . .'

Suzette looked at him steadily, then crossed her superb legs, the faint hiss of silk sliding over silk drew his attention. He recovered his self-possession and nodded his agreement with as good grace as he could manage. Suzette smiled and left him.

He waited the five minutes and followed the directions to her bedroom. It was large and pleasantly furnished with a view over the Bois, not that he had time or inclination for admiring the view. Suzette had undressed completely, except for a little camisole of blush-pink lace, so very flimsy and transparent it concealed nothing.

She lay on a broad bed of the most modern design, on her back, her knees up and her feet well parted. Her hands were under her head, she looked relaxed and comfortable. She turned her head to look at Remy when he approached.

'All ready for you,' she said sweetly.

'But I have brought nothing with me . . .' he said doubtfully.

He was staring in fascination between Suzette's open thighs. He was enchanted by her prominent and smooth-shaven charms – so much so he completely forgot his professional objections, if he really had any. He removed his jacket, folded it and put in on a chair. He turned back his white cuffs.

'It is better to approach more directly,' he said, 'not from the side but between the legs. Allow me to position you.'

'Of course,' she said with a noncommittal smile.

With careful hands he turned her across the bed, knees high, feet tucked back to her bare bottom. He brought a chair from by the dressing-table and placed it where he could sit very close to her smooth-petalled orchid. Suzette maintained an expression of indifference during these manoeuvres, but she noted his eyes seemed to glow and below the neat moustache his mouth was open a little.

He began his examination. His touch was delicate and his fingers moved over the smooth flesh between her open thighs, exploring the soft lips. It was immensely arousing, this gentle touch of fingertips on satin-smooth skin, little tremors of delight were running through Suzette's belly when at last he slowly pressed his finger into her.

He was becoming pink in the face, his breathing was a little faster than it had been before, but he remembered to ask most of the questions gynaecologists ask on these occasions. Suzette assured him there were no problems of any kind. To her mind all was in the best of order, as no doubt he would confirm.

'Yes,' he murmured, sounding breathless, 'the best of order – excellent order. It's a delight to see . . . I mean to see so very healthy and pretty a . . . I mean, so well-functioning a . . .'

He could have admired Suzette's superbly shaped breasts, the little camisole did virtually nothing to conceal them from him. But no, his interest was elsewhere, his gaze was fixed between her thighs, on her intimate nudity. He had parted the long pink lips to see her secret little bud – his fingertip touched it in a manner that sent shivers of pleasure through her.

Suzette was no longer observing his face. She closed her eyes and let the sensations ripple through her, content to leave all in Remy's hands now. She felt a finger deep inside her, probing gently, caressing rather than examining her. Was she a patient or something else now? she asked herself with a little grin. He was stroking her moist bud with such delicate skill that it was surely only a matter of half a minute more and she would reach her climax!

'It is necessary to change the position a little,' she heard him say. 'Remain calm and leave everything to me.'

His hands slid under her bottom and he pulled her towards him in a careful glide. Her legs parted on either side of his waist.

'Oh!' she said in surprise, but it was an exciting surprise.

'I shall test the reflexes, just lie still and keep your mind a blank,' he said, his voice blurred by a passionate obsession.

His fingers fluttered over her bud, maintaining the delicious suspense. She felt a certain trembling under her bare bottom, a tiny rhythmic shaking of his legs. She knew what it must be – he had opened his trousers and was stroking his own stiffness!

She had only to open her eyes to observe him in this fervent act of self-gratification. It was the tantalising beauty of her bare-shaven *jou-jou* that had forced him to this uncontrollable act! The thought intensified Suzette's arousal but she kept her eyes closed. The tiny spasms in her belly grew stronger and more demanding. Remy might pretend to be a doctor but in fact he was in the grip of his compulsion. In a moment it would all be over!

His caress brought her to an overwhelming crisis of pleasure. She moaned and writhed on her back and her dangling legs kicked on either side of him. She heard him gasp loudly and at last she opened her eyes – just in time to see him reach his orgasm. His hand-held stiffness strained upwards through his fingers to spurt its passion at her. And though he jerked backward in his chair he could not prevent his outpouring gushing warmly on to the soft lips he was holding apart.

'*Zut alors!*' said Gaby, when Suzette related these events to her. 'He's never done that to me, not yet anyway. But I've never pretended I wanted to be examined. Did you get him to do better later?'

'Naturally. When he'd got his breath back I told him I had no objection at all to his perverse little pleasures – I would let him *examine* me whenever he wished – but in return I expected to be properly thrilled whenever I felt like it. He was strangely embarrassed but eventually we came to understand each other.'

'Don't tell me you persuaded him to make love to you lying on your back!' Gaby exclaimed. 'I've never succeeded with him!'

'No, it was how you described it to me – he knelt on the bed and held me so I was very nearly upside-down. He couldn't slide all the way in like that but it was very exciting. Perhaps he has a mental block that stops him doing it the usual way. But I shall invite him round again, unless you object, *chérie.*'

'Have him all you want,' Gaby said generously. 'I'll hang on to him for the time being, I need him to take me out. But when I meet someone I like better, I shall drop him. Unless he drops me first, of course, for you.'

'There is no danger of that,' Suzette assured her. 'I have no intention of letting him *examine* me more than once a week or so – his perversities are amusing, but only occasionally, not as a regular routine.'

They were also in perfect accord, Suzette and Gaby, about the poet Michel. Suzette insisted he moved into the new apartment – it was too risky to let him loose like a homeless stray tomcat. She gave him a room of his own, with Gaby she took him shopping for new clothes and she gave him cash at the start of each week to pay for his meals in restaurants. For a more reliable person it would have been a monthly transfer into a bank account but she didn't trust Michel to cope satisfactorily with that. Banknotes in his hand once a week – that was best for him.

He responded well to his new circumstances, he was able to compose verses again! One of these new little poems of his that seemed to hold great promise was called '*Faubourg St-Honoré*'. It told of a beautiful woman in one of the impossibly chic shops there. As she looks at wispy silk underwear she thinks of her lover, will he take her in his arms and grow passionate with desire when he sees her wearing this?

And so on, a charming little poem. Michel had found his place in life. He adored Suzette to folly, he lived in her apartment, he saw her almost every day, she came to his room and made love with him when she remembered him. Michel had reconciled himself to never wholly possessing her, it gave an interesting touch to his verses.

When Suzette was too busy and forgot about him for a day, and Gaby was in the apartment, Michel made love to her instead. She had always liked him, though she never took him very seriously. Perhaps she viewed him as a type of big pet dog to pat on the head now and then. He had only to look at her with longing in his luminous dark-brown eyes and Gaby would smile and take him to bed.

As for Michel, he adored the slender blonde dancer, he kissed her perfect breasts with a devotion only second to that he felt for his beloved Suzette. In matters of the heart a man must be sensible, he cannot always be thinking of the woman he adores. When she is not available to him, then naturally he turns for a little consolation to another.

Needless to say, Jacques-Charles Delise was bitterly jealous of Michel's privileged position in Suzette's household. But not enough to want to move in, if he had been invited to – he would never quit his sordid room in a dingy Montmartre tenement, not for anything! Not that he was invited to move to the Boulevard Lannes, his constant drinking was too uncivilised.

But even his jealousy served a useful purpose – because of it he was determined to outdo Michel in what he took as a contest for Suzette's esteem. His tunes improved. And the other jealous idiot – Raoul de Montmilieux-Pontillard, as he called himself – visited the apartment most days. From his elevated position of commercial success he allowed himself to despise both of his collaborators, Jacques-Charles and Michel.

But he adored Suzette as they did and competed for her esteem and her smile of favour. In this respect, her smile was as much as he could hope for. She called him her big toad and though it was an endearment of a sort, it also expressed the aversion she felt at the prospect of any physical contact. She permitted him from time to time to kiss her bare backside, down on his knees, his round spectacles steaming up with passion as he pressed his wet lips to the satin flesh of a cheek!

He was well under control – Suzette had made him show her his shame, the male part that was only as big as his little finger and that at full stretch! He reddened and blustered on the day she fixed him with an unwavering stare – it was about eleven in the morning and they were in her sitting-room – and she ordered him to open his trousers and show her. He was on his knees at her feet, pudgy and awkward, he had been granted the privilege of kissing her bottom.

At that time of the morning Suzette hadn't been up very long. She was wearing an ivory silk negligee with an ostrich-feather trim round the neck and all down the front. She had one hand on the back of a white leather chair to support herself and with the other she hitched up one side of her negligee to hold it on her hip. Raoul had raised with a trembling hand her knee-length silk nightdress, to bare a perfect cheek for his kiss.

Needless to say, in this condition of partial exposure, there was more than Suzette's beautiful bottom uncovered.

Much more lay open to Raoul's admiration, perhaps even to his kiss, if he dare! But the strange truth was he dare not. He did not cast a glance at her greatest prize – he knew his level in her scheme of things. She despised him but he was useful to her.

Naturally, his male part was stiff and as big as it could be, hidden in his trousers. He was reluctant to reveal his secret, he resisted, he babbled objections, he defied her . . . in the end he gave in to her steady insistence and revealed it. He blushed as he did so, his face hot and his eyes downcast. He was certain she would sneer at his inadequacy!

But she didn't. She looked for a moment or two – which seemed to Raoul like an eternity – to confirm what she already had guessed about him. Raoul was fearful his stiff little part would wilt under her scrutiny from on high – shrink between his fingers to doll-size! But it remained hard, perhaps because he was so close to her that he could feel the warmth of her body – her beautiful creamy-skinned bottom was only ten centimetres or so from his perspiring face.

Without comment, she told him to put it away. Her voice gave no indication of her thoughts. But to have seen it was enough – like the Princess who knew Rumpelstiltskin's name, she was in a position of strength now. She turned toward Raoul and stepped a little way back from him, her silk negligee sliding down as she let go of it, concealing her naked beauty from him.

He gasped when she hooked a bare foot in a silver high-heeled slipper between his fat thighs, right up under his pompoms. She jerked her foot sharply upwards, he leaned backward to ease the sudden unbearable pressure! She jerked her foot up again – and again! Raoul squealed and fell on his back on a goat-skin rug, banging his head on the floor, his legs waving in the air.

The contempt of her gesture was enough to send him soaring to the summit of ecstatic sensation. He lay panting and squirming, his hot desire spurting inside his trousers.

'*Cochon!*' she exclaimed, and he moaned in delight.

He adored her, he knew she despised him, he knew he had to do everything in his power to make her a star. It was important to him to be brutally scorned and despised by the biggest star of them all, not just any woman. And then he would be truly happy, of that he was sure – this strange man who was once Raoul Lasse but who found it necessary to conceal his personality behind a grander though bogus name.

Gaby was not in accord with Suzette about Raoul. She disliked him for his arrogance and could hardly believe he became humble and submissive when alone with Suzette.

'He makes my flesh creep,' said Gaby with a shudder. 'I could never in a million years let him touch me. How do you stand it, being kissed by that slimy toad?'

'There's a superior type of pleasure from having a conceited pig like him on his knees begging to kiss my backside,' Suzette said with a grin. 'It makes me almost believe for a moment that there is justice in the world after all.'

It goes without saying that it was a celebrated French writer who observed that to understand women is to pity men – and that to understand men is to excuse women. Not that Suzette or Gaby had any knowledge of this observation, but they would both have recognised the truth of it immediately.

They had not been long installed in the new apartment before Julien Brocq made a surprise visit. It was in the early evening and Gaby was on the point of departing for the Folies Bergère but she lingered another ten minutes to make the acquaintance of Suzette's celebrated film-producer friend. Over a glass of cold white vermouth he told Suzette he was on his way home from his office and had the pleasant thought of looking in on her in the hope she would not be out . . . it was totally unconvincing and an expensive bouquet of scarlet roses in his hand made his explanation even less likely.

After Gaby had left, highly pleased because Julien had kissed her hand on her departure and remembered her name, he suggested to Suzette that she might like to have dinner with him – if she had no other engagement that evening, of course . . . just for old time's sake.

She was wearing the diamond bracelet he gave her the evening they became lovers – how long ago that seemed now! She wore it always, even when she was naked with another man. It had great significance for her, that bracelet, it had signalled the start of her sudden rise to success.

'Dinner? That might be nice,' she said, but with no promises of any type in her tone. 'I ran into Jasmin only the other day in the rue de Rivoli. We had a good long gossip over a cup of coffee.'

'Ah yes,' said Julien, with almost a sigh in his voice, 'dear Jasmin. Then I suppose she told you we have become friends?'

'She also mentioned Angelique Brabant and a certain apartment they now share in the rue Monge.'

'I see I have no secrets from you,' he said, sounding uneasy. 'Perhaps you disapprove of my little arrangement?'

That made Suzette laugh.

'Disapprove? What an idea! I am impressed by your stamina and appetite for life, *chéri*! You have chosen two exceptionally sexy friends in Jasmin and Angelique. I congratulate you and I wish you every happiness. You are a most enterprising man – as I have always known.'

'Enterprising . . . ah that, yes,' said Julien slowly, shrugging his shoulders. 'But to be entirely candid, as I can be with you because I know I can trust you, Suzette, it is no longer at all clear to me whose was the enterprise. The interesting *ménage* in which I find myself involved appears to have happened almost of its own accord.'

'Really? How did it begin?' she asked.

Julien, looking wearier than usual, was slumped in one of the white leather armchairs. He rubbed his chin and was silent for a moment or two while he assembled his thoughts carefully, then he related the sequence of events. It had started in the little bar near the Folies Bergère where he had gone to look for Jasmin after his return from America.

There were charming little dinners together and nights in the Hotel Ritz suite. Then came an astonishing evening when Jasmin brought her friend Angelique to dinner and afterwards they all three went to Angelique's apartment.

'Tell me about it,' Suzette urged him. She smiled to herself at the infinite gullibility of men when they were excited.

But he was unable to go that far, it was too embarrassing for him to do more than lightly sketch in the events of that highly memorable encounter. He touched briefly on the sofa, the large bed and the sunken marble bath.

'I've met the man who owns that bath,' said Suzette, amused by this account of Julien's adventures. 'His name is Chelle, I think, Jean-Jacques Chelle. He looks like a bank clerk.'

'Angelique left him for me,' said Julien with a note of

303

pride in his voice, 'although he is ten years younger. The pink marble bath was not enough to retain her affection. Nor his prowess on the circular bed with black satin sheets.'

'I am happy to see you in such good spirits,' Suzette said, a charming smile on her face to conceal what she truly believed – that Julien's principal attraction for her bare-breasted colleagues was his importance in the world of cinema.

'But that bath!' he murmured. 'If only I had words to convey the enchantment of that moment when I woke up to find my two delightful companions side by side in the perfumed water of the sunken pink marble bath! They were like water nymphs in a book of fairy-tales, their skin gleamed, their beautiful eyes glowed with affection . . . it may sound foolish to you, but in my heart I was twenty years old, I was the story-book Prince lost in a magic forest, who comes upon a clearing where a crystal brook flows – you must forgive my rambling, *chérie*!'

'You should put this pink marble bath scene in a movie,' said Suzette. 'A historical romance, perhaps. Did Madame de Pompadour lie about in a pink marble bath at Versailles? I'm sure Jasmin and Angelique would be very willing to strip off for the camera and splash about in scented water.'

'How interesting you should say that!' Julien exclaimed. 'Precisely the same thought had occurred to me! But not Madame de Pompadour, that's a little too *vieux-jeu*. I prefer a modern setting – I have set the best script-writer in Paris to work on the project.'

'I shall expect an invitation to the premiere. You look tired and in need of a holiday, Julien, you should go to the sea for some days to lie in the sun. There are dark shadows under your eyes. You have been working too hard. And not sleeping enough.'

'No,' he said with a rueful shrug. 'In the past weeks I have spent very little time working and a lot of time sleeping. The truth is my two charming little friends are wearing me out. I meet them after the Folies Bergère for a late meal and after a long night with them I sleep on into the afternoon of the next day. Sadly, I find I am not twenty years old – but it is impossible to give them up, I am besotted by them.'

'Then you must see them less often,' Suzette advised.

She had lost interest in Julien's problems. To her manner of thinking there was no problem. He ought to reduce his *ménage-à-trois* to a more usual two, himself and just one of the girls. But men were ridiculously vain about their sexual abilities, he would doubtless continue to frolic with the pair of them until he had worn himself to a thread.

When he again suggested dinner, she hesitated. She liked him but she was unwilling to endure an evening of listening to him on the subject of Jasmin and Angelique. He guessed what was in her mind and promised not to say another word about them for the entire evening. And he was as good as his word, he took her to a very good restaurant and, with no need to impress her, he was the interesting and amusing companion she remembered.

It was not late when a taxi dropped them off at the Boulevard Lannes, hardly eleven o'clock. There was no question at all in Suzette's mind – Julien was not staying. He could come in for a last drink if he wished but before midnight he was going to be on his way home. He needed to sleep, alone. She did not propose to become a refuge for love-worn men, however much she happened to like them. Their problems were their problems.

The lift up to her apartment was small, Julien smiled and put his arms round her, kissed her and smiled again.

'I know I am a fool,' he said. 'I devote myself to two women who have little interest in me other than what I can be cajoled into doing to prosper their career – while the simple truth is I have always adored you and still adore you now.'

Suzette smiled briefly and shrugged. Why were men so absurdly sentimental? she wondered. Someone ought to compel Julien to go away on a month's rest-cure – in the Alps, where he would have time and leisure to put his emotions in order.

The lift stopped at her floor and the door slid open. Instead of getting out to accompany her to her apartment, Julien stood close and slipped a hand into her silver-beaded evening jacket. He stroked her breasts through the coffee-coloured silk evening frock she had put on to go out with him. It was the lightest of caresses, his respect for her was apparent in his touch.

'If only I could,' he said, 'but it is beyond me at present.'

Whether he spoke the truth or not, he put his hand under her skirt and felt between her thighs. She shook her head at him.

'Julien, Julien, what is to be done with you?' she said in a lightly mocking tone. 'I am not your girlfriend, *chéri* – Jasmin and Angelique are waiting for you. But it would be better to go to your real home and sleep.'

'If we all did what was best for us, life would be impossibly boring,' said Julien.

His hand was inside her tiny silk knickers, he caressed the smooth lips between her legs with gentle fingers. The lift door began to close itself slowly, soon they would be carried down to the ground floor again. He halted the door with a foot, it was held about halfway open, the lift was immobilised.

'For the sake of old times together,' he murmured and he stroked her quickly but lightly.

'Julien . . . this is absurd,' she whispered. But because she had a great regard for him, she slid her feet apart to let him have his way.

Both hands were up under her frock now as he slid her knickers some way down her thighs and stroked the perfect cheeks of her bottom. Suzette leaned her back on the mirrored side of the lift and closed her eyes. She was thinking of a certain evening in Montmartre, where her singing career began, and a young poet in a roll-top pullover like a sailor, who made love to her in a doorway, standing up.

As for Julien, evidently he had overstrained himself until he was unable to do it. Let him have this substitute pleasure, the memory of what he used to do to her in those days when she went with him to the Hotel Ritz. The fingers of one hand caressed up and down in the crease of her bare bottom; the middle finger of the other hand fluttered over her secret bud, making it moister and firmer. She felt her orgasm hurtling toward her like a lift with a broken cable, accelerating as it fell.

'Suzette, do it for me now!' Julien whispered urgently.

'For you, *chéri* . . .' she sighed. Her legs were shaking and in her belly the golden spasms began. By a huge effort of will she opened her eyes and stared at Julien. His fingers ravished her through a long shuddering climax, his eyes fixed eagerly on her beautiful face as he sought for the past.

In this strange excitement he allowed his foot to slide

away from the door, it closed itself silently and the lift
began its journey down. Suzette sighed and shook in
ecstasy, thighs apart and Julien's hands up her frock
ravishing her, all the way down to the ground floor.

Gaby was of the opinion that Antoine Ducasse was
charming, as indeed he was, and ravishingly handsome.
But that was the limit of her acquaintance with him. He
called often to see Suzette at the new apartment but he
never seemed much interested in Gaby, however blondly
attractive. This was in marked contrast to Remy, the over-
anxious gynaecologist. In theory he was Gaby's boyfriend
but he was very willing to drop in when she was absent and
devote all his professional skills to *examining* her friend
Suzette!

To Suzette it seemed a long time since she went to the
cinema premiere with Antoine, the day they first met, but
it was less than a year. So much had happened! In the time
they had known each other she had learned about his
affaire with Leonie Laplace, first lady of the French stage.
Suzette thought him weak to tolerate Leonie's temper and
tantrums but she could commiserate to some extent. Poor
Antoine had to cling to the modest success he had, until
Fate or Fortune or Julien Brocq or another offered him a
possibility of moving from the theatre into films and so
become independent of Leonie's influence.

One afternoon, when Leonie was performing with her
accustomed *panache* at an interview, leaving Antoine at
liberty, he arrived with photos of himself to show Suzette.
She was alone, resting before an important engagement
that evening. Gaby had gone out for lunch with Remy and
would go from his apartment to work at the Folies Bergère,
having been *examined* all afternoon. Michel was at the
cinema, he adored American cowboy movies and the new

Gary Cooper epic was showing, dubbed into French, at the cinema on the rue de la Harpe.

Suzette felt comfortable with Antoine, they were at ease with one another. He spread out the many glossy photos of himself on the floor and they sprawled more or less upside-down on one of the white leather sofas to look at them. Suzette was in a black satin culotte suit, shiny and smooth. The effect was stunning! Antoine had thrown his expensive green tweed jacket on a chair, round his neck he had a paisley silk scarf, loosely knotted and tucked down into his shirt.

Suzette remembered he had once told her she was so beautiful he would like to have her picture taken nude and she had warned him nude photographs could very easily turn up in the Place Pigalle as postcards for tourists.

All the same, Antoine had found a photographer willing to take a series of pictures of him naked. They were professional, slick, well-lit and well-posed. And not in the least exciting. Suzette looked from one print to another, listening to what he was saying in praise of each.

She knew his body well, his slender hips and broad chest, his flat belly and long thighs. He was not an athlete, Antoine, but he was well-proportioned and the effect was pleasing when he stood in the usual athletic poses. He was wearing nothing, not even a small *cache-sexe*. The pictures could not be used for publicity, they had no purpose except to satisfy Antoine's narcissism. But why should they?

'There is one more,' he said, reaching for the oversize brown envelope in which he had brought the photos. He didn't put this one on the floor with the others, he took it from the envelope and handed it to Suzette.

The picture showed him full-length, facing the camera, hands on his hips and his feet well apart. His male part was not limp and small – it stood boldly up from the patch of brown curls at the join of his thighs, well-shaped and elegant. He could have been staring at the camera in pride, but in fact his eyes were directed downwards, admiring his own masculinity.

'Now that I like!' Suzette exclaimed, pleased at last. 'That displays you to perfection, *chéri*.'

'You really think so?' he asked, with a trace of anxiety. 'I mean, it's not too conceited?'

'Conceited or not, it is *you*, Antoine. You are learning to be yourself.'

Inspired by the photo, she slid the palm of her hand up along his thigh, feeling the comfortable warmth of his flesh through his trousers.

'It could not be easy,' she said, 'persuading it to grow long and hard with a photographer watching. And keeping it like that while the usual fiddling with lights and lenses went on. Did you take it in your hand and stroke it to make it stand up to have its picture taken?'

Her fingers told her Antoine was already stiff. She undid his trousers and slipped her hand inside. It was looking at his own photo that had made him aroused.

'It was not necessary to do that,' he said softly. 'Well, not very necessary, because I'd gone to a lot of trouble to find a woman photographer. She is not attractive but when she stared at me naked, it had the necessary effect – I went hard!'

Antoine had improved in one interesting respect since the day he made love to Suzette against the big mirror in his bedroom – he was much less passive now. He kissed the picture of himself and dropped it. He wriggled round on the sofa until he was able to stroke her belly through the shiny black satin of her suit.

Their contorted position was odd in the extreme – their heads almost on the goat-skin rug, bodies wrong-way-round on the sofa and legs in the air. Antoine's hand moved delicately, caressing Suzette with a *finesse* that sent shivers of delight through her entire body. Her hand moved dreamily in his trousers, along his warm and palpitating length of flesh.

There was no mirror here to admire himself in, but perhaps he was admiring the remembered image of himself in the photograph, triumphantly erect. Whatever the reason, he was aroused and he eased her out of her culotte suit – though with difficulty, for they were not all that far from standing on their heads. But he had her naked at last, her beautiful body bare to touch and to kiss, her smooth gleaming skin, her superb breasts!

When he penetrated her, the back of her head was on the floor – her raven-black hair against the long white goat-hair – and only her bottom was on the sofa. Her legs were stretched wide apart, vertical, feet pointing up at the ceiling. Antoine lay between her spread thighs, his head down near hers, kissing her ardently as he thrust with fast and nervous little pushes.

They reached their climax of pleasure at the same moment, she shaking in ecstasy, sobbing into his open mouth, while he thrust his hardness into her shaking belly and spurted his passion.

'Suzette!' he moaned. '*Je t'aime, je t'aime . . .*'

And when they were calm once more, she took him into her bedroom, not to make love again but to rest – this evening was her debut at the most important venue in Paris. She must rest for an hour and sleep a little to be ready. Dear Antoine had given her such pleasure – in body and mind and spirit she was refreshed and at her best –

tonight would be the performance of her life.

The hairdresser would be here at five. A limousine was coming at six to fetch her. Bathed and ready and beautiful, she would sit regally in it as it swept along the Avenue Foch, around the Arc de Triomphe, down the entire length of the Champs-Elysées, through the Place de la Concorde, up to the Boulevard de la Madeleine – and on until it drew up outside the Olympia on the Boulevard des Capucines!

She was a star, no one could doubt it. Tonight an audience of thousands would hear her sing at the Olympia – the very centre of the world for French performers! Mistinguett appeared here often in her great days before the War – *Miss* renowned for her legs as well as her singing. *Ah, but my nichons are better than hers ever were,* Suzette thought with a little tremor of pleasure as she cuddled up to Antoine on her soft broad bed and composed herself to sleep.

He was a very satisfactory lover, this Antoine, he had charm and style. Suzette decided to take him away from Leonie Laplace and keep him for herself. But only for as long as he continued to be amusing, naturally.

Headline Delta Erotic Survey

In order to provide the kind of books you like to read - and to qualify for a free erotic novel of the Editor's choice - we would appreciate it if you would complete the following survey and send your answers, together with any further comments, to:

Headline Book Publishing
FREEPOST 9 (WD 4984)
London
W1E 7BE

1. Are you male or female?
2. Age? Under 20 / 20 to 30 / 30 to 40 / 40 to 50 / 50 to 60 / 60 to 70 / over
3. At what age did you leave full-time education?
4. Where do you live? (Main geographical area)
5. Are you a regular erotic book buyer / a regular book buyer in general / both?
6. How much approximately do you spend a year on erotic books / on books in general?
7. How did you come by this book?
7a. If you bought it, did you purchase from:
   a national bookchain / a high street store / a newsagent / a motorway station / an airport / a railway station / other........
8. Do you find erotic books easy / hard to come by?
8a. Do you find Headline Delta erotic books easy / hard to come by?
9. Which are the best / worst erotic books you have ever read?
9a. Which are the best / worst Headline Delta erotic books you have ever read?
10. Within the erotic genre there are many periods, subjects and literary styles. Which of the following do you prefer:
10a. (period) historical / Victorian / C20th / contemporary / future?
10b. (subject) nuns / whores & whorehouses / Continental frolics / s&m / vampires / modern realism / escapist fantasy / science fiction?

10c. (styles) hardboiled / humorous / hardcore / ironic / romantic / realistic?

10d. Are there any other ingredients that particularly appeal to you?

11. We try to create a cover appearance that is suitable for each title. Do you consider them to be successful?

12. Would you prefer them to be less explicit / more explicit?

13. We would be interested to hear of your other reading habits. What other types of books do you read?

14. Who are your favourite authors?

15. Which newspapers do you read?

16. Which magazines?

17. Do you have any other comments or suggestions to make?

If you would like to receive a free erotic novel of the Editor's choice (available only to UK residents), together with an up-to-date listing of Headline Delta titles, please supply your name and address:

Name...

Address...

....

....